Mette Hansdatter

WHITE BIRD PRESS

Copyright 2024 by Phyllis Florin

All rights reserved. This book or any portion thereof may not be reproduced or used in any manner whatsoever without the express written permission of the author except for the use of brief quotations in a book review or scholarly journal.

ISBN: 979-8-870-12839-9

Author's Website: www.phyllisflorin.com

*I dedicate this book to my great grandmother,
Mette Hansdatter Oleson, whose life I've tried to imagine.
I share her grief.*

*Tröytte arbeidshender har no
lagt seg til kvile og striden er endt.*

Tired working hands have now gone to rest,
and the struggle has ended.

We shall not cease from exploration
and the end of our exploring
will be to arrive where we started
and know the place for the first time.

-T.S. Eliot, Four Quartets, "Little Gidding III"

Preface

I can't say that everything in here is true. Maybe if I'd been less self-absorbed at the age when I could have listened to my grandmother, I might have learned some things about her home in Norway and her parents, especially her mother, whose story this is. But by then, fifty years after immigrating, my grandmother's memory wouldn't have been too fresh either. In fact, when my sister asked Grandma about her mother when she was eighty-five, she said, "I don't remember so much…"

And who knows how much she preferred to forget.

She told my mother about the twins, that is something she remembered, or more likely, could never forget, but none of the other siblings had heard the story, so I don't know if it's true. I can't believe that either of them would have made up such a thing.

Why should I even care about my grandmother's mother, this woman I know so little about, who lived so long ago? And the answer is: she has seeped into me. I've only seen one picture of her, taken around 1896, when she was in her late thirties. She looks far older. The photo is badly damaged and half her face has been obliterated, as though burned. Her hair is parted in the middle and pulled tightly back. I can't see her eyes well because of the damage. She has no expression. She likely wouldn't have known what to make of having her picture taken. I imagine she was instructed to sit still and that is what she's doing. Synneva, her loyal daughter, stands next to her, her elbow resting on her shoulder.

I have read many stories and books from that time to understand how they lived, but there is no book, and no person, to tell me about her, what she thought and felt. Did I feel her near at times? Was it she who gave me that nudge, that thought out of nowhere, a feeling of being pushed in a certain direction? Did she put it in my head that despite everything, she had loved deeply and dearly?

I went to Norway, to the parish of Nornes. I stood on the shore where she stood, and looked across the fjord to Fimreite. The buildings were razed long ago and grass has grown over everything, but sheep grazed nearby and gulls and divers swam on the fjord, just as they did when she was there. The mountains rose above me. It is a beautiful place. I was there in June when it was green and lush and there were wildflowers everywhere. I made a small bouquet for her— Johnny jump-ups, wood roses, buttercups. She's buried in the church cemetery, her bones deep in the earth. On her marker, which is just a square of limestone embedded in the ground, are the words: *The struggle has ended.* That is where I lay the flowers

Mette Hansdatter

1922

"Mette?"

Someone called her, but she didn't want to leave the tree. The wind ruffled her feathers and she tipped her head into it. Her robin friend had just hatched her babies and the two birds talked of the difficulties of raising children, of feeding and mothering. Mette said she worried when the time came for the babies to leave the nest, that was the part she dreaded the most. The mother robin assured her they knew what they're doing. *But there are so many things out there that can get them,* Mette said.

"Mother?" A different voice. She cocked her head. Her daughter?

The sun was warm and felt nice. How good it was to be free, to have wings, to have no cares, to just sit and look out at the fjord, or if she wanted, to fly away to another tree, to anywhere.

"Mette?"

That other voice again, the one she didn't know. She turned to see who it was. *En gubbe*, an old man with little hair and a white moustache, stood beside her chair.

He put a hand on her shoulder and when she stiffened, he quickly withdrew.

"It's been a long time, I know," he said. "But don't you remember me?"

Her eyesight was bad, she couldn't make him out.

"Mother, it's Finn Olesson," Eva said loudly in her ear. "Dad's brother from America."

Finn Olesson. Finn Olesson. She turned the name over in her head like a squirrel with an acorn. There was something there, something. It made her uneasy, the way he assumed she should know him. She rubbed her brow.

From America? She squinted at him more closely. She had known someone named Finn a long, long time ago when she was a girl. The man talked to her daughter and she saw that they were both looking at her. Her hand went up to her mouth, and she let out a little cry. *Finn.*

She reached out to him.

1867

"The end will come like a thief in the night. We know not the day or the hour." The minister towered over them in the pulpit, dressed in a long black robe with a stiff white ruff around his neck. He had a black beard and spectacles and spoke sternly as if scolding them. Mette fixed her eyes on the picture of Jesus above the altar. He wore a blue robe and cradled a lamb, with two lambs sitting at his feet. Mette, too, took care of lambs and calves and baby goats.

"Not even the angels of heaven, nor the Son, but the Father only knows. On that day, all will be judged." He swept an arm to encompass all the congregation, including little Mette. "*All* will be judged," he repeated, as though to say, *even you, Mette Hansdatter.*

"The sky will open up and God will come down on his majestic throne." He raised his open arms to the ceiling so his sleeves looked like wings, then lowered them and peered at the congregation. "And when He does, those who are not in the book of life will be cast into the lake of fire." He paused to let the terror of that sink in. "You must be prepared," he admonished, "you must live as though God's judgment is coming this very day, as it very well might."

Mette looked up at her mother who nodded at her. Her mother wore her best head scarf made of thick white wool, and Mette would have liked to hold it and press it against her face, for the softness, the comfort of it. She did not want her mother to see how frightened she was, she would think her foolish. She tucked her hands under her legs and swung her feet until her mother clamped a hand on her knee.

That the world could end at any moment made Mette feel as if she had worms in her stomach. She could be at the summer pasture, away from her mother when the sky opened, or she could be sleeping, or in a boat on the fjord. It was not something she wanted to think about, but now it was in her head. She looked around at the rest of the congregation as the collection plate was being passed, but no one seemed alarmed. Old Peter Johnsson caught her eye and frowned at her. Mette quickly looked away. It won't be as scary when I'm grown up, she thought. That gave her some comfort even though she felt eight was old enough to understand these things. She wasn't a baby.

She didn't think she wanted to see God coming out of the sky on his throne in his white robes, glowing like the stars and sun were in him. She tried to swallow but she had no spit.

"Mette, look who's here," her mother said, nudging her. While she'd been imaging the end of the world, the service had ended. Walking past them as they were leaving the church, was Ole Ellingson from Nornes parish and his five sons, Finn, Erik, Elling, Lars, and Ingebrigt. She smiled shyly at her friend Finn who smiled back. She was afraid of Ole Ellingson. He looked a bit like an owl with his beak nose and bushy eyebrows over stern eyes. His thick gray beard fit around the bottom of his face like a scraggly ruffle. Finn's mother, Kristi, who also wore a white wool scarf tied under her chin, smiled kindly at Mette. Mette and her mother were in service to Kristi's brother, Niels Larsson and his wife, Elin of the parish of Fimreite. Now they all stood to join the others departing the church.

"*God dag, god dag,*" they said to one another.

"And what did you think of the sermon today, Mette?" Kristi asked her.

"*Det var fint,*" she said shyly, looking at her shoes. It was fine.

"You must be a good girl and do as the Bible teaches, so you will be in God's book of life," Kristi said.

Mette nodded and looked down at her shoes. She would be a very good girl.

1873

The shadows stretched long across the summer pasture, and the air cooled even though the sun was still well above the horizon. The call of the *lur* sounded across the mountain. The low musical tone of the birchbark horn and the dong dong of the cows' bells assured the world that all was well, the cows were coming home. The dairymaids sang to them and held out handfuls of salt to lure them to the *sæter*, the summer hut. The creatures lumbered over, their bellies full from a day in the pasture. *Kom nå, kom nå*, Mette sang to her two cows, and Sommerleaf and Freya came to her side, pushing their heads against her, their tails swishing away the flies.

Mette pulled a stool up to Sommerleaf and pressed her forehead against the cow's soft warm belly and patted her, but her thoughts were on Finn Olesson who would be there soon. He said he would come Saturday, and it was Saturday. Finn, with the flaxen hair and blue eyes.

Her friend Anna lead her cow near Mette and sat down beside her. She studied Mette for a moment and said, "Mette, just putting your head on Sommerleaf will not bring the milk, and I believe there should be a bucket under her."

Mette blushed and attended to her work. But soon she was back to thinking about Finn. Her work slowed, and Sommerleaf stamped her foot and turned to look at her balefully.

Anna sighed. "They say a dairymaid who doesn't sing while milking must be in love. When is Finn coming?"

"Soon."

"Saturday night is my favorite night," Anna said cheerfully and started humming as she pulled on the cow's teats. "Tor will also come." Mette stole a look at her friend as she milked and sang. Tendrils of her fair hair were wispy around her face, a single braid hung down her back. Even though there was much to do and the work was hard at the summer pasture, Anna made it better.

Mette was afraid that Finn's father would not let him come. She bit nervously on the inside of her cheek. Ole Ellingson was a crabby man and didn't think she was good enough for his son. Mette touched each of the buttons on her blouse and spit for luck. When she wanted something as much as she wanted to see Finn, she feared something would happen to make it not so. Why should a dairymaid get what she wants?

She spoke softly to the cow. "He'll come, won't he, Sommerleaf?" She ran her hand over the animal's warm hide.

After they finished their milking, the two friends trudged over to the cottage with their full pails and gave them to the girls who were separating the cream from the milk. In exchange, the girls handed them two empty buckets from the previous dairymaid that had to be washed. As they knelt at the brook scrubbing the pails, someone came behind Mette and hands covered her eyes.

"Who am I?" a voice asked.

She swallowed. "Is it Finn Olesson?"

"You are right," he exclaimed, as though astounded by her prescience. "And look at what I've brought you." He held a cap in front of her.

"Raspberries! Where did you find them?"

"I'll show you, but first, you must catch me." And off he ran.

"Wait," she called after him. "Wait! I must finish my chores."

Mette quickly finished, returned the pails, neatened her hair, then pulled her kerchief back up.

He had come.

"May I go?" she asked Randi, the head dairymaid. "I've finished the milking and washed the buckets."

Randi smiled. "I thought I saw Finn. Yes, you may go."

When she caught up with Finn, he took her hand and led her a short way down the mountain and off the path to the raspberry bushes.

"Look what else I have for you," he said, opening a cloth to reveal brown goat cheese and flatbrød. That he would do this for her filled her with an anxious joy, as if now something bad was going to happen because she was too happy. She smiled and looked up at him and their eyes held. He led her to the edge of a small tarn he had once christened Mette's Lake where they sat down to eat. From their mountain perch, they could see Jonsbrygga, Finn's family farm by the Sognsdalfjord, the buildings small as toys. Smoke rose from the chimney so they knew Finn's mother was preparing the evening meal. Across the fjord was Finn's uncle's farm in Fimreite, where

Mette was in service with her mother. Beside them, in the field of heather and buttercups, the goats sat chewing their cud, blinking into the lowering sun.

"I remember the first time you brought me here," Mette said.

"You were afraid we were lost," he teased.

She bowed her head. "I was more worried Randi would scold me for running off, even though I was with a herd-boy."

"I was a good herd-boy, wasn't I?"

"Finn Olesson, that is not for you to say," she said, and then jumped up and grabbed his cap. "Now you have to catch me," she said. Dagny, her favorite goat, who was almost like a pet, kicked his hind legs in the air and took off with her, and looked so funny, she laughed and tripped. Finn caught her from behind with both arms and swung her around so they both fell. They lay on the ground, breathing hard. The fir trees loomed above them, dark and shadowy. He turned on his side and propped his head up with his hand, looking down at her.

"Who is this that appears like the dawn, fair as the moon, bright as the sun...?"

Mette squirmed and couldn't meet his eyes. He seemed to remember everything he'd ever read. She wished sometimes he would be more like her, and not so "high minded," as her mother said of him. She wished, too, that she could read better, but she didn't have the time. Her mother didn't see the need for her to learn to read or write more than what she'd been taught in school. The minister does the reading for us, she reminded her.

"But what if I want to write a letter?" Mette had asked.

"And why would you want to do that?"

"If I should go to America," Mette offered.

"You?" She grunted and shook her head. "America is not for you."

Ole Ellingson often scolded Finn for spending too much time with books. "Books don't plant or pick potatoes," Finn would say mimicking him, parading up and down, stroking an imaginary beard. "Books don't put food on the table," he said. Mette had to admit she agreed with the old man, although she would never say so to Finn. She wasn't sure why since they spoke of almost everything.

"That's from the Song of Solomon," he said to her. "Remember?"

She closed her eyes and nodded. Everyone in her confirmation class knew about *that* book of the Bible, with its mysterious verses of love and wine and the man's fruit being sweet to the woman's taste, a part she remembered. Since it was not a chapter the minister read in confirmation class, she had struggled to read it herself but she did not understand it all.

Now with Finn so close, his breath on her cheek, she felt warm between her legs. She thought that the Song of Solomon had something to do with that feeling. If it was in the Bible, it must be good, she thought. Finn leaned closer and said, "May I kiss you then?" She looked into his eyes which were so blue it was as though the sky were in them. Was it wrong? She wasn't sure. He kissed her softly, lightly on the lips and then a little harder. He pulled back and looked at her, pushed the hair from her forehead. Then he moved on top of her. They had done this before. He had told her that this was what married people did, and they were almost married. She liked it but even though they kept their clothes on, she felt there was something wrong about it. Still, there wasn't anyone around. It was just them and the goats and the quiet swishing of the trees. He put his head on her shoulder as he pushed against her, breathing hard. The warmth in her rose and intensified. She held him close, breathing hard, too, and then suddenly he groaned and stopped.

He fell on his back and they both lay silent. In the distance a curlew cried.

After a while, when his breathing had slowed, she asked, without looking at him. "Is this a sin?"

"No," he said quickly, turning to her. "God knows what is in our hearts. He knows we're going to marry."

"When do you think that will be?" she asked, turning on her side and propping her head up.

"First, I must get some land."

"When will..."

"I don't know *exactly* when," he said, cutting her off. "Mette," he said more gently, turning on his stomach and raising himself on his elbow. "I'm third in line for the farm. *Third*. Somehow, I am going to have to earn enough money to buy some land, *if* there is any land to buy, and then I will have to build a house. All that before we can marry." He sat up, pulled a tuft of grass and threw it.

"That's why we must go to America. We will have a better chance there." He turned to her. "Think of it, Mette. Our own land, our own farm."

Mette did not have her Viking forebears' desire to see the world. Indeed, her thin lips tightened if she had to go as far as the village of Sogndal, nine kilometers away. Christiana or Bergen were much closer than America, but even so, she doubted she would see either city, yet she sat wide-eyed in wonder listening to stories from those who had. Bergen was at the edge of the sea, halfway to America, a long, long way from Fimreite. The master's wife, Elin, had been there several times, and had told her of the harbor, of the big ships from different countries, of the hotels and theaters and shops, and all the people scurrying to and fro, the fashionable ladies in their big hats. One part of Mette longed to see it for herself and another part feared all the things that could happen to her in such a strange place.

Whenever Finn talked of America, her arms instinctively went around her thin body. Traveling across the big ocean to an unknown place scared her almost as much as knowing the world could end at any moment. Even if it was just talk. It wasn't that far-fetched, that was why. People like her went to America all the time.

"Finn Olesson, where would I get that kind of money? I have no one in America to send me a ticket, and every kroner I earn I need for myself and my mother."

He thought on that, pulling more grass. "God will help us find a way," he said finally. He turned to her. "Would you go then?"

She looked at him and then at her hands folded in her lap. "If it is God's will, then of course I would go."

ଓ

The next morning Ole Ellingson and his four sons sat at the table eating their porridge. Ole sat in the high seat at the head of the table, his rightful place as master of the farm, and, in order, Erik, the oldest, sat to his right; Ingebrigt, the next in line, to his left. Finn was next to Erik, and Elling, the youngest, across from him, beside Ingebrigt. They were dressed in their Sunday clothes, vests and knee pants, their hair wetted and combed down, ready for church. No one spoke. There was just the sound of porridge being spooned in mouths and the slurping of coffee. Kristi, the mistress of Jonsybrygga, peeled potatoes for the Sunday midday meal. She would eat when the men were finished.

"On the mountain yesterday, were you?" Ole grunted at Finn. Finn had felt his eyes on him since he sat down. He shifted in his seat and sipped his coffee. He didn't want to fight with the old man, not on the Lord's Day. Everyone in the room knew that Ole Ellingson did not approve of Mette. He didn't call her by her Christian name, just referred to her as "that dairymaid."

"Yes, *far*, I was on the mountain," Finn said, bracing himself, as did the others. When his father bent over his bowl, Finn beseeched Ingebrigt with raised shoulders, but Ingebrigt was expressionless. Erik shook his head slowly at Finn meaning, *"Don't."*

"Visiting that dairymaid," Ole said, with a snort. "Do you think I don't know what you're doing?"

Finn stiffened. "I was merely visiting the maids along with the others."

"Are you courting that girl?"

Finn pushed back from the table, and stood. "I'll get the carriage ready."

"*Sitt*," barked Ole Ellingson, and the room tensed like a fiddle string wound as far as it would go. Finn sat back down and brazenly looked his father in the eye, but inside he trembled.

"You will not court that girl," Ole said, glaring at him. "I won't have it."

"It doesn't matter," Finn said, standing again. "We're going to America." This was the first time he'd said that aloud, and he liked the sound of it. To be free of the old man was reason enough to go.

Ole Ellingson stood, angrily pushing away from the table. Father and son faced each other, their hands in fists by their sides. "It will be all the worse for you if you keep this up," Ole said, coming right up to him. "*I'll* get the carriage ready." Kristi and the brothers looked at Finn as though he were a wild animal just come into the room.

Kristi moved first. She quickly swept the peels into the slop pail, then picked it up to take to the critters, but Finn took it from her. "I'll do that, *Mor*," he said.

"Not America," she said to him gently, her hand on his arm. "One is enough." She referred to the eldest son Lars who had immigrated two years earlier, and upon whom Finn pinned his hopes for a ticket. Finn gripped the handle of the pail, his jaw visibly tensed. "It's what I want most," he said.

Outside, Ole Ellingson harnessed Mœrkei, his pipe clenched in his teeth. He brushed the horse's flank, patted him on the rump, talked to him. The horse raised his head and neighed. His father was fonder of the horse than of his sons, Finn thought.

After a few spoonfuls of porridge, Kristi tied her Sunday scarf under her chin and picked up her Bible, and followed the men folk to the carriage. Ingebrigt helped her up and the rest of them piled on, everyone silent, no one wishing to disturb the fragile peace. Ole Ellingson clucked to Mœrkei and they set off towards Ølmheim, to *Norum Kyrka* where they would worship the Lord, their refuge and strength, from whom all things came, who held them in His hands and protected them from evil.

ଓଃ

Mette reclined in the meadow near her cottage, propped up on her elbows, and gazed across the fjord to Nornes. She hadn't seen Finn in two weeks. Jonsbrygga was too far away to see anything as small as a person, so she made a tunnel with her fist and peered through the hole. In her tiny telescope, she spanned east to the white steeple of Norum Kyrka which rose above the trees like hands in prayer, then further up the mountain to the summer pasture, abandoned now in September, and behind that, snowcapped mountains.

She imagined how the fjord would look if it weren't filled with water. Like a deep valley, she supposed, as deep as the mountains were high. It made her a little breathless to think about standing on the rim of so deep a chasm. The fjord, she knew, had been carved by a glacier when the world was made of ice, and then filled with sea water. The water that separated her from Finn was the same water that separated Norway from America. That was almost too big to think about.

Finn's dream of going to America was going to cause trouble, she knew. She and her mother were poor and had to work hard for the little they had. Mette's mother was a cotter, a farm laborer, and they lived in a small cottage on the land of Niels Larsson, Finn's uncle and their master. Her mother said she wouldn't allow her to go to America, but Mette was seventeen and did not need her mother's permission. She had been confirmed; she was an adult. But she also knew the fourth commandment: *Thou shalt honor thy father and mother.* She would surely get a black mark in the book of life if she abandoned her mother.

Her mother, Synnøve Hansdatter, from the parish of Ølmheim, had come to Fimreite, to the farm of Niels Larsson, to work as a dairymaid when she was fourteen, her first position after confirmation. Synnøve had lost both parents at an early age and had been forced to look after herself. She was good at spinning, and as she became more proficient at it, Elin, the master's wife, requested that she do more of that. She had acquired a reputation for her fine lace-weight yarn. When she wasn't at the wheel, she was growing, harvesting and preparing flax, and cleaning and carding wool. Her hands were knotted and calloused and her fingers stained from making dyes. She had been in service all her life, and now she had little to look forward to but the pain of a lonely old age.

Synnøve never spoke of Mette's father. There wasn't much to say since she herself barely knew the man. She was thirty, he was sixteen, when they found themselves in a bunkhouse trying to keep warm on a cold November night. Mette knew only that he, Hans

Hanssen, had been a transient who found work on the Larsson farm; that he had left before he knew Synnøve was pregnant; and that she had never seen him again. Synnøve had told Mette she regretted how much Mette looked like him. Same brown hair, same blue eyes. Mette suspected he might have gone to America, and maybe if she went with Finn, she'd meet him there.

Synnøve had nothing good to say about girls who abandoned their parents, especially those who went to America. She preached of the sinfulness of that country, that it was a wicked place. How she knew anything about America, Mette did not know. *You can't speak English*, she said to Mette. *Imagine all the bad things that could happen if you don't know what they're saying.* The country was full of heathens, Catholics who worshipped the Virgin Mary and even people who didn't celebrate Christmas. *How would she like to sit alone on Christmas Eve with no family and no lutefisk?*

Mette repeated the worrisome things to Finn, but he brushed them aside. No immigrant speaks English at first, he said. He also assured her there were plenty of Norwegians in America, especially where they were going.

"Your mother is an old woman with old woman worries," he said, knocking lightly on her head. "She'll say anything so you won't go. Don't listen to her."

But Mette did listen. She feared the long voyage and being seasick or worse, of having no money, of dying of hunger or disease, of not being able to find her way and unable to ask anyone for help. What if she were separated from Finn? Worse, what if something happened to Finn and she couldn't get help? She worried about men taking advantage of her, of people laughing at her. Mostly, she feared being away from her home, from everything she knew, from Norway.

She blew on the dandelion fluff and watched the seeds fly away. She wondered what Finn was doing now. Fishing, digging potatoes probably, or haying, or chopping wood. There was always wood to be chopped. She should be cutting the grass she was lying on, but she'd been at it all day and was tired. She lay back, her hands under her head, and closed her eyes. She imagined she had magic powers that would let Finn know she wanted him to come to her. She pictured him looking up, like a deer in the forest hearing the crack of a branch, sensing her call. He would have magic powers, too, and be able to cross the fjord in just a minute. Then he'd be there, beside her, and....

"I see you think the grass will cut itself," her mother said, startling her.

Mette quickly stood. "I was just taking a little rest."

Synnøve had an armload of just-pulled flax. She jutted her chin towards Nornes. "Dreaming about Finn?"

It unnerved Mette when her mother read her mind.

"Do you want to know what I think?" Synnøve asked.

"I'm sure you will tell me whether I do or don't."

"Remember who you're talking to, *pike*. That old bear Ole Ellingson will never allow Finn to marry you. You must remember, too, that Finn doesn't have much of a chance getting a share of the farm, being third in line. He would be cut off entirely if he should be foolish enough to go against his father's wishes. If this talk about America is true, and Lars sends him a ticket, well, that's the end of it, isn't it? Either way, it's best to stop now before you've gone too far."

Mette pulled the sharpening stone from her pocket and began to hone the blade of the scythe.

"Unless I go with him to America."

Synnøve frowned and looked off. "I would not pin my hopes on that." She looked up at two pelicans flying overhead, and then turned to head back to the house, but stopped. "Did I ever tell you about the owl?"

Another one of her stories. Mette started to cut the grass, but her mother stopped her.

"Listen. I've told you before that I shouldn't have been at the summer pasture when I was carrying you, but I thought I'd be back before you came. What a day that was, lying on the floor in that rickety hut, and no birth helper near, only the dairymaids." She shook her head as she remembered. "I thought I was going to die. But I don't think I ever told you about the owl. A white owl sat in a tree nearby and hooted for the longest time, as though warning us of something. It made all of us nervous, especially with a baby there. It would fly away and then come back. An owl, you know, means misfortune."

"What are you saying?" Mette asked.

"A girl who has had an owl appear at her birth should be very careful." She looked intently at her daughter.

Mette felt a little prickle at the back of her neck. "But you don't know that it was meant for me. It could have been for one of the others, even you."

Synnøve looked at her. "*Ja, ja sann.* Who knows who it was for? Finish up here and then we'll do the milking."

☙

Mette beat the weft-threads up into the cloth she was weaving, then stood back and looked at what she'd done. She was pleased with the pattern. Different sized green squares, yellow diamond shapes in between, like the sun shining through the trees, then brown for the earth. Elin, her mistress, had asked her to weave a coverlet for the carriage and so far her work pleased her.

Mette had taken to weaving, much as her mother had to spinning. She had a natural ability it seemed. Like every girl, she had had to learn this task at an early age, but for Mette it wasn't so much a chore as something she wanted to do. She took to it like a bird to the air, her mother had said. Some found the work tedious, and it often was, but Mette found the process calming and felt strengthened by it. It was hard to express what she got from it, but it was both mysterious and satisfying.

"It's like painting a picture with wool and thread," she had said to Finn. "That's silly, isn't it?"

"I know what you mean," he said. And she knew he did.

Suddenly Elin was behind her and startled Mette, who hadn't heard her come in.

"*Uff*, you're jumpy," Elin said. She inspected what Mette had done so far and nodded, which meant she liked it. "Needs red," she said. Mette thought so too, but she did not like to be told what to weave.

Elin was a large woman and strong. She ran her household with a firm hand and had no time for idlers. Her hair, pulled back in a bun, and her complexion were dark as a Sami's. It was unfortunate that she and the master Niels had not had children, but she was not one to dwell on what could not be changed. Instead, she put her vigor into keeping up the household which included, besides her and Niels, her aged parents, and the other farm laborers who came and went. She was kind enough to Synnøve and Mette, but she let them know when their work was not satisfactory. She expected them to work hard in exchange for their cottage.

"Now why did I come here?" Elin asked herself. She sat down heavily and her weight pushed the chair back. She kicked off her shoe and pulled a foot up to her knee to rub it as she inspected the small room which was rightfully hers. The spinning wheel and loom took up most of the space. There was a bed where Mette and Synnøve slept, a stove for heating and cooking and a cupboard in the corner.

"Where's your mother?"

"In the *eldhaus*."

"I hear Finn wants to go to America," she said.

So that's why you're here, Mette thought.

"He hopes to, yes."

"And how does that sit with you?"
"I'm not sure."
"You're not sure. Hmpf. Does he want you to go, too?"
"Yes."
"But you wouldn't, would you?"
"I...I don't know. Perhaps."
"Bah. You would leave your mother? Come, Mette, you know God commands us to honor, obey and serve our parents."
"Yes, *fru*," she said.
Elin grunted. "It's not good that so many young people are leaving Norway. If I had children, I'd forbid them to go. I'm going to have a talk with Finn."
That was Elin, not just running her household, but everyone else's as well. Mette didn't want Finn to go, but it wasn't Elin's business.
"I wanted to talk to Synnøve. She's in the *eldhaus*?"
"Yes, *fru*," she said with a nod.
On the way out, Elin looked again at the weaving and muttered, "It would be a shame if you went to America."

ଔ

Ole Ellingson put his foot down on the fork and pressed it into the soil, then pulled it out and sifted for potatoes. If Finn thought their exchange about the dairymaid that Sunday was the last word on the subject, he was badly mistaken. To have his son disrespect him so openly, with no regard for the consequences, deeply angered him, even if part of him admired his son's courage. He tossed the potatoes into a basket and pressed the fork into the ground again. Had he worked so hard to raise five strong sons and to keep the farm thriving, just so they could run off to America or marry a cotter's bastard?

He had been devastated when Lars emigrated. What did that say about Jonsbrygga, when his firstborn, the one who could have the farm, didn't want it? What did it say about Norway, that its young people were leaving the country because there was no place for them? Ever since that first ship sailed away from Stavanger to America, when ordinary people like himself could up and sail across the ocean, everything had changed.

Yes, it was hard carving out a living in the rocky soil God had given them, but it was their land. Jonsbrygga had been in the family for four generations, over a hundred years. They weren't living off someone else, like the *husmann* and the *cotters*. Those poor souls were going to America in droves and that was understandable, that was their only hope for any kind of life.

And now this business with Finn and that *dairymaid*. He had nothing against the girl and her mother as long as they stayed in their place. Service, yes, but God in heaven, not to wed. All she could bring to a marriage would be a few pots, bed linen, a spoon. He did not agree with Kristi that a man should marry whomever he pleased. He feared Finn would do something foolish, get the girl in trouble, and then be forced to marry her. He stopped digging to wipe his brow, and saw Kristi coming towards him with a jug of water.

He took a long drink and wiped his mouth. "What do you know about this America notion?" he asked, squinting out at the fjord.

"He's said nothing to me," she said. "Lars could use a brother over there, I suppose, but I hope it won't come to that." She took a drink. "I think he's wrong about Mette Hansdatter though. She's not the kind to emigrate."

"Why do you say that?"

"She's a nervous girl, I've noticed. She doesn't even like crossing the fjord on her own. I don't know, I just sense it."

Ole nodded. "That's what I thought. He just made that up." He felt a small relief that Finn was probably bluffing, but he also saw that he could no longer stand by and merely hope that Finn would use the head God gave him. He had to do something. If Finn met a better prospect, he would see he had other options.

"I wouldn't meddle if I were you," Kristi said. "She's a good girl."

"Attend to your work, woman, and I'll attend to mine." He drove the fork hard into the ground.

☙

At nineteen, Finn was a good-looking man. He was not tall, but not short either, with fair hair, "fine as a goat's beard," his mother said, his father's blue eyes, and pronounced cheekbones. His nose was his best feature which was thin and straight and just the right size, at least that's what Mette thought. As often happens, the father's father appears in the grandson, and Ole Ellingson said Finn was the exact likeness of his father. Since there were no pictures of him, they had to take his word for it.

Finn and Mette had grown up together. Whenever the Olesson family crossed the fjord to visit the Larssons, Finn ran to find Mette. Ole Ellingson had not seen what was going on right under his nose. He had not seen how drawn to the shy Mette Finn was, how protective of her. If Ole had opened his eyes, he would have seen Mette follow Finn around, how delighted she was with the stories he told her, stories of kings and trolls, princesses and elves. He would have seen them go off together, exploring, and might even have worried how long they were gone.

By the time Ole Ellingson realized what was going on, they were in far and deep.

Ole Ellingson seemed to be the only person in the county of Sogn who did not see Mette's many virtues. Even though she was illegitimate and born into service, all who knew her thought her to be a kind, pious girl; timid, perhaps, but that was not necessarily a bad thing in a woman. She was a hard worker, a good weaver, and a great blessing to her mother who had no one else but her in the world.

Ole wasn't interested in whether Mette was a good girl or not, he was only interested in what she could bring to the marriage. He went ahead with his plan of finding a better prospect for Finn and found one in the nearby village of Slinde. A young woman named Berit Persdatter whose father was a well-to-do landowner.

Finn and Erik were chopping wood when Ole came over to them and clapped an arm around Finn's shoulders and announced that he'd made arrangements for him to meet the woman.

Finn wiped his brow with his arm and squinted at his father. "You did what?"

"It's arranged for next Sunday afternoon, and you'll be there if I have to take you myself."

"It will be a waste of my time," Finn said. "And hers."

"You'll do as I say," Ole said. Finn took a step toward him, but Erik held him back. Finn stood for a moment trembling, then threw his ax down and fled. He expected Erik would follow, and it wasn't long before he heard the crunch of stones behind him.

"Brother," Erik said, clapping him on the shoulder, which made Finn want to punch him, he was so wound up. "You can't win a fight with the old man."

Finn picked up a handful of stones and began throwing them into the fjord. "You should have let me try."

"You wouldn't be standing here now."

Finn wasn't sure that was true anymore. Erik was six years older than Finn, and Finn looked up to him. Of all the boys, Erik most resembled their father, stocky build, straight brown hair that was already receding, and tired blue eyes. When Erik was ten, he'd seen his older brother drown, and it had changed him. He had turned inward, become quiet, and ever watchful. His mother feared he'd put his need to protect his brothers ahead of a wife, as he was in his twenties and showed no interest in marriage.

"The way to deal with *far* is to make him think you're doing what he wants, if you see what I mean," Erik said, pitching a stone that arched high, then splashed in the water.

Finn frowned at him.

"Berit Persdatter may not have any interest in you either, so you go there, do your duty and that's the end of it. You've pleased the old man, but nothing will come of it, do you see?"

"What if there is interest? On her part, I mean."

Erik thought for a moment. "Well then, tell her the truth, which is what I'd do anyway."

"And if he arranges another?"

"Go to that one, too. It's not something he likes doing, and he will soon tire of it. By then, maybe your ticket will have arrived."

The two brothers stood side by side, casting stones into the fjord.

"Why does he not do this for you or Ingebrigt?"

"He's given up on me, I think. There's still time for him to meddle with Ingebrigt and Elling though, so perhaps they'll be calling on the Slinde woman next." He squatted on the beach and squinted against the sun. "You've gone against him with Mette. He can't have that."

It was late afternoon. The smell of the sea was calming, and they both breathed it in, almost tasting the rich algae brine. Finn would have liked to get out the boat and row, anywhere, just to be on the sea, but there was still work to be done, there was always work to be done.

"I'll be glad to leave here," Finn said as they started back to the farm.

"This?" Erik swept his arm out towards the fjord. The afternoon sun glinted off the surface of the water where two grebes floated. Fimreite mountain rose on the other side, now thick with cloudberries, and the air was rich with the smell of the sea and the sweet musty fragrance of the hay that dried in the fields.

Finn looked up. "No, this I will miss."

03

Finn thought on these things as he made his way to Slinde that Sunday afternoon to pay a call on Berit Persdatter. Even though he detested the mission, he couldn't say he minded the ride. The *cariole* was in good working order after he'd tightened both wheels. It was fine being alone, just he and Mœrkei, who also seemed to enjoy the trip. A small waterfall cascaded down the rocky slope into a pool beside the road, and Finn felt the fine spray. He thought about not going and saying he did, but that would get back to the old man. He hung on to the hope that Erik was right.

As he rode up the hill to the gaard, the farm estate, it was obvious that Per Andersson was a man of means. The house was two stories, timber built, red-tiled roof and a covered porch. The buildings and grounds were well kept, and the tilled lands and rolling pastures butted up to a forest of birch and juniper. The buildings of the gaard were all neatly trimmed with a carved design and formed a square with an inner courtyard that he now drove into. Red flowers tumbled from window pots. Berit sat on an elaborately carved bench, knitting as she waited.

She was a plain girl, older than Finn by a year or two, he estimated. Her complexion was fair, and her ashen hair was pulled back in a single braid. Her eyes were narrow, like a Lapp. She had a large bosom and Finn's eyes were drawn there.

"*God dag*," Finn said as he stepped down from the cariole.

"*God dag*, Finn Olesson" she said, putting her knitting down and coming towards him. "I am Berit Persdatter." They shook hands. "Let us rejoice in the day the Lord has given us." She did not seem shy in the least, and was not nearly as uncomfortable as Finn. It crossed his mind that he probably was not her first suitor.

"It is a blessed day," he responded awkwardly.

She took the reins from him and led Mœrkei to the trough so he could drink, and ran her hand over his flank.

"*Takk*," he said.

"Will you come in?" she asked, pulling her shawl around her.

He assumed her parents were in there, waiting to pass judgment on him. "As you say, it's a beautiful day. Would you like to walk?"

She cast a glance towards the house and then nodded. "As you wish."

They walked down the hill towards the pond. Finn was impressed by the many cows and sheep that were grazing in the pasture nearby. There must have been twenty cows at least and two dozen sheep.

She asked after his family and how he was faring, then got to the point, "You didn't want to come here, did you?"

"Is it so plain to see?" He looked down, embarrassed. "My father refuses to believe I am going to America."

"Oh, you're emigrating?" she asked. "I didn't know that."

"I hope to. I'm waiting for my brother Lars to send me a ticket."

"So many are leaving," she sighed. "Two of my cousins went last year. I miss them very much."

"How about you?"

She looked off wistfully, and somewhat sadly. "No, no. That's not for me. I could never leave Norway, and I'm fortunate that I don't have to." She turned to him. "So it seems this is a waste of time for you, Finn Olesson, to make the long trip over here. I am surprised you came at all. Aren't you seeing your uncle's dairymaid?"

Finn stiffened. He wasn't sure if she was looking down on him or not.

"Where have you heard that?" he asked, leaning on the fence and not looking at her.

Berit touched his arm. "Your father said something to my father. I make no judgments. I leave that to the Lord. Well then, I will tell my father that we are not a good match, as I already knew."

"How did you know?"

She gathered her shawl more tightly. "My father will not accept that I do not wish to marry, so I must go through this every once in a while. I do so to please him."

Finn breathed a sigh of relief and silently thanked Erik. "So, neither of us wanted this meeting."

She smiled. "I am glad to meet you, but I'm sorry to say that is true."

They chatted longer about the herds and the price of milk and the good haying weather. He respected her knowledge of the workings of a farm. With no brothers, she had had to be more responsible. They walked back slowly and she offered him coffee, but he wanted to go. When they got to the carriage, she pulled a sugar cube from her pocket and offered it to Mœrkei, then stroked the horse's neck.

"Your friend, is she emigrating with you?" she asked.

Finn looked down. "I hope so, if it's God's will."

"Then I hope so, too," Berit responded. She held out her hand.

"*Gud være med deg*, Finn Olesson." God be with you.

They shook hands. "And also with you...and *takk*."

He climbed into the cariole and clucked to Mœrkei. As he drove off, he wondered what it would be like to live on a place like that, to have such herds and land and a big comfortable house, and a wife who knew how to run a farm better than he did. And then the distant thought: maybe his father was right.

"Finn," she yelled after him. He stopped and looked back.

"May you find your fortune in America."

He raised his hand and waved.

He wished he could tell Mette about this. That's what he wanted right then, to see her. Even if he could have such a *gaard*, it would not be the same without her.

☙

Not long after his visit with Berit, Finn and Ingebrigt went to Fimreite to cut birch branches for sheep fodder. It was past Michaelmas, the haying had been done and winter was getting closer. But on that autumn day, it was warm, the air smelled of dried leaves and reindeer moss, and of the flatbrød Mette and her mother were baking over an open fire outside the cookhouse. When Mette looked up, she saw the two brothers nearing the shore. Even at that distance, knowing one of them was Finn, her heart jumped. If her mother hadn't been there, she would have dropped everything and run down to meet him. But Synnøve looked at her sternly. "Tend to your work," she said.

Mette was dusted with barley flour. Synnøve pointed to her face with her elbow, indicating there was some there. She wiped her face with her bent arm, but when Finn saw her, by the way he grinned, she knew it must still be there. Ingebrigt, too, grinned. She blushed and looked down.

"God bless your work," Ingebrigt said, eyeing the tall stack of flatbrød they'd made which was meant to last the Larsson household for at least six months. Judging by the many balls of dough, they still had much to do.

Mette liked Ingebrigt well enough. He had a bit of a limp from being kicked by a rutting billy goat when he was a boy, and he was self-conscious about it. He was a kind, serious man, but she just didn't have much to say to him. Once she caught him staring at her and Finn and when she returned his gaze, he quickly looked away.

Finn said they were headed to the house to get his uncle's cart, and that they would need to make two trips. Synnøve offered them a piece of flatbrød with newly churned butter which they wolfed down so quickly, she offered them another. They devoured that, too. It was evident that if she kept offering, they would consume the entire stack.

"I'll bring you water later," Mette piped up.

"*Takk*," Finn said cheerfully. Synnøve nodded. She could hardly disapprove of a service for her master's nephew. As they were leaving, Finn walked past Mette and his hand very lightly brushed against hers.

After they left, Mette sprinkled the table with flour and started to roll out another ball of dough, but the rolling pin stalled as she stared off. Her mother scowled at her. She pressed the dough thin, but not too thin. When done, she slid a flat stick under the center and gently lifted it, the dough hanging over the sides. She carefully lay it on the round flat stone over the fire. While that baked, she began the next one.

The time dragged by until she said nonchalantly to her mother. "They'll be thirsty by now, don't you think?"

"Finish the one on the fire," Synnøve said.

She ran to the pump to fill the jug with spring water. While there, she washed her face. Then she ran back to the house to get a bottle of bilberry juice and tumblers, which she put in a sack. Nothing made her happier than doing something for Finn. All she wanted was to serve him all the rest of her days.

She found the men hard at work, already with a full cart. The cut branches were piled up, white stalks and yellow leaves, and it caught her eye. She wanted to weave something like that, the white and gold, the black lines on the bark. She made a mental note of it.

"*Hallo,*" Finn said, coming towards her.

"Look what I brought," she said pulling out the bottle of bilberry juice.

"*Takk, takk,*" Finn said with a big smile. She poured juice in each tumbler and then filled them with water.

"*Skål,*" they said, raising their glasses. After a second glass, Ingebrigt went back to work.

"Come with me later," Finn said, low in her ear. "Ingebrigt isn't coming back with me to pick up the second load so we can be together."

"To Nornes? But what about your father?"

"*Far*'s in Bergen and won't be home until tomorrow."

"But you'd have to make a special trip to bring me back here," she said. "It's too much work."

Finn flexed his arm to show his muscle. "I could row twenty times across the fjord if I had to," he said.

There was nothing she wanted more than to be with Finn but she had chores. "After we finish the bread, we have to do the evening milking," she said sadly.

"I'll have you back in time. My aunt won't even notice you're gone."

She didn't want to show too much excitement. "I'll see what *mor* says."

She ran back to the cookhouse. *Thank you, dear God.* A small prayer. *Thank you for this.* Alone with Finn on the fjord on a day she thought she'd be endlessly rolling out flatbrød. Now she just had to get her mother to agree.

"That took longer than it should have," Synnøve said when she returned. Mette picked up the rolling pin and returned to the task. As she pressed down on the dough, she said very casually, "Ingebrigt can't come back for the second load and Finn wondered if I could help." Her mother checked the bread baking on the stone, flipped it over, then narrowed her eyes at her daughter.

"Finn can't do it himself?"

"Many hands make light the work," Mette said and immediately regretted it because of course....

"That is true here, too," her mother said.

Synnøve looked up at the sky and judged that the time was mid-afternoon. There were eleven balls of dough left to roll out. "Do half of that, and you can go, as long as you're back for the evening milking."

She had just placed the fifth one on the fire, when Finn wheeled the last load of branches to the boat. She wanted to help him, but Synnøve pointed to the sixth ball with her stick. "You don't go until that's done properly," she said. Never had Mette rolled out a ball of dough as quickly as she did that last one.

After she rinsed off her hands and face, she met Finn at the boat and at least helped load a few of the branches. She wished they were carrying hay so she could lie back on it, but with the branches taking up half the boat, it meant she could sit closer to Finn. She let her kerchief fall to her shoulders, and the breeze felt good on her damp head. Finn pushed off and jumped in the boat.

As he pulled and pushed the oars evenly and surely to Nornes, he'd glance behind him every now and then to make sure he was on course, then he'd look at Mette, and then return to his thoughts. She admired his face, the creased brow, his manliness, but she could see there was something on his mind. When he caught Mette staring at him, he smiled, and looked down.

"Are you giving me the eye, Mette Hansdatter?"

"I am, Finn Olesson."

He began to sing.

Eight pots of cream
Four marks of butter.
If you'll cook coffee,
I'll carry water.
If you'll be the wife,
I'll be the husband...

Finn would often start a song to get her to sing. Their voices blended and the breeze took the song away across the fjord. A grebe swooped down and landed on the water, followed by another.

"That's us," Mette said, "husband and wife. If we had wings, we could fly to America, and then we could fly back whenever we wanted to." She watched the birds glide about on the water in the mountain's reflection. *Behold the birds of the air: for they sow not, neither do they reap, nor gather into barns; yet your heavenly Father feedeth them.*

Her fingers trailed in the water, and the oars made a soothing splash. If only it could always be like this, the two of them forever in Norway.

"Have you ever seen the *gaard* of a wealthy landowner?" Finn suddenly asked.

Mette's heart darkened. "No. Have you?"

"I have. My father sent me to...well, it's not important. It was something to see. That kind of wealth is not for you and me, at least not here. I'll never have a proper farm here unless I marry into it."

She felt the shame of her station and afraid of what he was getting at. Was this why he asked her to come back with him? To tell her he was marrying someone else?

"That's why we have to go to America, Mette."

We have to go to America. *We.*

"Tell me again where we'll go," she said.

"Wisconsin," he said. "Where Lars is."

"Vis-con-sing," she repeated.

"There are plenty of Norwegians there, so you will not feel lonesome."

"But it's not by the sea," she said.

"That's right, it's not by the sea, but it is near water almost as big as a sea."

"But you know that a Norwegian can never be far from the sea."

"I think we shall survive," he said.

"Will we still have herring to eat?"

He mulled that over as he rowed, and said they probably would not have fish as much as they did in Norway, but that there was plenty of other food.

"Oh," she said. "Will there be rommegrøt?"

He said, of course there would be, since America had cows and grain and that's all one needed to make rommegrøt. He said everyone was equal in America, you didn't have to take off your cap, even if you met the president. There was so much land, he said, the government gave it away to anyone who wanted to work. There was gold there, too.

"We'll be rich," Mette said, enjoying the story.

It was like being told a fairy tale of finding treasure. "We'll build a big house with two stories and many windows so we can look out over all our land. Our son will become President of the United States. You will have a maid to help you so you can just weave and cook. No farm work for Mette Nornes!" She blushed when he used what would be her married name.

"Will there be trolls there? Will they try to steal our gold?"

Finn laughed. "No trolls, Mette, only taxes, just like here."

She knew he was having fun, but she also knew part of him believed that they could have whatever they wanted. She wished she had his sense of adventure and determination, but she worried that Finn didn't have his feet on the ground. His dream was too big, he had read too many books that told of things that could not happen to people like them. He didn't seem to understand the dangers that could befall them.

"The creatures will be wondering where I am," she said to Finn. She didn't want to talk about America anymore.

As they neared Jonsbrygga, she became more anxious. Even if Ole Ellingson weren't around, she didn't like being there. Ingebrigt and Erik came down to the shore with the cart to help them unload and she felt herself redden as if she'd done something wrong. She pulled at her skirt, and tightened her scarf.

"I should get back," she called to Finn. Not just to her chores, but back to her home, to her place, to where she belonged.

☙

Winter. The arctic wind came down from the north, cold and sharp. Ice formed on the edge of the fjord and snow lay heavy on the pines. The creatures huddled together in the barn and munched on the sweet summer hay. At the darkest time of the year, just before Christmas, when it seemed as though they'd never see the sun again, there came a letter from Lars. It was Elling who brought it home from the post office. He removed his gloves, pulled it from his inside pocket and handed it to Ole. Kristi took the porridge she was preparing for the midday meal off the stove, and sat in her rocking chair. The brothers gathered around, waiting, as Ole pulled his *tollekniv* from its sheath on his belt, and slit the envelope open. Would it be good news or bad? Would there be money? Finn could hardly wait. Would this one hold the ticket?

When Ole unfolded the letter, something fell to the floor and Finn lunged for it. When he saw that it was exactly what he hoped it was, he could only stare at it. There was a picture of a ship in an oval at the top with the words *Cunard Lines* under it. It was in English but he recognized the words Bergen, Hull, England and New York. Passage for one.

"It's a ticket," he said. "A real ticket." He looked at them to see if they comprehended what he'd said. "A ticket to America." Kristi nodded and bowed her head. The brothers patted him on the back, but with little feeling. They all wanted to get a look at it, but Ole Ellingson grabbed it from Finn's hand and brought it to the clouded window's light to examine its authenticity, then thrust it back at him.

"If Lars has money like that," he grumbled, "why can't he send some home?"

"It's not a gift, *far*," Finn reminded him.

"Read the letter," Kristi said impatiently.

Ole held the letter at arm's length. *"Dear Family..."* he began, then pulled the paper closer and squinted. He handed it to Finn.

"He writes too small and with a clumsy hand," he said.

Finn took over. *"Dear Family,"* he read, *"I send you greetings from..."* He paused, then showed it to Erik.

"Duluth, Minnesota," said Erik.

"I sit on my bed at a ...." He gave the letter to Erik. "You try."

"Well, for heaven's sake," said Kristina. "I don't remember having trouble like this with his other letters."

Erik looked over the letter, and then read the whole thing.

I sit on my bed at a logging camp thinking of all of you. I wish I could fly home like the swallow in the song, and be there for Christmas. It's been hard this winter and while I am making good enough money logging, sometimes I wish I had not come here. There is a bad fellow in this camp who doesn't like Norwegians or Swedes for any reason I can tell. I will be glad to have Finn over here, as I get very lonesome sometimes.

They all listened quietly as Erik read the words that came from so far away. Lars had been gone five years. Would they still know him if he came to the door? Kristi pressed her apron to her eyes, and Elling, who had been the closest to Lars, blew his nose. All that was left of Lars were his words. He was becoming a stranger to them, someone they used to know.

When Erik was done reading, he folded the letter and put it back in the envelope and handed it back to Ole, who put it in the box above the door with the other valuables.

Kristi went back to the stove and ladled out the porridge into a communal bowl, and they all took their places at the table. No one spoke. Any excitement or despair about the arrival of Finn's ticket was second to the remembrance of their departed son and brother.

ଓ

Ole Ellingson still bristled over the Berit issue. Finn had spoken honestly to him of his visit, that Berit had been pleasant enough, but that she had made it clear she did not want a husband. Finn had thought of her since that day, and wondered if it weren't for Mette and if he weren't going to America, if something might have happened between them. Idle thoughts for idle moments.

Ole had calmed down, but at the beginning he'd stomped around so it seemed the plates might fall from their racks and crash to the floor. He couldn't just set something down, he had to throw it. He didn't believe Finn when he said Berit was not looking for a husband. He was sure it was because he said he was going to America. He reminded Finn that it hadn't been easy arranging that meeting, that he had to practically beg Per Andersson to allow a meeting with his daughter. *And then, like a lunatic, you up and tell her you're going to America.* He clamped down on his pipe and shook his head. *En galning!* A lunatic!

Who is the lunatic now? Finn wanted to ask. But he was discovering it was one thing to dream about going to America, and another to have a ticket in hand. Money was worrisome. He'd put aside what he could ever since he'd hatched the plan two years ago, from fishing and selling pelts and working on neighboring farms, and he had built up a small savings, but he worried it wasn't nearly enough. He didn't dare ask the old man for a loan. Mette's worries now became his. "What if this happens or that, what if I run out of money, if I get lost, if I can't find lodging...if, if, if, if." Then he'd shrug it all off, and think, "I'm young, I'm strong, I'm a hard worker, everything will be fine. I have enough to get me to Wisconsin." But doubt would creep back in, and lines of worry crossed his brow.

ღ

The Olesson family piled into the boat and Erik and Ingebrigt rowed them to Fimreite to have the Christmas meal with the Larssons, and that included Synnøve and Mette. Finn was nervous about telling Mette, but he hoped that with the good feelings of the day, the celebration of the birth of the Lord, that Mette would be more receptive to the news, more understanding. Anyway, it should not come as too much of a surprise since it had always been his plan that he would go first and then send a ticket to her.

The seven of them entered the warm house bringing the cold in with them, stomping the snow from their boots and brushing off their coats. The house smelled pleasantly of the juniper strewn on the floor. After taking off their coats, they paid their respects to Elin's aged parents, Jakob and Petra, who sat grim as corpses in their rocking chairs. They took their turn shaking their hands and greeting them, yelling into their ears, wishing them a *god jul*.

The table was laid with a white linen cloth, woven by Elin's mother long ago, and set with plates that came out only on special occasions. Four long white tapered candles in brass candleholders burned brightly. Plates of lutefisk and pickled herring sat on the sideboard. While Niels poured glasses of brandy, Finn went to find Mette, who was at the stove stirring the rommegrøt. She was so pretty in her Sunday finery, her hair neatly pulled back in a thick braid, that Finn felt a pang in his heart that he would soon leave her. She wore a lacy white blouse with a high collar, a gift from Elin, and a black homespun wool skirt. When Finn took her hand, he saw she had scrubbed her hands and nails and smelled faintly of verbena.

"*God jul,*" he said, extending his hand which she shook. "You look fine today, Mette Hansdatter."

"*God jul*, Finn Olesson," she said, and when she smiled, she showed her chipped tooth, then covered her mouth. He had been with her the day that happened. She was ten and they were running along the shore when she tripped and fell and hit her mouth on a rock, knocking out a corner of her front tooth.

"I have something to tell you..." he began, but just then his uncle called out for everyone to gather round for a toast. Finn knew his father would announce the news after that, and he wanted Mette to hear it from him first.

"Mette, before we..."

"Come, come everyone," his uncle said.

"It came," he blurted out. "The ticket, from Lars." The smile immediately left her face. She kept stirring the rommegrøt but now all her attention was on the pot.

"Mette..." He reached for her hand.

"Go. I'll be there as soon as I can."

He turned to leave, then said, "Will you walk with me after the meal?"

She nodded, but he had never seen her look so stricken.

As soon as Niels gave the toast, Ole announced that they had had a letter from Lars, which he would read later, and then said, very solemnly, that he had sent Finn a ticket. A shadow fell over the festivities. Synnøve looked at Mette, but she looked down. Elin turned abruptly and went to attend to the meal.

"This is what I want to do, what I must do," Finn said as if realizing what he was doing for the first time. "I am leaving Norway. You all knew I was counting on Lars for this. It will be hard, I'm not fooling myself, but I have to think of the future."

Elin came back into the room, stern and formidable. "I do not approve of this, Finn. Your parents have already lost one son to America, yet you want to bring more grief down on them. And don't think you're going to drag Mette with you. Her place is here with her mother."

At the mention of her name, Mette left the room.

Finn respected his aunt, but knew her to be a meddler and one who liked to push her ways on everyone else. She was not the first person to fill his ears with all the reasons he should not go. "I have prayed on this, Aunt, and I believe I have God's answer. You may say what you think, but I do not need your approval. You would not go to America, that is clear, but that does not mean I shouldn't."

"You will pay a price for your foolishness," she humphed.

Finn knew it was pointless to argue with her. "Whether Mette goes or not, is up to her."

"What is it? What's wrong?" old Petra asked, and Synnøve went over and yelled in her ear that Finn was going to America. "Well, why shouldn't he?" she said. No one answered.

Before they ate, Niels gave the blessing and then added, "We ask that you watch over Finn, protect and guide him on his journey to America. Amen."

After the meal and clean-up, Finn and Mette slipped away. It was early evening and winter dark, their only light a half-moon, but the stars were out, thick and bright. Finn pointed out the hunter Orion and the North Star.

"When I'm in America," Finn said, "I will see the same North Star as you."

But Mette wasn't looking up, she was looking down, and now the tears came rushing out.

"Be careful," Finn said, teasing her. 'They'll freeze on your face."

She wiped them away with her scarf. "What will I do?"

"It won't be for long. As soon as I get work, I'll put away something for your ticket. I promise, Mette. Maybe I'll find gold there."

Once that amused her. "That could be a long time. I know how that goes."

He stopped and faced her, took her mittened hands in his. "You know I want you to be my wife. Being apart will be hard for both of us, but when we're together in America, you'll see, it will all be worth it."

"How can you know that?"

"I have faith, Mette, as you should. Faith that God will be with us."

"It may not be God's will."

Finn looked up into the starry sky, then closed his eyes while he gathered patience.

"Let us pray that it *is* His will then."

"But doesn't it bother you what Lars said? That people don't like Norwegians there?"

It did bother Finn, but it certainly was not going to stop him. "I will not let one bad man ruin our plan," he said.

He heard the shouting of good-byes, his family was leaving, and his father called to him.

"Finn, *kommer sammer na.*" Come along now.

His father had been surprisingly tolerant of Mette since the ticket had arrived. Finn supposed it was because he assumed he didn't have to worry about her coming into the family anymore, but also, because Finn's emigrating made everything else unimportant.

"We have four months," Finn said to Mette.

"Only four months! Does this have to be, Finn? Must you go?"

Ole Ellingson called out again. "Finn! *Kom!*"

"*Ja, ja, jeg kommer,*" he shouted.

Then he joked to Mette, "You see, I have to go now." He looked into her eyes. "You know I must go, and so must you." He kissed her. "Good night, my girl." She kissed him, too, and he ran off into the dark, the snow crunching under his feet, the stars shining. When he got in the boat and looked back, he could just make out her figure in the dark as she trudged back to the house.

☙

The time went quickly, as Mette knew it would, and every moment with Finn was more precious than her *solje,* the silver brooch Synnøve had given her for confirmation. The round dangling discs hanging from it were supposed to reflect harm away from her, but it had not done its work. Perhaps the Old Ones did not want to be involved in this America business. Or perhaps they did not consider the situation harmful. It was hard to know exactly what the Old Ones thought, but Mette felt their presence. She felt them as women in pure white head scarves, tall and straight as pillars, protective and watchful.

Finn came to see her every Saturday evening if the weather permitted, and they usually saw one another on Sundays at church. There were not many places they could be alone, so they walked if it wasn't too cold, or just sat in the cottage and drank coffee. Sometimes Synnøve would go to the main house to give them privacy. They lay together with their clothes on, as those who courted in days past used to do, and sometimes he'd move on top of her, and she had no objection. In fact, it was what she desired.

One evening, Finn lifted her skirt and began opening his trousers. She pushed him.

"Finn, *nei,*" she said. "We can't start a baby."

"Just once." He groaned and pressed his mouth to her ear. "Just this once."

"Finn, *nei*," she said more firmly and pushed him away. Finn rolled to the side and rocked against her, unable to stop. When he was through, he lay on his stomach.

"Remember on the mountain when I asked if this was a sin, and you said it wasn't because we were to be married."

"Yes."

"What if we do not marry?"

Finn thought on this. "Why do you think we may not?"

"So many things could happen, things neither of us can know. I may not get to America."

"That's it, isn't it? You're already preparing for that."

"Finn, fie! There's nothing I want more than to be your wife."

"Then it shall be. God knows what is in our hearts."

"That's what you said that day, too."

"It's true, isn't it? He alone knows."

It was getting late and Finn had to go. As he left the house, he turned to Mette and said, "Wed or unwed, we are one."

☙

In late March, when the snow had melted and life outdoors was possible again, the Fimreite parish had a farewell dance for those leaving for America. It was not often Mette got to dance with Finn, and she thought she might take wing, her feet were so far off the ground.

She wore the same blouse and black wool skirt she'd worn at Christmas, this time with an embroidered vest of her *bunad,* the dress of Fimreite. He wore a waistcoat and vest, and was as handsome as she'd ever seen him. Mette and Anna, both flushed with the warmth of the room, sat side by side. Anna linked her arm in Mette's.

"It will be hard for you when he goes." Her eyes were on Finn who stood with the other boys. "But then you will join him and all be well," she said cheerfully.

"But who knows when that will be," Mette said.

"I can't wait to go to America."

"Yes, I know, so you can marry a rich man."

"Yes, and I'll never have to shovel manure or work in that stinky barn again. No more field work. I'll be a lady who tells the servants what to do." She gracefully put out her hand as though waiting for it to be kissed.

Tor was suddenly in front of her. He said nothing, just awkwardly stood there, then slightly bowed. Anna smiled at Mette, then stood and curtsied to Tor, and off they went as the fiddle played.

Finn and Mette danced almost every dance together. His hand was on her waist and then her back, her hands on his shoulders. They'd part and come together, their faces so near, almost touching, round and round, twirling, her skirt flaring out. She was sure she would never be as happy as she was that night.

He walked her back to her cottage. It was a mild night and there was the flicker of the aurora borealis across the sky, pulsating bands of blues and greens and yellows. They stopped to watch the show, their arms around one another.

"It is God's gift to us," Mette said. "He reminds us of His Presence."

The air smelled of fresh soil and new growth. Almost all the snow was gone, and a full moon cast their shadows in front of them. She wasn't ready to go in, the dance was still in her blood. They walked near the edge of the fjord, the dark water lapping at the shore. They held hands, then stopped to kiss, then walked more, lingering. She knew that evening was something she would never forget. She sniffed.

"Mette," Finn said. "You musn't."

"I can't help it." He was leaving in fifteen days. It was too much to bear, that she might never see him again. She started to run as they used to, then ran faster. She was always the fastest runner. Maybe she could outrun the fear, or she could run back to when they were children, run away from America. Her skirts caught around her legs and tripped her and he was there to catch her, but they both dropped to the ground.

"Mette, this is what we want," Finn said after they'd sat for a while, catching their breath.

"No. It's what *you* want. I want to be with you *here*." She placed her gloved hand on the ground. "*Here*. In Norway."

He put his hand over her hand. What could he say that he hadn't said a hundred times before?

"I'm going, and you're going to follow me. That's the end of it."

"You could stay." But she knew even as she said it, that it was too late. He was going. Whether she followed was up to God and to Finn, too, and in the end, to her.

He stood and offered his hand to help her up. They were near the woods at the end of the peninsula, and as she stood, she first heard its call and then looking up, saw it sitting on a pine branch lit by moonlight, not three meters from them, a pure white owl. She pulled on Finn's coat and motioned for him to look, putting her finger to her lips. Goosebumps rose on her arms. Did he speak to her?

"*Hoo hoo*," Mette called and the owl hooted. She did it again and the owl answered. She dared to hope that maybe this was her *fylgja*, her guardian spirit. Perhaps the same one that was at her birth. She did not believe, as her mother did, that the owl was always a messenger of misfortune.

Finn looked from her to the owl and back again.

"*Jenta,* it's just an owl searching for prey."

"Perhaps. But he looks so intently at me, as though he knows me."

"They all look like that," Finn said.

The owl pushed off the branch and silently flew over them, close enough so they felt the draught of its wings. Finn instinctively ducked. They clung to one another and gasped in wonder.

"Maybe that *was* something...." Finn said.

But Mette was sure of it. It was a sign, but of what? Was he protecting her? Or was it a warning? Her heart fluttered as though it had its own wings. She reached for Finn's hand. The clouds on the horizon lit by the moon looked like ships, ghost ships on their way to America. If the owl were her guardian spirit, she wished Finn would stay in Norway. That's what she wanted most, and that's what she could not have.

April 18, 1877

It rained the day he left, a long hard spring rain, as though the heavens, too, wept. People from the parish stood on the shore in the early morning to see them off. Some wore oilskin coats, a few held umbrellas, some, like Kristi and Ole Ellingson, just let the rain drench them, as though that was the least of their suffering. Ole had made his peace with Finn. It was hard to read anything on the old man's face, but the slump of his shoulders showed it was a heavy weight he carried. Kristi wore a black scarf of mourning on her head and held a black handkerchief to her face.

Three others were going that day. Peder Madson, Bente Olesdatter, and Astrid Jonsdatter all had made the decision to leave their homes for the unknown, and had found the means to do it. Only time would tell whether they were brave or foolish. Astrid cried so shamelessly in front of everyone, with no ability to control herself, that Mette went to her and grasped her hands. She knew she was with child, that the father had left without knowing it, and now she was going to join him.

"I hope to see you one day in America, Mette," Astrid said. "You must go to Finn when he sends for you. Will you promise?"

"I do not know what God intends for me."

"You would let Finn marry another? You must do what's right as I am."

"But I do not have the means and my mother..."

Astrid looked pitifully at her. "You would let your mother come between you and Finn?"

Ingebrigt pulled at Astrid's arm. He was becoming impatient. He had volunteered to row them to Hermanswerke where they would catch the steamer to Bergen. "*Kom,*" he kept saying. "*Kom, kom.*" He told them to hurry up, herded them and their bags on the boat.

Finn was at her side. Her heart and throat ached, her legs so unsteady, she was afraid she might crumple to the ground. If she could have, she would have locked their arms together.

Hold deg. Stay.

As impossible as it seemed, they could be saying good-bye forever. But this happened all the time. It was not many who got what they wanted in this life. When they embraced awkwardly in front of everyone, she felt his fist on her back and in her ear, "I will see you there."

When the boat pushed off, Kristi cried out, "*Gud være med deg.*" God be with you.

Sørg for å skrive," others cried. Be sure to write.

Være godt. Be well.

Come back. Don't go.

They waved their handkerchiefs as the boat grew smaller and smaller. When they could no longer see it, when it had disappeared into the gray sheet of rain, the crowd slowly broke up and the people stumbled back to their homes, rain-soaked and heavy with grief. Mette went back to Fimreite with Synnøve, Niels and Elin. The only thing spoken was from Niels who said, "*En annen borte.*" Another one gone.

When they reached Fimreite, the rain had stopped, and Mette quickly climbed out of the boat and thanked them. Instead of going to the cottage, she went to the mountain, and picked her way along the narrow path, through birch and juniper trees until she came to a small clearing with a large boulder where she could sit and see over the fjord. There she let out her pain and grief, crying until her throat was raw and she could scarcely breathe. She rocked back and forth, said his name over and over, and then yelled it out loud in case he could hear her.

☙

The worst was not knowing if he'd made it, if he was well. She knew she shouldn't expect a letter for at least a month, but a month had come and gone, two months, then three, and still no word. The leaves of the birch turned yellow and fell. A cold wind picked them up and swirled them in little eddies. The darkness of winter approached, eating up a little more sun each day until soon there would just be a few hours left. Mette filled her days with work and when her chores were done, she wove her sorrow into cloth at the loom. When it was time for bed, she fell asleep as soon as her feet left the floor.

Everywhere she looked, she saw him—on the fjord, in the barn, in the house, at church. Not long after he'd left, she'd gone with the others to the summer pasture, and that had been somewhat better, because she was kept busy from dawn to dusk, but he was there, too. She heard him in the wind and in the brook, and when she lay in their secret place, she felt him next to her.

In early autumn, Ingebrigt came by. Mette saw him through the window walking toward the cottage from his uncle's house. Even if she couldn't make out his face in the gloaming, she knew him by his walk. She was used to his coming by, which he did every now and then to see how she was. She liked when he did. He was the next best thing to Finn himself. As brothers, their voices were similar and they shared the same laugh. Both set their forearm on the table when they drank their coffee. His face was ruddy from the wind and she thought it made him look almost handsome that evening. When he sat down, he gave her a look, as though searching her face for something, which made her self-conscious. He nodded to Synnøve who sat in her rocking chair knitting by the fire. Mette poured him a cup of coffee and he at first took two lumps of sugar, she noticed, then put one back.

"We've had a letter from Finn," he said and reached into his pocket, his eyes on her.

"A letter?" Her voice rose in pitch and her eyes brightened. She looked at the letter as though it was sugar cake. "May I see it?"

He let her hold it. It was addressed to his father, in his handwriting. "To think it came all the way from America," Mette said, "with only those words." She pointed to the address: Ole Ellingson Nornes, Slinde, Norway, which was the nearest parish with a post office. She shook her head at the wonders of the modern world. She held it to her nose hoping to smell Finn, then gave it to him, and sat forward.

"Will you read it to us please?" she asked, picking up her knitting. Ingebrigt straightened out the page, there was just one, and began reading in a low monotone. *Dear Mother and Father and friends at home....*

"Speak up," Synnøve barked.

Ingebrigt cleared his throat and read louder. "*I am here in Wisconsin...*" he began. Finn wrote of the voyage, a storm that made him fear for his life, the wretched sea-sickness. Ingebrigt stopped and looked up at Mette. *"Tell Mette I was glad she made me take the flatbrød. It was the only thing I could keep down some days."* Oh, that made her heart swell, his mention of her. She couldn't look at Ingebrigt.

He wrote that he had felt God's hand in his journey, even during the storm. He had to take three trains to get to Wisconsin from New York, but he had tracked down Lars in Madison, and found work on a farm for a Norwegian family, two dollars a day. Lars worked on a different farm, but he planned to move to Minneapolis for the winter. *The land here is hills and woods, but not as beautiful as Norway. I get lonesome, especially in the evening, so I must keep busy. The same God that watched over me in Norway watches over me still.* It wasn't a long letter but at the end when he said to greet everyone, Ingebrigt paused again, and looked at Mette. *"I hope to get Mette here soon."* Synnøve's needles stopped clacking for just a second, then began again. The fire snapped and sparked.

He hadn't forgotten her. He still wanted her to come.

"Me in America," she said and tsked.

"So he's there, then," Synnøve said. "Well, that's what he wanted."

Mette felt Ingebrigt gauging her reaction. She pulled a long strand of yarn from her basket and continued knitting.

"*Takk for det*," she said. Thank you for that.

He nodded. "Will you go to America then?"

"If it is to be," she said and pulled more yarn. "But what about you, Ingebright? Don't you have America fever?" She knew the answer.

"Me?" He pulled back and scowled at her. "Never," he said and grasped both his lapels as though he were about to give a speech. "I was born here and I will die here. To pay that kind of money and go that distance to a place where a man can't be sure he'll even have a bed to lie in, much less land to farm...that money could be put to better use right here in Norway."

Mette smiled. She and Finn used to joke about Ingebrigt's sternness. Finn would strut around grasping his lapels, just the way Ingebrigt was doing now, and make up things. *Why, if we don't get the hay in the barn before Michaelmas, the sun will fall and all the stars will go out. And then where will we be? In the dark, that's where, in the dark.*

"May I see the letter please?" she asked. She wanted to touch the paper Finn touched, to see the words formed by his hand, to press them to her lips.

ଔ

Kjare Finn. Mette wrote in a slow and careful hand. *Dear Finn.* There, she'd started a letter. She held it up and admired what she'd written. The wind rattled the shutters and the candle flickered. It was a foolish thing to do, waste a whole candle just so she could write to Finn, but she had purposefully waited until her mother went to bed so she could write without her looking over her shoulder. Not that she could have read it, but she always had something to say.

Kjare Finn. She pressed the end of the pen to her cheek, and looked up at the rafters, then back at the pen she had borrowed from Elin. It was very fancy with its black casing and gold tip. She was grateful to Elin. If she hadn't loaned her the pen and stationery, she would have had to buy it herself out of the money she was saving for America and she needed every kroner of that.

Even with no one around, she felt self-conscious and even a little ashamed. Who was she to put words on paper? She was not the kind to write, not like the ladies of Bergen at their pretty desks writing letters all day long.

Mette had attended school for six years, from when she was eight until she turned fourteen, which gave her just enough instruction to be confirmed. School was usually held in winter for two months because it was the best time for the boys, but girls didn't have that same slack time, so she was often absent, and sometimes it was just too cold. Her school was at the home of Birgitte Jonsdatter and meant a two-mile walk in each direction. She liked being with the other children, her friend Anna especially, and she was excited about learning to read and write. She hadn't liked the schoolteacher though. His name was Lars Fondenes and he looked like a troll with his big bushy beard and big lips, and breath that smelled like sheep dung. He was very strict and kept a birch whip by his side to slap the fingers of those who misbehaved. She'd never been struck, but she could still remember the sound.

Kjare Finn. I was glad to get your letter? But *she* didn't get the letter, it hadn't been sent to her. *I was glad to read your letter.* But that wasn't true either since Ingebrigt had read it to them, although she had read it herself later. She stood up and paced. This was harder than she thought. The candle was going to burn out before she had written the first sentence. You have to just say what you would say if he were sitting there, she told herself. She imagined him then, smiling at her across the table. She sat down again and wrote.

Dear Finn,

I am happy to hear you have arrived safely and that you are in good health. We are in good health here, too. Ingebrigt read your letter to Mother and me and it was good. I think of you every day. The days on the mountain after you left were long and lonely without your visits. I looked to see you come up the path. I look for you now to come across the fjord. It is good you've found work and that you are saving your money. I pray we will be together soon. Now I will stop as the candle is about to burn out. May God be with you always. Mette.

She added a little flourish to her name, just a little curl at the end, then sat back in the chair very pleased with herself. She held up the letter. She wasn't sure if she'd spelled everything correctly and there were a few blotches from holding the pen too long to the paper, but she thought Lars Fondenes would think she had done well. She waved the paper back and forth to make sure the ink was dry, then folded it in half and slipped it into the envelope and addressed it as Ingebrigt had written down for her. Tomorrow she would give the letter to Niels to post when he next went to the village. She hoped Finn would write back just to her.

෨

It was late to be on the fjord, dusk was quickly turning to dark. As Ingebrigt rowed back to Nornes from Fimreite, he thought of the long-ago battle between two Viking kings that took place on that very spot. Deep beneath him on the sea floor were the bones of the thousands of men who died that day, piles of skulls with empty eye sockets. He pulled harder on the oars and began to whistle.

He thought of Mette whom he'd just left, her dark hair and blue eyes, the way her blouse pulled across her bosom when she leaned back in the chair. He gripped the oars a little tighter. She'd said he was a good man. He looked up at the starry sky and smiled broadly. When she thanked him for coming, she said, *"Du er en god mann."* It could be that she liked him more than Finn. The oars splashed as they came up and out of the water and then back, and his hands stung from the cold and wet.

She would not go to America, he would put money on that. He credited himself with understanding her better than Finn. As he had come to know her, it was plain to see that she did not like being too far from home, and she had a strong sense of duty to her mother. Even though she often complained about Synnøve, he could not believe she would abandon her in her old age, and he commended her for that. All those girls running like lemmings to America and leaving their parents did not sit well with him.

At first, he just went to sit with her, to provide some comfort over Finn's departure. He'd always been a little envious of them, how easily they got along, how happy they seemed together. He wanted that with her, too. He wasn't much for conversation, but it was different with her. She seemed interested in whatever he said, and sometimes he even made her smile. She was good with her hands, with knitting and embroidery, and especially with weaving, women things. She was good to cook and good to do her chores. Best of all, he believed she was content to stay put, something he considered a virtue in a woman.

There were obstacles to courting her, of course: Finn and his father. He was also older than her by seven years, but he didn't think she was bothered by that. When he put his thoughts in her head, it all seemed to work out well. She had to know there was little chance of Finn sending her a ticket and even a smaller chance of him returning. He was just being sensible. As for his father, he would deal with that when the time came.

The moon shone on the dark sea as he plowed the water. Almost home. A light shone in the window of the house. He saw no reason to wait. If Mette agreed to his courting her, and as she was a sensible woman, she would, it could still be as much as two years before he had the resources so they could marry. Ingebrigt stored the boat in the boathouse and walked towards the house. The stars seemed to nod and wink at him, as though in agreement with his plan. He would prevail. He felt strong, as though God were walking beside him; invincible, as though His arm were around his shoulder.

෴

He went to her the next Saturday. After a short visit at his uncle's, he walked slowly towards her cottage, hoping she'd see him and come out. He didn't want to see her mother. Soon the door opened and Mette stuck her head out.

"What is it then, Ingebrigt," she said. "Have you lost something?"

"Oh, Mette, I'm glad to see you," he said.

"So, it's me you're looking for?" she asked.

"Can you come out?"

She hesitated for a moment, then went back inside and returned wearing a kerchief and a heavy shawl.

"It's a bit chilly," she said.

"Shall we go to the woodshed and sit?"

"Why don't we go in the house?"

"I have something to say, and I'd rather not say it in front of your mother."

When they got to the shed, he closed the door, and twisted his cap as though he were wringing water out of it. "Have you guessed why I'm here?"

She looked uncomfortable. "*Nei,*" she said, her head down, but her eyes looked up suspiciously. "Perhaps."

"I will be forthright. I would like to formally visit you on Saturdays if you will permit it. Finn is gone now, Mette, and we are here." The wind picked up suddenly and whistled through the cracks. Mette tightened her shawl and looked down.

"If you say no, I will stay away," he said.

She looked at him as though he were someone she should know, but couldn't place.

"I am confused, Ingebrigt. You know I am going to marry Finn."

"How long will you wait? A year? Two years?"

He moved to take her hand but by the look on her face, thought better of it. "You're like me, Mette, you belong here in Norway. It'll take years for Finn to save enough to buy you a ticket and by then you'll be an old woman."

"How you talk!"

He took her arm, a bold thing to do. "I am looking for a wife, Mette, and if it is not to be you, then I will have to go elsewhere."

She pulled her arm away and took a step back. He had not seen it before, but he saw it now: she did not feel as he did. For a moment he thought she might laugh at him. She pressed her lips together and bowed her head, then looked up at him.

"And what do you think Finn would say to this?" She crossed her arms, waiting for an answer.

"Finn is a million kilometers away," and then he added a little more gently, "And he is not coming back."

"You don't think you are betraying your brother?"

"No," he said. "It's not a betrayal if you two are not together."

"But we don't know that yet. It will be different if he does not keep his promise, but as you are in a hurry to find a wife, then I'm sorry, but I must say no." She touched his sleeve. "But, Ingebrigt, I wish it didn't have to be so."

She must not understand what he was saying. He suddenly took her by the shoulders and pulled her to him, making her stumble forward. His intent was to kiss her, but his lips landed to the side of her head. Horrified, he quickly released her. "I'm sorry, I don't know why I did that. I hope I didn't..."

Mette adjusted her kerchief, which had slipped, and stared at him, her face red. Ingebrigt wanted to flee. She put her hands out so as to prevent him from coming near, then backed to the door.

"I think of you as a brother, Ingebrigt, that is all. *God natt.*"

Ingebrigt watched her enter the house and close the door. He spun around and slapped his cap against the wall. "*Dumming,*" he said under his breath. *Blockhead.* He walked down to his boat. It was dark now. Even the stars seemed to mock him. *Dumming, dumming,* he muttered. He hoped to God that that wasn't the end of it. He hoped he hadn't ruined his chances forever.

☙

Overnight the snow had banked against the house, covering the window and making the little cottage even darker. Mette reluctantly rose from the warm bed, keeping the quilt around her, lit the lantern and adjusted the flame. Before dressing, she shoved what was left of the kindling into the stove and got the fire started. She blew on the flame, and added the last log. Satisfied that it was going to take, she quickly got dressed. She chipped at the icy surface of the water in the bucket. Once the water was heated, she poured it over the coffee grounds from the day before and heated that. After she'd done the morning chores and cleared the snow from the house, she would have to gather more wood since there wasn't much left in the shed either.

It was hard for Synnøve to get up. Her arthritis bothered her in the cold, and she moved with difficulty. She was fifty, a *gamel jente*, an old woman. Mette watched her with sadness and resentment. The more infirm Synnøve became, the harder it would be for Mette to abandon her. Sometimes she suspected her mother's groans were more for her to hear than from actual pain.

On those hard cold winter days when their provisions were low, Mette slipped away to be with Finn in America. She sat near the stove, gripping her shawl with one hand and sipping weak coffee with the other. She warmed herself with *dagdrømmer*, daydreams. It snowed where Finn was, of course, but in her daydreams, not as much. The days were not as dark, the cottage not as small, the wood more abundant, and easier to chop. In America, cutting wood would be Finn's job, not hers. The house would have a room for cooking, one for sitting and one for sleeping, with a stove in each one, and no draughts. She imagined herself stirring a pot of rommegrøt on a modern wood stove in a room lit with electric lights, a fat baby in her arms.

"Cows," her mother nudged her. She swore her mother knew whenever she thought of America.

There was a pounding on the door, then it suddenly opened and snow and wind whooshed in as well as Erik.

"Erik," Mette exclaimed, jumping to her feet. "*God morgen.*"

He nodded to them. "We got a letter two days ago. I thought you'd want to hear it," he said, but he immediately noticed the empty wood box. "You need more wood," he said and went out to get some. When he returned, Mette saw by his grim expression, that he'd assessed their fuel situation.

"Is Ingebrigt also coming?" she asked, quickly pouring him a cup of coffee.

"No, it's just me today." He sipped the coffee. "*Takk.*"

She hadn't seen Ingebrigt since his pronouncement, almost two months ago. True to his word, he had stayed away. Synnøve badgered her with what she'd done to scare him off, but she pretended not to know.

"You'd be a fool to let him get away," Synnøve hissed. "He'll take care of us."

Mette had hoped Finn's next letter would have been just to her, but maybe there was still one coming.

She had nothing to offer Erik but flatbrød.

"I've eaten," he said, putting both hands on his knees. He left his hat and coat on since it was still cold in the house.

"The letter then?" she asked, unable to conceal her eagerness.

"Oh yes!" he said. He took out the letter and put it on the table, then lit his pipe. The fragrant scent of tobacco smoke relaxed her a little. There was no ticket. She felt both discouraged and relieved. Finn had been gone seven months. Was Ingebrigt right? Did he even think of her anymore?

Kjare broder, Erik read. Dear brother. Mette sat with her hands folded in her lap listening intently. There was good news first. He had found work for the winter at the same logging camp Lars had worked at, and was making good money. The work was hard, but he was making a go of it. He'd made a Norwegian friend so it was good to talk about the old country. In the spring he hoped to find work on a farm near Madison and then look for his own place. Lars had decided to move west to look for gold. Erik read: *Already, I am doing better than I ever could have done in Norway. Most people are kind and help a man when he needs it. Not a day goes by that I don't think of all of you and Norway, but I'm glad I came, and I hope others will join me.* He didn't specifically say her name, but Mette felt sure he meant her. He said to greet everyone and hoped they would write soon. That was all, no message for her, so she wondered if that was because he was sending her a letter of her own.

Erik folded up the letter and put it back in the envelope.

Mette straightened and smiled. *"Takk,"* she said.

"The milking," Synnøve grunted and nudged Mette again.

Erik pulled on his gloves and slapped his knees. "Come now," he said. "Let's get you some wood." Mette bundled up and followed Erik out the door. Whatever news came from Finn, good or bad, there was work to be done and there was no end to it.

ଓ

April came and went and still no ticket for Mette. Ingebrigt lay awake listening to the drone of the family snoring. His bad leg ached, which is what woke him, and he rubbed it. Mette came into his thoughts, as she often did at night. He liked when she reached back to tighten her braid because it pushed her breasts out. He shifted towards the wall, his back to Erik, and let himself think of her completely, how he'd unbutton her blouse and put his hand inside, then lift her skirt and pull her to him. His breathing quickened and when Mette opened to him, he could not stop himself. Erik snored on.

He wasn't sure what to do now that a year had passed. He regretted his proposal. More precisely, he regretted the timing of the proposal, it had been too soon, he saw that now. But even more he regretted saying he would find someone else if she wasn't interested. He didn't want anyone else. He had looked at other girls, not that there were that many. He had even visited Berit Persdatter in Slinde, but it was obvious she was not interested in him, cutting off the conversation in ten short minutes. He called on Sophie Olmheim, and she was nice enough, but all she talked about was her weaving, and he hardly got to say a thing.

He knew he wasn't a prize catch with his bad leg and his impatient nature, and now he was getting old. He couldn't help it if he thought things should be done right. Mette was the only one who seemed to share his view of things, who appreciated all he did.

He turned to the other side, pushed Erik's leg away from him, then rolled on his back. He feared he was going to end up alone, like Jon Pedersson down the road, that crabby old man, as sour as vinegar. When sleep seemed impossible, he crawled over Erik as deftly as he could and went outside. He used the privy, then sat on the bench by the house, his head in his hands.

He was twenty-five years old and he wanted a wife; specifically, he wanted Mette for his wife. He wondered if he could go back and ask again now that a year had gone by, or if she would give Finn another year. If he did nothing, she might think he'd lost interest or found someone else, and if he went, she might reject him again. *"Jeg vet ikke, jeg vet ikke,"* he said aloud. I don't know, I don't know.

The door opened and his father came out.

"What are you doing out here?" he growled.

"Same as you."

Ole eyed him. "Something on your mind?"

"No."

"Woman problems, eh?" he said with a low chuckle, and went on to the outhouse.

A pale dawn lit the horizon casting the dark mountains in silhouette, the fjord below them. When Ole returned, he squeezed down beside Ingebrigt, forcing him to move over. "Have someone in mind, do you?"

The last thing Ingebrigt needed was for Ole to take an interest in him. He leaned forward, his elbows on his knees, debating what to say.

"Mette Hansdatter," he finally said.

Ole blew his nose and bent forward to stuff the handkerchief into his back pocket. "Well?"

"I said, Mette Hansdatter."

Ole looked at him dumbfounded. "You don't mean it."

"Yes, *far*, I do mean it."

Ole slapped his hands on his knees. "Is she the only woman in Norway? Look around, boy, you can do better than that."

"I have looked around, *far*. I fear she will go to America if Finn sends her a ticket."

"That's right," he said. "You can't count on that one. Better let it go." He got up to go inside, then turned to say, "I suppose if I'm against it, you'll go to America, too."

"Could be." He had no intention of going to America, but it was something he could hold over the old man.

"Hmph," Ole grunted, and left him.

Ole's fear of losing another son to America was stronger than his disapproval of Mette, so Ingebrigt didn't think he would stand in his way. But there was still the problem of how to approach Mette. Perhaps she would come to him, although that was about as likely as finding a pot of gold.

He rubbed his face with both hands, then sat back, crossing his arms over his chest. Maybe if he thought very, very hard, concentrated on her, she would sense it. He looked towards Fimreite, summoned her face, then squeezed his eyes closed and thought hard. *Mette Hansdatter, come to me.* No, that wasn't right. *Mette Hansdatter, vær min kone.* That was better. *Please be my wife. Please be my wife,* he thought over and over, with her face in his mind, aiming at the place right between her eyes, although his eyes tended to slip down to her bosom and he had to pull them back up to her face.

"What are you doing? Does your head hurt?" He hadn't heard his mother come out. He jumped to his feet. "Just thinking, *mor*. Just thinking about what needs to be done." With that, he hurried into the house, leaving Kristi shaking her head.

଼

Mette held the letter in her coarse, chapped hands. She had been on her knees scrubbing clothes when Niels returned from the village and came towards her. "You've got a letter from Finn," he said. She dropped everything and stood. "I hope this doesn't mean you're going to leave us," he said with a sad smile. She wiped her hands on her apron and took the letter. It was addressed in Finn's handwriting to Mette Hansdatter Fimreite, Fimreite, Norway. She looked from the letter to Niels with an expression of wonder and appreciation, but couldn't find words.

"Give us the news after you've read it," he said, and left her.

"*Takk*," she said, calling after him. "*Takk*." He waved. She was grateful that he was not going to wait for her to read it in front of him.

She should finish the wash and then read it, but she couldn't wait. She found a shaded place to sit, under the eave of the house, and said a little prayer before opening it. She unfolded the letter which was two whole pages written front and back, and there it was: the ticket. Her hand flew to her mouth. He'd kept his promise. Now it was true, she was going to America. She looked up to see if there was anyone near to tell. But there were just the chirping birds and the water lapping at the shore. She pushed her kerchief off her head and ran her hand across her hair.

Kjare Mette,

I'm sorry I haven't written sooner, but I have been waiting until I could send you a ticket. We will be together soon! But first, many thanks for your fine letter, which brought me great joy. You wrote a letter! You must be very proud of yourself, Mette Hansdatter. Mette smiled as she read Finn's words, almost breaking out into a laugh. She could hear him, the way he teased her. *As you see, dearest one, I have kept my promise, and now I am eagerly awaiting your arrival. It is all going just as we planned. I beg you, don't let your fear stop you, Mette. We will have a good life here in America. There are many Norwegians in these parts to keep you company. You will be lonely at first, but that will pass. I am pleased to say that things are going well, Mette. I made good money logging, enough to buy a little bit of land, and I'm about to start building a house. I hope you will come soon, perhaps in July or August.*

But that was in just a few months.

Finn went on to tell her what she should bring. She shouldn't bring her trunk, he said specifically. She would have to carry her bags, sometimes for a good distance, so she should pack lightly. They would send for her trunk later. He told her there would be many people to help her when she arrived in New York, people who spoke Norwegian. They would help her to get on the right train, get food, and whatever else she might need. They were there just for that purpose. She didn't need to be afraid.

But she was. The old fear settled heavily on her shoulders.

The letter was long because of the instructions. In closing, he wrote, *Please greet everyone for me. We will be happy here, Mette, we will. Your always devoted, Finn.*

She held the letter in her lap and looked out at the mountain. He had kept his promise. He still wanted her. When she looked up, she saw her mother coming quickly towards, her, almost running.

"Niels told me. Is it what I think?"

Mette nodded and showed her the ticket. Synnøve reached out to grab it, but Mette quickly yanked it away.

"What do you mean to do?" Mette said, surprised at her boldness.

"God will punish you if you go."

"You know well enough that you have a place here even if I go."

"And how will I fare without you?"

Mette wasn't sure. Would Elin and Niels take in her mother when she could no longer work?

Synnøve looked at her hard, her face dark and cold, her eyes sharp. "Think hard on this, daughter."

ଔ

She was at the spinning wheel when Ingebrigt burst through the door. He didn't knock and he startled her. He didn't care, all was lost now. For a second, their eyes held and it crossed his mind that maybe by her stare, he *had* reached her with his mind. But then she quickly looked down.

"*God dag* and God bless your work," he said brusquely, taking off his cap.

"*God dag and takk*," she said, self-consciously running her hand over the front of her blouse. He wanted to run to her, drop to his knees and grasp her hand. He wanted to tell her how much he'd thought of her, how he had hoped that letter would never come, that he wanted another chance. But, instead, he took her in for a moment, just for a moment, before he said what he came to say. He looked down at the floor to collect himself, then said, "I hear my brother has kept his promise."

When she stood, Mette almost knocked over the spinning wheel, which she quickly grabbed to keep upright. "Yes, I...."

"You are now one of the lucky ones," he said with a small tight smile. "I was wrong about my brother."

"I can hardly believe it. He must be very rich to afford such a thing," she said.

"He could have taken a loan."

She looked at him, her lips parted, her eyes wide. "You mean, maybe he can't afford it?"

"No, no, I don't know. It's as you say, he's rich, he saved his money. What's important is he has done what he said he would do."

She seemed shaken by that offhand comment. He hadn't meant anything by it, just that maybe to keep his promise, Finn might have had to borrow money. It's what he would have done.

"Well now," she said. "Yes, America. Everything will be so different. *Mor* is..."

"Where *is* your mother by the way?" Ingebrigt asked, looking around the room.

"At the house," she said. "She is worried and angry with me, and I am worried, too." She wrung her hands and tried to smile.

"Mette," he said starting towards her, "You don't have to go just because he sent you a ticket. May I see it?"

Mette took the Bible down and retrieved the letter.

Ingebrigt looked at the ticket and said, "It's as I thought. There is no name on it so anyone can use it, and there are plenty who would want it."

She turned away from him, her eyes filling with tears, which she quickly wiped away. "No, he sent it to me, and I...I want to be with him."

He held his tongue. It didn't look to him like she wanted to go, but he was not going to interfere. He wanted to sit down and take the weight off his aching leg, but he didn't know if he should.

"*En kopp kaffee?*" she asked.

"*Ja, ja, takk,*" he said gratefully, and sat down.

She brought the coffee to the table, a cup for each of them, and sat.

"I'm glad you've come, Ingebrigt." When she looked at him, his heart surged. She dropped her head and shook it. "To think I, a servant girl, am going to America. God does indeed have a plan."

"But..."

"I know I don't *have* to go, but I must go, I must. It is a chance for a better life." She was repeating what Finn had said.

He gathered all his courage. This was the right time to say something. He held the edge of the table with both hands, and looked at it as if he were measuring it, and said, "If you should decide not to go, I will...I will be..." He wanted the right words. "I will be just across the fjord."

She smiled. "*Takk,* Ingebrigt. *Tusen takk.* There's so much to do now. Maybe you can help me with these instructions," she said, pulling the letter from her apron pocket.

"Of course. But I mean it, Mette. Should something happen...I mean should you decide...well, I want you to know, what I said before, it still is true."

She nodded her understanding. "When do you think I should go?"

༄

After Ingebrigt left, Mette looked around at the cheerless room which now was the most precious thing on earth to her. The rows of chipped plates slatted against the wall, the rusted cookstove, the bed in the corner with a coverlet she'd woven, one of her first, her rosemaled trunk, the wooden shoes beside the door. How many times had she cursed the draughty place, its rotting wood and leaky roof? Now that she could leave it, she didn't want to.

She was glad she and Ingebrigt were friends again. She felt comfortable with him, which came as a surprise to her. She felt a certain safety with him, that he understood her, and would do whatever he could for her. When they sat at the table, she had almost put her hand on his, but then feared he might take it the wrong way. She was leaving after all.

She looked out the door to see if her mother was on her way home. They weren't speaking and it was hard to be around her. Elin also was angry with her. She had stormed in the last time she'd brought her the basket of mending, and put it down hard on the table. Mette's ingratitude for all they'd done for her was disgraceful, she'd said. If it weren't for them, she'd be a waif on the road begging for øre. Going to America and leaving her mother alone was pure selfishness, and she could be sure God would give her a black mark for it.

Mette tucked the envelope back into the Bible, and pulled her coat from the peg.

How blue the sky was, how beautiful was God's work. She squinted against the sun's glare off the cold, quiet fjord. The sheep were grazing outside and she looked fondly at them in their dirty gray coats, as though they were her children. She whistled to them and they turned to look at her. The ewe she called Bralina, bleated. She would not see the summer pasture again or dance at the midsummer bonfire. She would never see her mother again. She sucked in a sob. To whom did she owe her allegiance, she asked herself, to her mother or to Finn? She blamed Finn for making her choose. She blamed her mother for not having more children. She blamed herself for everything. She prayed, *Thou art my rock and my shield. I will trust You and not be afraid.* But she was more afraid than she had ever been in her life.

She turned to go back to the house and saw her mother returning home. They regarded one other. Synnøve wouldn't talk about it. She just repeated under her breath: *Du forlater mor.* You leave your mother.

◌

Mette sat upright in bed calling out for help, waking Synnøve, and probably those in the main house, too.

Synnøve shook her hard. "*Pike, pike*, wake up."

Mette's eyes opened and she looked at her mother, trying to get her bearings. She looked about the room and fell back on the bed, clutching the blanket to her chest and breathing hard.

"I couldn't hold on...there was a storm...and I went into the water. No one could hear me." She started to cry. "*Mor*, I was drowning, there was no one to help me."

"God speaks to you, child. He sends you a warning." Then she lay back down. "It's as I said."

Mette lay trembling. It wasn't the first time she'd had the dream, but it hadn't wakened her before. Foreboding swelled in her chest, and she pressed the heel of her hand against her heart to slow the beating. She had told no one of this fear, but she wondered if she should or if they'd think she was mad. *I am going to drown.* They'd say it was nerves, but she knew it was more than that: she was being warned.

Worse, when the fear bloomed, it overshadowed the joy she felt of being with Finn again. Even if she didn't drown at sea, if she managed to make it there, would it be the same with him? More than a year had passed since she'd seen him. Would he see her differently through his new American eyes? Was he a gentleman now? He had dropped Olesson from his name and now was just Finn Nornes. Would she have a different name in America? These thoughts stuck in her head.

She had decided to go in July with two others. It gave her great comfort knowing she did not have to travel alone. The newspaper printed which ships would be in Bergen harbor and when they were departing, and Finn said she had to arrive at least two days before to get things in order and do the necessary paperwork. That made her almost lose breath, having to find her way in Bergen, and staying in one of those emigrant hotels. She'd be with the others, but still, she'd heard bad things about those places.

Anna helped her practice English from the guidebook that got passed around the parish. They could say and understand, "Hello" and "good-bye," "good day" and "thank you." She felt a little proud of that, that she could speak another language. It didn't mean she was better than anyone else. No, Mette Hansdatter would not let herself get puffed up about something like that, especially around her mother. Synnøve regarded her with a cold eye when she repeated the simple phrases. But she felt very grand when she could understand and repeat, "Wake up. We are in Chicago." *Vak oop. Ve ere in Chicago.*

༒

There were days when Mette's fears subsided enough so she felt more excitement about going, especially seeing Finn again. Anna was a big help with that. She came across the fjord from Ølmheim to Fimreite, as her work allowed. Mette was always cheered by her friend's visits, but Synnøve left in a huff whenever Anna arrived, and made a point of inquiring after Anna's mother. Was she well looked after?

One day as they were deciding on what Mette should take with her, Anna said, "You need a hat."

"I can't afford that."

"You'll be the only woman in America without a hat."

Mette smiled. "Well then, that's what I will be."

"Mette, I want to give you a gift..."

"Anna, no! I could never accept..."

"Will you listen to me please?" She stood in front of her friend and put her hands on her shoulders. "I want to give you something to remember me by. I have saved a few kroner, and it would make me happy to do this for you. In a way, a part of me will go with you then."

Mette kissed her friend on the cheek. "You are so kind. You make me feel ashamed. *Takk.*"

"We'll make a trip to Sogndal," Anna said. "We'll have one last adventure before you leave."

What could she do? That her friend would spend her hard-earned money on her made her want to weep. Anna put her arms around her.

"Then it's settled," she said.

༒

Mette had been to Sogndal only twice in her life, both times with her mother and Niels and Elin, to buy provisions. It was a big village on the east edge of the fjord, with many shops and houses packed close together, and was very different from the countryside. Mette tried many times to talk Anna out of it, but she wouldn't hear of it. They planned to walk with the hope of catching a ride from a passing carriage.

Elin made a list of things she wanted from the village, and as the news of their trip spread throughout the parish, other neighbors stopped by with letters and parcels and requests for purchases. Ole Olesson asked if they could purchase a bottle of cough medicine for him, Fru Halverson and Fru Johannson asked if they would please mail some letters and drop off a package at the post office, and Erik, too, asked if she would be so kind as to deliver a payment to the bank.

The day they set out was warm and promised to be hot. Along with the various packages and letters, they brought flatbrød and a canteen of water, which they carried in a basket on their backs, and, of course, their knitting. It would not do to waste the day. They knit as they walked, gossiped, talked excitedly about the approaching midsummer's eve bonfire, and made plans for when Anna came to America. Mette insisted that she stay with her and Finn until she found her own place.

They'd walked half an hour or so when a carriage came by, and the rather taciturn driver jerked his head towards the back which was piled with sacks of seed potatoes. "*Komme inn da*," he said grumpily. It was not very comfortable but better than walking.

The long dusty road followed the fjord. Sometimes it was on the same level and sometimes it ascended and the fjord was a long way down, separated by a fence made of rocks and boulders. The road narrowed and widened as the geography demanded, and cascades splashed down the rocky hillside spraying them with mist. They passed a mill and the two owners waved to them and they waved back. The air was spicy sweet with the scent of pine, but as they got closer to Sogndal, there were more birch and apple trees. After an hour's drive, the driver indicated that he was turning north and he left them there. The village was two kilometers ahead.

"*Tusen takk*," the girls said as they climbed down. He nodded and drove off.

Mountains loomed protectively above the village and straight ahead was the famous Jostedal glacier which glistened in the sun. So many carriages and people on the street. Mette's eyes darted this way and that, afraid they might be accosted by someone. Everyone looked suspicious. That man there, with the goat, what was he up to? She didn't like how he looked at them. Two men passed by, doffed their hats and said, *God dag.* The girls nodded and clasped one another's arms. They located the post office, easily identified by the Norwegian flag flying above it, and dropped off the letters and parcels that had been entrusted to them. The kindly post agent directed them to the milliner's shop.

"*Gud dag, jenter,* may I help you?" the shopkeeper asked when they entered, as though they might be lost. Anna elbowed Mette.

"*Gud dag,* madam," Mette said nervously. "*Ja, takk,* I must have a hat to wear to America." Why did she say to America? She didn't need to know that.

"Going to America, are you?" She looked at Mette with a bit more interest. Madam had a tape measure around her neck, and a pin cushion on her wrist, like a bracelet. She came from behind the counter and looked at Mette from her head to her shoes.

"*Ja,*" Mette said with a little bend in her knees, not at all sure why she did that. She didn't think one had to curtsey to a shopkeeper. "Just a plain hat."

"Plain, hmmm," Madam said. She looked around at the hats on display in her small shop, some elaborate with many flowers, feathers and ribbons, some small, some with veils, wide-brimmed and narrow-brimmed. For someone who had never owned a hat, Mette couldn't believe how many different kinds there were. The shop smelled of perfume and was so fancy, it made Mette feel out of place and homesick. She wanted to flee back to Fimreite, but Anna had her firmly by the arm.

"I think this would suit you," Madam said, walking over to the wall and removing a hat from the hook. She held it aloft and turned it around. It was called a boater, the woman said, straw with a brim to keep the sun out, a light blue satin ribbon around the short crown and a flat bow on the side.

"*Komm,*" the milliner said, directing her to a mirror. She placed the hat on Mette's head, made an adjustment, secured it with the hat pin, and turned Mette to face the mirror.

Mette swallowed. Was that her? Could a hat change a person that much? She looked fashionable, she looked pretty.

"Mette, you look very nice," Anna said.

"How much is it?" Mette asked.

"Three kroner. It's a good price."

"That's too much," Mette said. "Do you have anything cheaper?"

The shopkeeper sighed. "I'm afraid not."

"Let me see if I can...." Anna started to say but Mette interrupted her.

"No," Mette said to her. "That's too much."

"You might try mail-order. You might find something for less."

"*Takk,*" Mette said.

The girls left the shop downhearted. That was not how the day was supposed to go. They did not know hats were so expensive.

But as they were crossing the street, the milliner called to them.

"*Jenter, kommer,*" the woman said, and motioned for them to come back. "How much can you afford?"

"I had hoped no more than two kroner," Anna said, a bit embarrassed.

"Fine. You shall have it for two kroner. I should like one of my hats to go to America."

"Two kroner," Mette said. "But that's still too...."

"*Takk*," Anna said. "*Mange takk*."

"Well, you are a pretty girl," she said to Mette, "and my hat makes you even prettier. You could do with some nicer clothes though."

Anna spoke up again. "We're going to the dressmaker next."

Once outside, they broke into laughter. "We're going to the dressmaker, are we?"

"Yes," Anna sniffed. "You shall have a dancing frock."

Mette and Anna splurged on day-old sweet rolls and ate them while they walked through the town looking in shop windows and doing their errands. So many things to see in the village, so many people coming and going, stylish ladies and men in suits, boats arriving and departing. Flowers spilled from the window boxes of white houses, and everything was neat and clean.

"Think of it," Mette said, "this must be what Bergen is like, only bigger." She began to feel heartened that if she could do this, she could manage Bergen and after Bergen, New York City.

The church tolled two bells, plenty of time to get home. They said good-bye to Sogndal, and Anna, at least, promised she would be back soon. She wondered if the milliner could use an assistant. As *Stedje* church was on their way, they decided to go in and sit for a while. It was cool in there and they both had much to be thankful for. They prayed that a kind traveler would give them a ride as they were laden down with packages. Back on the road, Anna began to sing as she walked, and Mette joined in, her hat box bumping against her leg.

ଓ

She didn't sleep the night before; she couldn't. She gazed at the fading stars through the small window, and remembered what Finn had said, that when he was in America, he'd see the same stars. Now she imagined them falling from the sky as God said they would at the end of the world.

She got up quietly although her mother was probably already awake. She prayed as she dressed by the dim light of the pre-dawn. *The Lord is my shepherd, I shall not want...* She fastened her *solje* at her throat and fingered the tiny discs. *Yea, though I walk through the valley of the shadow of death, I will fear no evil, for Thou art with me, Thy rod and thy staff comfort me...* As he had done with Finn, Ingebrigt was going to take her and the two others by boat to Hermanswerke, to catch the ferry to Bergen. Panic like black ink seeped across her chest and into her throat and she held a handkerchief to her mouth and gagged. She checked again that she had the ticket, which was in an envelope she had pinned to the inside of her dress.

It was going to be a hot day. She went outside to use the toilet and then washed up. She looked at herself in the mirror that hung in a cloth sling, brushed her long dark hair and tied it into a neat braid, then put on her new hat. It didn't bring her the same pleasure as it had the day she bought it. It was just a hat.

Synnøve poured coffee for her and set out porridge and flatbrød. Mette wasn't hungry but she sat at the table and sipped the coffee, nibbled the flatbrød, while she stole glances at her mother, not knowing what to say. What was there to say? The lines in Synnøve's face had deepened overnight it seemed. Her hair was pulled tightly back in a bun, and she wore a black scarf around her neck. All the times Mette had wanted to get away from her, now she couldn't believe she would never see her again. The rocker creaked as Synnøve rocked back and forth, back and forth, a clutched handkerchief to her face. The knock at the door startled them.

"Well now," Ingebrigt said as he came in. "Today is the day." He shook hands with Mette, then with Synnøve. He looked at her hat, but didn't mention it. "Are you ready then?"

Mette stood. "*Ja, ja,* I am ready."

"Are you all right?" he asked. "You look ill."

"I'm fine, just a little nervous," she said.

He picked up her valise which she had moved to the door, and the bag of provisions Synnøve had prepared for the trip—flatbrød and dried mutton, a bottle of bilberry juice, and two jars of cloudberry jam. The time had come, the time she had dreaded since Finn first said the word "America." She stood awkwardly at the door. "*Mor...*" she began.

"*God være med du, datter,*" Synnøve said, coming to her. God be with you. She put her rough hand over Mette's, and then suddenly, "Don't forget me."

"*Aldri,*" Mette cried. Never. She threw her arms around her mother. She could not hold the tears back any longer. She could not be leaving home forever. She could not.

"*Adjø, mor, adjø.*" She wiped her face and held tightly to Ingebrigt's arm. Synnøve walked with them down to the shore, holding on to Mette as though she'd never let go. Niels and Elin waited for them. Elin stood sternly, nodded at her, and Niels held out his hand which she shook. Ingebrigt put the bag in the boat and turned to offer his hand to help Mette.

She had one foot in the boat when Synnøve called to her, then collapsed to her knees. Elin tried to help her stand, but the woman was broken by grief. Mette turned to go to her then she, too, buckled. Ingebrigt got his arm around her just as she began to go down.

"Mette," he said. "What is it?" He walked her to a place where she could sit.

"I feel sick." She turned her head and vomited, then pulled her handkerchief from her sleeve and pressed it to her mouth. The others ran down to her, but Ingebrigt stretched his arm to stop them. She retched again.

"I...I...the ship..." she murmured to him.

He put his ear next to her mouth to hear better.

"What do you mean? What about the ship?"

"I can't go. Finn will have to understand. God help me."

He hesitated. "But Mette, there's still..."

"No," she cried. "No, I can't go. I will die." She gripped his arm and pressed her head against it.

He looked at her in alarm. "Die? Why do you say that?"

"God has shown me! I will drown!"

He waited for a moment, aware that time was ticking by. "Are you sure you want to do this?"

"Yes," she said through tears, and then resolutely, "I am sure." With those words, the weight she'd been carrying ever since Finn first spoke of America, lifted just a little.

Anna came. She had rowed over from Ølmheim to say goodbye. She jumped out of the boat, pulled it to land, then ran to Mette.

"Mette, what is it? What's wrong? Are you ill?" She put her arm around her friend's shoulder.

"I can't go, Anna," Mette sobbed. "I can't."

"But you promised Finn..."

"*Nei*, Anna, I couldn't promise." She reached up to pull out the hat pin, and took off the hat.

"Here," she said, handing it to Anna. "I want you to take this back."

"*Nei, nei*, Mette. It's still yours."

"It will always remind me of today. You wear it to America."

Ingebrigt brought her valise to her. She felt sorry for everything in it—the dress, the skirt and blouse, two pairs of bloomers, a pair of stockings, her nightgown, her carding combs, a coverlet, her Bible and hymnal. She felt sorry for Anna's hat and for the milliner who had wanted it to go to America. But it was for Finn she was most sorry.

"God must have His reasons," Ingebrigt said, searching for the right thing to say.

Synnøve and Elin came towards her, but Mette turned her back to them. She wanted to see Ingebrigt depart. She watched him push off, then hop in the boat. He lifted his cap. She held Anna's hand and rocked back and forth. She was not the person Finn thought she was. She had never been as brave as he was. She wanted to pretend she was on that boat, on her way to him, that this was just a bad dream, one she would wake from in America with Finn at her side.

െ

Kjare Finn,

Now I am writing to tell you what I think you already knew, and may always have known. I cannot go to America. But you see that by the ticket you now have in your hand. If you were here, you would see me on my knees, my hands clasped together, begging you to forgive me, begging you to understand that I do not have the courage. You must believe me when I say that I truly meant to go. I did as you said. My suitcase was packed, I had provisions for the trip. I even had one foot in the boat. Finn, please believe me when I say that there is nothing I want more than to be your wife, but going to America is not God's will for me. He made me see that the journey may not take me there. I must stay in Norway, it is what God wants. I remember when we were children, when we crossed a stream, how you would go first, then reach back for me and help me across. But this time I cannot follow you. I think of you building our house, the house we imagined. Putting up the walls, pounding the nails, making a home for us. My tears do not stop. I'm sorry, Finn. I'm so very sorry that I have betrayed you, but I believe I am doing God's will. I send you my love, always true. Mette.

A letter from Finn crossed hers in the mail. He had evidently sent it at the same time she'd sent hers. It was a photograph of him. He sat in a chair and looked to be in his Sunday best, in a jacket and tie and a newsboy's cap angled rakishly to the side. He looked directly at the camera in seriousness, but she could see merriment in his eyes. On the back, he wrote: *This is so you'll recognize me when I come to fetch you in Madison. Until then! Yours, Finn.*

1878

Who is this that appears like the dawn, fair as the moon, bright as the sun? Mette lay in bed beside her mother remembering when Finn had said that to her. What would he think of her now? She looked over at her mother who slept soundly, her mouth open, her cheeks sunken from lost teeth.

She had not bled in two months. She clutched her nightgown in a ball at her chest and searched the darkness. God had not heard her prayers or He was punishing her. She pressed a hand to her belly. It hadn't been the same with Ingebrigt as it had been with Finn where it was more like play. With Ingebrigt, it had been real, the way babies are made. She groaned softly thinking of it, and tears started.

She blamed the dance, the music, the way it emboldened them. She remembered it as one remembers a dream. The fiddler's music, the swirling skirts of the girls, the crack of the boys' boots on the wooden floor of the parish hall, the windows frosted from the cold. She saw Ingebrigt in his waistcoat coming towards her, the slight limp in his left leg.

He wasn't as handsome as Finn, but, like him, he had his father's blue eyes and his mother's high forehead. His hair was already thinning and his ears stuck out a little, but she really didn't see those things so much anymore. Ever since That Day, as she thought of it, when she stepped out of the boat, he had been gentle and kind to her. He didn't push, but he offered help, and his visits were comforting. More than comforting, reassuring. She looked forward to them. It was soon known to everyone that he had begun courting her in earnest, even though Ole Ellingson was against it. She had not refused him. Why should she? He was her best, and probably only, hope.

She was surprised he could dance. When he stood before her offering his hand, she took it in hers, keeping her eyes down, and followed him. They walked in time together, his arm around her, then she twirled under their raised hands, just the fingers touching. He wasn't the best dancer in the parish, but neither was she. They did well enough. The fiddler played and they danced many times that night. She had smelled beer on his breath, but he didn't seem drunk. His face was flushed in the heat as was hers, and they went round and round, so she felt a little dizzy.

Afterwards, he walked her back to the cottage in the cold fresh air. He put his arm around her waist and she let him. It was pleasant to have the attention of a man. When they got to the barn, he stopped and pulled her inside. Before she could say a word, he took her in his arms and kissed her. He had kissed her before, but not like that. She felt him hard against her. He'd waited so long, he said, he wanted to lay with her.

He kissed her on the mouth again and again, and then he pressed her down onto the hay. She didn't resist when he lifted her skirt, and when his hand went to her breast, she felt the same desire she'd felt with Finn. He grunted into her ear as he undid his pants. She promised herself it wouldn't happen again, but it had. It was as though they couldn't help themselves. They were drawn to the other like the bull and the cow.

Gud i himmelen, kan du hjelpe meg. God in heaven, please help me. Her crying woke her mother.

"What is it? What's wrong, *pike*?"

"Mor, jeg beklager." I'm sorry.

Her mother looked at her hard, searched her face. "*Pike*, what have you done?"

ଓଃ

She'd betrayed Finn and lain with his brother. It wasn't exactly sin as it used to be the custom, bundling, that way of becoming acquainted while courting. But now the church spoke against it. Too many illegitimate children, too many men fleeing when they found out they were to be fathers and too many poor women forced to raise their children alone. Mette chewed on her lip. She was lucky, she had work, she had a home, such as it was, and she worked for a good family. She would not have to beg if it came to that, and she was sure Ingebrigt would not forsake her.

As for Finn, his response to her letter had come swiftly. It was short and Mette felt his anger.

Dear Mette,

I will answer your letter which was hard to take. I might have known this was coming, but I held out hope that once you had the ticket, you would overcome your fears, and see the opportunity this country offers us. This is a rich country, Mette, and we could have made a good life here. We still can, if only you were willing to try. There is not much else to say to convince you. I've said all I could and even sent you a ticket. If you are content staying put, then so be it. I must believe you know what is best. May God bless you. Finn.

She had read the letter over and over, and thought of burning it so she'd never have to see it again, but then decided to keep it because every word, every letter from him, even that one, was precious to her. She wrapped it and his other letters and picture in a small linen cloth she had woven just for that purpose, and placed them at the bottom of her trunk. She believed, she had to believe, that she had done what God wanted. She couldn't say how much Ingebrigt had to do with it. Perhaps knowing he would marry her and they would stay in Norway, had allowed her to say no to America. She believed he was honest in his love for her, and she would be a good wife to him. But he would never take Finn's place in her heart, never. God did indeed work in mysterious ways.

She was going to have to write another letter to Finn to tell him herself that she was pregnant and was going to marry his brother. She hoped he would understand, even give them his blessing. But maybe that was too much to ask.

☙

Mette studied her reflection in the mirror, turning her head from side to side. She didn't look any different. No one would know she had a baby inside her. Before long, the whole world would see her growing belly. The thought of it made her turn red with shame. She planned to tell Ingebrigt that night and that made her nervous. Would he be angry? Blame her? She believed he would be fair, that he would claim the child as his, and that their intention to marry would be announced, and, once married, the baby would be legitimate. She had many worries, but the biggest was Ole Ellingson, who had not changed his mind about her.

Behind her was the click click click of the spinning wheel as her mother spun wool into yarn. Mette wove her hair into one long braid and tied it with a ribbon, then wrapped a floral kerchief on her head, tied it under her chin, and tucked in the loose hairs.

"Ingebrigt is coming?" Synnøve asked.

"Yes," Mette said.

"Remember..." Synnøve started to say, but Mette pulled her cloak from the hook and hurried out the door. She did not want to hear another lecture.

There was a mist over the fjord and the waves were choppy, but she could see Ingebrigt's shape and the movement of his arms as he approached. When he reached the shore, he walked to the prow of the boat as skillfully as a dancer and jumped out without so much as getting his heel wet, and pulled the boat on land. "*God aften*," he said, taking off his hat and bowing. She smiled at his courtliness, and took his offered arm. They walked along the edge of the fjord, toward the wood, the Fimreite mountain loomed over them. This is my husband, she thought, *min mann*, and gave him a shy side-glance, and then she thought of Finn, even though she no longer pretended Ingebrigt was him.

They walked in silence as she gathered her courage.

"I believe it will rain tonight," she said, feigning great interest in the sky and clouds.

"Yes, I think you may be right," Ingebrigt said and looked up. They walked on quietly for a while. Occasionally Ingebrigt would pick up a stone and hurl it into the fjord.

"I think we ought to get married soon," she blurted out.

Ingebrigt smiled as he threw another stone. "That we will soon enough. But there are many things to be done."

Mette pulled his arm to stop him. "I think perhaps we should make it a little faster because..." She looked down at her belly and mumbled, "...because I am on the way."

"On the hay? What did you..."

"*Way.* I'm...it's..."

It was impossible to speak to a man of these things. With her hands, she made a rounding motion over her belly.

He stopped then, took her arm and turned her to face him. "You mean...?"

She nodded, clenching her lips together, and looked down.

"When?" he asked.

"November, I think."

He appeared to be calculating in his head as he stared out at the sea. "The devil," he said. He slapped his cap against his leg. "The devil in hell." He turned her towards him and said, "Are you sure, Mette Hansdatter?"

"As sure as I can be."

"Maybe you've made a mistake, you could be just..."

Mette turned away from him. She would not discuss how she knew.

"I know," she said firmly.

"Am I...?" He hesitated. "Am I the father?"

She felt as though he'd struck her.

"What do you mean?"

"Did you and Finn?"

"Finn! No, we..." A crack of thunder sounded so loudly it startled them. Both peered up at the sky. Even at her age, she still thought of

Thor driving his thunderous cart across the heavens, lashing the wild billy goats, their hooves flashing with lightening. It still frightened her.

But this. She couldn't guess how much he knew about her and Finn.

"You are the only man I've...known."

"Do you still think of him?"

"I will say that I don't."

It began to rain then, lightly at first, but then harder. Neither of them moved. They hadn't even made it halfway to the wood.

Finally she said matter-of-factly, "We don't need to get wet," and began to walk back. More thunder rumbled across the heavens.

"Mette, wait."

The rain was coming down now. Her kerchief was plastered to her head and her clothes were giving off an unpleasant odor. She turned and looked at him through the veil of rain and said, "You can be sure of me, you must know that."

He reached for her and pressed her to him. "It's just that I...I don't have anything," he said, low and anguished, into her neck. "I can't marry you until I have enough money and we have a place to live, and I don't know when that will be. And you know father, he won't...well, you know father."

Yes, she knew the old goat, and she knew he would be hard on Ingebrigt when he learned of this. But Ingebrigt was going to have to stand up for himself, and she knew his father would not want to see him fail.

She was soaked through and through and just wanted to get out of the rain, but, instinctively, almost maternally, her arms went up and around Ingebrigt's shoulders and she returned his embrace. "It's you and me now," she said. "Until death do us part."

As far as Mette was concerned, they were married that day with the rain pouring down on them like holy water. How it would become official, she did not know.

ೞ

Ingebrigt could only blame himself. He had practically forced himself on her, but he had been patient for so long. Finn's memory was too strong at first, but as they got to know one another and she grew more comfortable with him, she allowed his arm around her, then a kiss on the cheek, then on the lips. What happened in the barn came almost six months after he'd formally began courting her.

He was going to be a father. Even though this was not the way he would have wanted it, he couldn't help but smile that everything was in good working order, and with Mette, too. She would give them children. If it was a boy, all the better. He was going to have to announce his intentions. That meant speaking to his father, and he would rather hold his hand in boiling fat than do that. With a child involved, it was possible Ole Ellingson would be more lenient. Ingebrigt couldn't hold America over his head this time, as even his father would know he would never abandon Mette in her condition. His second thought was to have his mother there when he spoke to him. She'd always liked Mette and would stand up for her. He watched his father to see when the best time would be, when he was most relaxed, and that seemed to be after the evening meal, after they'd read from the Bible and a story or two had been told.

That gave him an idea.

One warm spring evening about a week after Mette had given him the news, after everyone had eaten and the dishes had been put away, they did as they usually did, sat at the table, smoking their pipes. Kristi sat in her rocking chair with her knitting. After Ole read from the Bible, Ingebrigt said he'd like to tell a story. They all turned to him with interest. Ingebrigt put a hand on each knee and leaned forward.

This is the story of a prince who was looking for a wife. His father, the king, had arranged many meetings with the finest ladies in the land, but none were the one for him, so one day he got on his horse and decided to look for himself. He left the castle disguised as a peasant in the dark of night.

Ingebrigt searched their faces to see if any of them had figured out what he was doing.

He went up the mountain and down the valley, across the fjord and over the hill, and had many fine adventures but no luck. But one day, while he was up on a mountain, he chanced to pass a summer pasture and when he stopped, a kindly dairymaid offered him a cup of milk. He was struck by her beauty, her long flaxen hair, her fair face, and, her, here he hesitated, *uh, womanly ways. The milk she offered him was delicious, tasting of the sweetest clover and alpine grass. She poured him another when he'd finished the first.*

"*Where is your home?*" *he asked her.*

"*I live in a little cottage in the valley with my poor father.*"

"*I am a prince,*" *he said,* "*and my castle is over yonder behind the mountain, and I should like to make you my princess, but my father will not allow me to marry a dairymaid.*"

Ole Ellingson stood. "I see where this is going," he said.

"Father," Ingebrigt said and also stood. "I must ask you again for your permission to marry Mette Hansdatter."

"And you know I will not give it."

"But now you must because she is...she is..."

"She is what?" He peered at him sharply.

Was he to say it in front of everyone?

All eyes looked down, the knitting stopped, the room silenced. There was no need to say anything.

Ole spoke first. "She's a clever woman, getting herself in a fix so you will have to marry her."

"I must ask you not to speak of her like that. I am the one to blame."

"Are you sure you're the father?"

"Yes, I know I am."

"No man knows for sure."

"I do, *far*."

"I predicted it would come to this," he boomed. "The farm will never prosper if I allow such matches. Two of my sons have run off to America, two don't even bother to *look* for a wife, and now you want to marry a milkmaid! What is to become of Jonsbrygga!"

"*Far*, Mette will help the farm prosper. She's a good worker, a good woman and now we have a child on the way. *Far*, please, I beg you, please give us your blessing."

Ole looked at him for a bit, then sat down. "How did you plan to end your story?"

"With the king's blessing. But that only happens in fairy tales."

ଙ

Mette began her last letter to Finn. When she thought of him now, it was more as an old friend, mixed with shame and a little resentment. He shouldn't have left. He shouldn't have put her in the position of having to choose. It was his fault. But, no, it wasn't his fault, it was her fault. She was the disappointment. But then she had never completely agreed to go, she had never promised. She went round and round in her head with these conversations, what she said or didn't say, what he said, what could have been, what was.

She hadn't been honest when Ingebrigt asked if she still thought of Finn. She did still think of him, not all the time, but he had her heart first, that would always be true. She poised her pen over the square of blank paper and pressed her lips together, thinking of the best way to say what she had to say. At least she didn't have to look him in the eye when she told him.

Kjare Finn,

Well now, it has been a whole year since I last wrote. I hope you are in good health and that your farm is doing well. I pray that you have forgiven me. Now I am writing to tell you that Ingebrigt and I are going to be married. He has been kind to me since you left and when it was clear I would stay here, he asked if he could visit me. Not before then, I want you to know. Now I must tell you something else so you hear it from me. I am expecting a child in a few months. Your father is not pleased as you can understand and we are still waiting for his permission. We hope to marry in a year or so, when Ingebrigt has saved enough money. I hope you will understand. I hope you will find a good Norwegian woman who will make you a good wife. May God bless you and keep you. Mette.

A tear fell on the paper and made the ink run. She quickly blotted it with her apron. "A good wife" was smeared, but it could still be made out. She thought of copying the letter on a new piece of paper, but then decided the tear was true and she let it be.

ଓଃ

In the dark of winter, the cry of the newborn was like a shoot of green. Mette opened her eyes. She was in the chamber in the main house. She had not died. *Gud ske lov.* Praise God. She heard the fire crackling in the stove so the others were up. The light was dim, the sun barely made it over the horizon in November so even though the day had begun, it was dusk light. Her child was beside her, squirming and crying to be fed.

Overnight, everything had changed.

Mette ran a finger over her son's cheek and picked him up to look at him in the dim light. She unswaddled him and felt his hands, kissed his little fingers and his tiny fingernails. She cupped his feet in her hand, happy that he had all ten toes. She checked his organ, just to make sure. God had given her a fine little boy who looked very much like his father, even Ole Ellingson would be able to see that.

She wrapped him up tightly again so he looked like a caterpillar, and held him to her warm breast, kissed his forehead. He was an angel come from God and a bearer of His light. She felt the silver cross her mother had sewn in the hem of the swaddling fabric. The child would need constant protection until he was baptized, until then he was at great risk, not least from the *hulderfolk* who, if they got the chance, would exchange one of their ugly babies for hers. She felt a dark wave of fear when she thought of all the things that could happen to him. She held him closer, then awkwardly helped him find the breast and soon the crying stopped. She would be a good mother to him, she promised. She already could feed him, that was something.

How she wished Anna were there. She hardly saw her anymore since she moved to Sogndal, and she missed her awfully. Anna would have many good things to say about this little one. She would be his godmother, Mette decided.

"Of course you're hungry," she crooned. "You've come so far, all the way from heaven, haven't you, *lille* Ole?" It felt strange calling him that. While it was the custom for the first son to be named after the father's father, Ingebrigt had not completely agreed to that, or rather Ole Ellingson hadn't. She feared what would happen if they couldn't name him properly. She kissed the infant's forehead and hoped he would not grow up to be like his grandfather, and then asked God to forgive her for thinking that.

Yesterday seemed like years ago. She had been sitting by the hearth in the cottage carding wool when she felt the first pain. Terror shot through her. While she believed with all certainty that if she died, her soul would go to heaven, she wasn't quite ready to die. When the first pain passed and she was fine, she thought, *that wasn't so bad*. But then another one had come, and another, and soon they were very close together. Synnøve ran to Elin, who told her to bring Mette to the house, and then Elin sent for Gudrun, the minister's wife, who was a healer and the *hjelpjente,* birth helper. Even though the women at Fimreite could handle the birth themselves, it was the law that a *hjelpjente* be present so there wouldn't be any "accidents." Gudrun was a big woman and kind, with gentle hands. She was never without her black bag, which held her potions, salves and tinctures, and always sweets for the children. Mette thought of her as a kindly mother bear. She swayed when she walked and seemed to fill the room when she entered it.

Mette knew a little something about pain, but nothing like what was to come. It was startling how huge it was and what power it had. She made herself concentrate on a task, like weaving or embroidering, and do it step by step. She counted stitches in an imaginary knitting to keep her mind straight. She breathed, she tried to think of the birds flying high in the sky, she thought of the owl in the wood, her friend. She squatted on the floor and held on to the side of the bed as though she were careening down the mountain on a toboggan. She grunted and cried out. "Push," Gudrun said, her hand on her back. "Push, Mette."

Now, with her child in her arms, it all seemed like a murky dream.

"Who is the father?" Gudrun had asked. It was her responsibility to report the birth to the parish.

"Ingebrigt Olesson Nornes is the father. He will say so."

She was hungry now. She hoped her mother had made porridge. She could eat a tub of it. A cup of coffee with thick cream and sugar would be good, too. When the child was through suckling, she buttoned her blouse and got up, thinking she would get dressed and make the coffee, but she wasn't as strong as she thought. She sat back down.

"*Er du våken da?*" her mother said as she poked her head in the room.

"*Ja, ja,*" she said.

"*Ingebrigt er her.*"

She made herself stand, held on to the wall until she felt steady. She brushed her hair and quickly tied a neat braid. She pulled on the skirt that was lying on the chair where she'd left it, and an apron over that.

"*Kommer da,*" she said. She heard the heavy thud of steps and there he was, bringing the outside cold into the room. He carried a lantern and set it down on the table, then pulled off his hat and gloves, and dropped them on the bed. Mette picked up the baby and held him near the light so he could see.

"God has given us a son," she said. She held the child out to him, but he shook his head.

"I'll make him cold." He studied the tiny face of his son and smiled.

"A fine, healthy boy, that's good." He looked at her. "God be praised. I'm glad to see that you are fine then."

"I am well enough."

"Good, that's good." He cleared his throat, but said nothing.

"Is there something you have to say?"

Ingebrigt sat on the bed beside her and clutched his cap. "*Far* has said we cannot name the child Ole. As we are not married, he…can't be sure…"

Mette interrupted him, "That the child is yours?" Her honor was being questioned again. She shook her head in disgust. Ingebrigt's face was filled with anguish, so she thought he might cry. She put her hand on his. "He need only look at the boy to see he is his grandson."

Ingebrigt peered at the sleeping child. "That may be true, but he will not budge on this."

"The Old Ones say a child will resemble the one he is named for, so perhaps it is not the worst thing for him not to be named after that…man." She didn't want to speak ill of him and bring further misfortune on her son. "Still, he must know that he puts the child at risk by not naming him properly."

"What if we named him after your father?"

"I wouldn't name a goat after that man."

They were both quiet as they looked at their son. Finally, Mette spoke. "The feast of Andrew is this month. What if we named him Anders after the Lord's first apostle."

Ingebrigt smiled broadly and shook her hand. "*Ja, ja,*" he said. "That is a good name." He touched the child's forehead in blessing. "May Saint Andrew guide and protect you, Anders Ingebrigtson, my son."

"*Our* son," Mette said.

☙

The birth of his first grandson was a dilemma for Ole Ellingson. He felt an inclination, a leaning towards the child, but the whole thing was disgraceful. God would want him to be merciful, to forgive them, to agree to the marriage, but that was more than he could do. He had put his foot down and Ingebrigt had as good as stepped on it.

Ingebrigt had gone to the pastor and requested the baptism, and with help from his mother, they planned a small celebration in the spring. By doing this, he made it known to the parish that Anders was his child, and that he meant to make Mette his wife. Even if he was against it, Ole had to admire his son for that.

Ole was noticeably absent from the baptism, and Kristi had forbidden him to attend the party if he could not be civil. "Do not offend God with your anger and hatred," she said. So when the others were gathered together in the house, he stayed in the woodshed, dark and cold as it was, where a small stove gave some heat. That is where Niels found him sitting with a knife and a stick, whittling.

"There you are," Niels said, clapping a hand on his shoulder. "Congratulations on a healthy grandson. The Lord has blessed you."

Ole snorted. "A bastard."

"Only because of you. The boy and girl should get married."

"Did Ingebrigt send you out here?"

"No. Look here, Ole, you must do something. I don't want to lose Mette, but they ought to be together, and it's up to you as Ingebrigt's father to give them a bit of land so they can start their life together. That is the proper thing to do."

Ole Ellingson glared at him from under his bushy eyebrows. "You should mind your own business."

"I feel this *is* my business as it concerns Mette."

"I'll run my farm and my family the way I see fit."

Niels squinted at him. "Well then, what if Ingebrigt were to move across the fjord with us?"

Ole sized him up, to see if this was a real offer or if he was just judging his reaction, decided it was the latter, then went back to whittling. "The problem is not where they should live. It's that she's a servant."

"We've all been in service at some point, Ole, even you. It's honest work."

"God damn it! You know what I mean. He can do better than that. What does she have to offer? A carding comb?"

Niels pulled over a stool and sat. "Ole, have you forgotten she is one of the finest weavers in our parish? Her mother is skilled at spinning. Think of what that brings to your family. And if that's not enough, then remember, she also has your son and your grandchild."

Ole glowered at him and thought for a moment of grabbing him by the neck. Niels instinctively drew back.

"Ask God for His help, Ole. Just as he has forgiven your sins, so must you find it in your heart to forgive Ingebrigt and accept Mette and their child into your family."

"Leave," Ole snarled, getting to his feet. "Get out of here."

Niels slowly stood. "You have already lost two sons to America and now you threaten to exile another. Is that how you run your family, as you say? They're going to marry anyway, now that there's a child. It will make all the difference if they do so with your help and blessing."

Ole sat in the shed long after Niels had departed, even after the guests had left. He sat by the dim light of the lantern, whittling and thinking.

✿

One Saturday afternoon about a fortnight after the baptism, Ingebrigt put on his best suit and rowed across the fjord to Fimreite. He was not good with words, but he felt the occasion required him to say something memorable. *Today we begin a lifetime together, so with this ring...* As he thought that, he quickly touched his jacket pocket to make sure he had remembered it. Yes, it was there, his grandmother's gold band, given to him by his mother. He was the first of her sons to marry, she'd said, and wanted Mette to have it. Normally, one would wait for the wedding to give the bride a ring, but he decided he wanted her to have it now, as his promise to her, so she wouldn't lose faith in him. And because they had a son.

He still was not sure this wasn't some form of trickery. How had his father changed his mind? And would he change it back? His mother said it was the doing of her brother, Niels. That he'd talked to him at the baptism and made him see that giving his blessing to the marriage was the Christian thing to do, and had also reminded him of Mette's reputation as a weaver. Evidently, Ole had taken his words to heart because not long after that, he'd said to Ingebright that he would not stand in his way. It wasn't exactly a blessing, but at least he said that much. It meant everything to Ingebrigt.

As it was the first warm day of spring, he found Mette sitting outside the cottage.

"Ah, it's you," she said putting down her knitting. "And so dressed up. Are you going somewhere?"

"It is a special day," he said. "Would you like to walk?"

"Anders will be wanting to be fed soon," she said. "You seem pleased with yourself."

Ingebrigt reached into his pocket and drew out the ring and held it up.

"That can't be for me," she said, pulling back.

"This ring was my grandmother's and her mother's before that, and now it goes to you as my wife."

"You mean..."

"Yes," he said. "A miracle has happened. *Far* has agreed to our marriage."

"But how?"

"My uncle, we think. *Far* came to me yesterday and said, 'Do as you must.'"

"Master Niels spoke to him?"

Ingebrigt nodded. "*Mor* said he did, the day of the baptism. I think he's the only one who could have changed *far's* mind. Your skill as a weaver might have come into it."

Mette's face was a study of joy and bewilderment. Anders began to wail as though he had something to say about it, too.

"As I thought," Mette said. "I must go to him."

"Wait a while," Ingebrigt said. "I have something to say." He cleared his throat and held the ring up. "This ring means...." He looked at her, then out at the fjord. What was he going to say? "Today, we begin a lifetime together and...uh..." Then he remembered what she'd said to him the day in the rain when she told him she was pregnant. "It means that you can be sure of me," he said, lifting her hand to slip the ring on. "It means that you will be my wife."

"A gold ring," she said quietly.

Ingebrigt knelt beside her. "We'll have a proper wedding in a year or so." He took the ring from her and tried to put it on her finger. It was just a little too small, and as he tried to jiggle it over the knuckle, she stopped him.

"Let me," she said. She put the knuckle in her mouth to moisten it, then with just a little wiggling, she slipped it on. She held out her hand to admire it, a hand far too coarse for a girl of twenty. *Det var bra.* It was fine.

"*Takk,*" she said to him. "*Mange takk.*" She shyly kissed his cheek.

"Mette Hansdatter, I have finally won you," he said, and kissed her back. "Now then, let's tell our son."

ଔ

The weaving took over her thoughts, waking and sleeping. With the wedding date set for the following May, Mette had begun the *åkle*, the cover for the marriage bed. It was one of the most important things she would weave, and into it she would put her hopes for a good marriage, for children, for protection from the Ancients and from God. Synnøve had offered the yarn, a generous wedding gift, and one which Mette had difficulty accepting. It meant more work for her mother, and it pained Mette to see her rub cod liver oil into her hands each evening to ease the ache. And then, she carried some guilt for all the times she put the blame on Synnøve for keeping her from going to America. It was unfair, but in her darkest moments, it seemed that if it hadn't been for her mother, she'd be in America now. But those times were becoming less and less, and mostly they kept a civil peace.

The central motif of the coverlet was to be the tree of life, with roots deep in the earth and long branches extending to the heavens, which Mette felt was strong and holy, as she hoped their marriage would be. She'd seen a similar design in a shop in Sogndal, when she and Anna were there, and had studied it. Then she'd thought it would be for her and Finn. She wanted to include the owl, her guardian spirit, or so she believed, and the rose, the most beautiful of flowers. The border would be the cross and lily motifs and she was going to weave Ingebrigt's and her name into it, too. Her mother had dyed the yarn in Mette's choices, red, brown, yellow and green, and knew, from skill and experience, just how much yarn should be dyed in each color.

Mette began weaving in October when the work moved indoors. She did all her other chores quickly so she could get to the loom. She placed the cradle nearby so she could tend to Anders who watched his mother with curious eyes.

Her fingers moved as she slept. In her dreams the owl was the shuttle, flying in and out of the threads, the pattern appearing in its wake. Some nights she had to climb the tree higher and higher to continue weaving. The owl, made of linen and wool, would sit on her shoulder, and she had to instruct him to go back into the weave. The tree branches flowered where she hadn't woven flowers. The roses, the beautiful roses, bloomed in each corner so Mette could almost smell their perfume. When she woke, she felt as though she'd been at the loom all night.

When she tied up the last of the strings and the coverlet was finished six months later, she knew she hadn't done it alone. God's hand was in the weave, the owl's, the ancient ones, too, who spun the threads of life. Her mother had seen the work emerging with little to say about it, but when she saw it finished, she patted Mette's back and said, "well done," which made Mette glow inside. Mette hoped Ingebrigt would be pleased. She even dared to hope that Ole Ellingson might think she brought something of worth to the marriage.

1880

Hup! Hup! Hup! The fiddler sawed away on his fiddle and the Norwegian flag snapped in the breeze. Everyone wanted to dance with the bride for luck, and for that honor, they put an øre or two in a box. Mette was dizzy, and had to stop to catch her breath, but then there was someone else, so on and on she went, dancing, dancing into the warm night.

The day was a blur. She had had to hold tightly to Ingebrigt's arm to keep steady. She remembered the scent of wood roses as they rode to *Norum Kyrka*, Anna beside her, her reassuring words, the coolness of the church, the minister's black robe and stiff white ruffle, of him speaking of the duties of a married couple as they knelt at the altar, of the holy lives of Zacharias and Elizabeth, and urged them to have the same kind of faithfulness. She remembered his hand over their heads in blessing and the look of joy on Ingebrigt's face when they rose from the altar to walk out as a married couple. *A mighty fortress is our God*, the congregation sang. Ingebrigt tightened his grip and Mette smiled at her husband with happiness and gratitude. He was very handsome in his wedding finery.

She did not wear the crown, but no matter, it was well known that she and Ingebrigt had a son. She wore a white wimple, as white as the brightest cloud, made for her by Anna who had pursued her plan to be a milliner. From that day on, she would wear her hair up. Her dress was the traditional Sogn *bunad*, a skirt of homespun black wool with a crisp white linen apron, a green linen blouse, the traditional bride's color, and over it a black vest embroidered by herself over the long dark winter months, in bright colors, red, blue, green and yellow. Three ribbons hung from the scarlet wedding belt, yellow for her baptism, red for her confirmation and green for her marriage, each with a silver bell, which tinkled as she walked, to ward away any spirits who wished them harm.

She had dreamed of Finn the night before. They were young, herding on the mountain and he'd begun dancing, spinning around, kicking his legs in the air. He'd grabbed her hand and she danced, too, and the two of them twirled round and round, and then, with just a little hop, they were off the ground and in the air, higher and higher. It was so easy to fly, she wondered why they hadn't done it before. They flew together over the trees. She'd awakened with an ache in her heart. She missed him as much as she had right after he left. *Finn*, her heart cried. *Finn*. But she pushed all that down, and put on her best face for her husband.

The guests had brought enough food to last for days. Fruit soups, mountain fish in cream, baked cod, roast mutton, pickled herring, cheese, and soft rolls, and many bowls of rommegrøt sat on the long table; alpine strawberries and raspberries, cream waffles, cookies and cakes, and lots of good strong coffee sweetened with sugar and thick cream. Several bottles of homemade brandy were passed around as well as plenty of home-brewed wedding beer made by Ole Ellingson. While he was not happy about the wedding, he was not about to let the guests think he was poor.

Anders, who was already two, was a miniature Ingebrigt in his little suit and white leggings. He held his mother's hand and danced, played with the other children, and chased away the magpies that swooped around the food. By early evening, he was asleep on his grandmother Synnøve's lap, his little suit rumpled and dirty, his leggings more gray than white.

Drunk as an auk, Ole Ellingson came up to Mette and clapped a hand on her shoulder. "You got him, didn't you," he said thickly, just inches from her face, his eyes bleary. The smell of brandy on his breath was strong, and Mette instinctively pulled back. His arm felt like a great weight pressing down on her.

She tried to think of something kind to say, but just then Anna arrived. She grabbed Mette's hand and pulled on it.

"Ole Ellingson, you must come, too. Gunnar Hansson is going to dance the *halling*."

"*Takk*, Anna," Mette said and squeezed her hand.

"Be strong, Mette. It would do him no good to harm you."

They ran to the meadow where everyone was gathered in a circle. Erik hung a cap on a long pole, stood on a chair, and extended it into the circle.

"Higher," everyone called. He raised the pole a bit higher. "Higher," they called again, and he raised it even higher, higher than the height of a man.

Gunnar stood in the center of the circle and grinned. He motioned to Erik when the pole was at a good height. The fiddler played and Gunnar began to dance around the circle as though taking a stroll, his arms straight out, twirling around. Then he suddenly dropped to a squat, bounced up, strolled again, kicked up one heel, then the other, and slapped them. Round and round he danced. He passed by the cap again and again. But just when everyone thought the pole was too high, that he wasn't going to be able to do it, suddenly he leapt in the air, swung his leg up, kicked the cap off the branch, dropped to a squat, and then leapt to his feet. Everyone clapped and hooted, and slapped him on the back. Ingebrigt brought him a stein of beer, which he drank in one long swallow.

Tears came to Mette's eyes. She stood between Ingebrigt and Anna, and looked around at the circle of her family and friends. She'd done that, too, hadn't she? She had managed to "kick the cap" with her marriage to Ingebrigt. She had married into the family of a landowner, she was no longer a servant. The music cut sweetly through the night, the bonfire blazed. *Good-bye, Finn. Good-bye, America. This is where I belong, this is my place.* She would care for her mother in her old age. She would be a good daughter and a good wife.

⋈

"Cloud," Mette said to Anders, pointing to the sky.

Anders pointed, too, and repeated, "Clud."

"Sky," Mette said.

"Sky."

"Sea." She pointed to the sea. The little boy squealed with pleasure.

Mette stood at the shore with her trunk by her side. She and Anders waited for Ingebrigt, who was going to take them to Nornes where she would finally join him at Jonsbrygga. Synnøve would follow in a few weeks, as soon as the Larssons had found laborers to replace them. It was understood that when Mette moved, Synnøve would move with her. Ole Ellingson was not pleased with this arrangement, but that was how it was. The wife's mother would always have a home with her daughter. And then, too, Synnøve's spinning skills would be an asset to Jonsbrygga.

"See papa," she said and lifted his arm to wave at Ingebrigt. He raised both arms over his head.

"Papa," Anders said.

It was a fine warm day, the sky was the blue of her child's eyes, the clouds like washed fleece on the horizon, the sun glinted off the water. The wooded slope above Nornes was green and met the hazy blue of the mountains behind it. It was beautiful, yes, but more beautiful was land of her own, her own house, a promising future where they had it good, and her children would never be hungry.

She admired the shoulders of her husband and his strong arms as he pulled toward the shore. She saw by his grim expression that he was not in a good mood. This errand was taking him away from his work. She had learned something about Ingebrigt and that was he had a fair bit of his father in him. She nodded in greeting, and said little as he helped her in the boat along with her trunk. She had acquired more things in the past few years, the bed cover, of course, more wool, eiderdown, another dress, two aprons, some good homespun cloth, a linen sheet, two burlap sheets, and other things that would be useful as the wife of Ingebrigt Olesson. And under all that, Finn's letters and his photograph.

Mette thought Ingebrigt seemed a bit surprised and pleased at the weight of the trunk. He took Anders from her while she got in the boat and then placed him in her arms. They pushed off from the shore of Fimreite, and headed towards Nornes. The words of Ruth came to her, *Thy people shall be my people.*

She held her son tightly on her lap as he babbled on. She hadn't anticipated her feelings for the boy, how fiercely she wanted to protect him from any harm. She thought how deep the water was, of the many who had drowned. She held him tighter. It wouldn't be long before he, too, would learn to row.

Mette looked back at Fimreite, her cottage, and her days of service. She turned to look forward to Nornes where she would be in a different kind of service. The oars splashed up and out of the water and down again, and Anders clapped his hands gaily. Underneath the pretty sunny day and the sparkling blue-green water, and all that lay ahead of her, she felt a dark layer of fear. She pressed her face to Anders' neck. She was going to have to prove to Ole Ellingson that his son had made a good choice.

☙

Nine months after the wedding, almost to the day, their second child was born, and appropriately named Kristina after Ingebrigt's mother.

1882

It was just a matter of time; still, when she heard the words, *I have taken a wife,* Mette dropped a stitch in her knitting. What foolishness. Finn had been gone over two years.

Her name was Telma, a Norwegian from Stavanger. She had emigrated with her sister about the same time as Finn, and worked on a neighboring farm. A daughter had been born just three months after they were married. Well, Mette thought, she was the last one to cast a stone. Why shouldn't he be with a woman after all this time? Her thoughts flew to her and Finn on the mountain, side by side, him brushing her hair away from her face. More foolishness. She was twenty-three and still thought like a young girl. You must act like a woman, she told herself.

The family had gathered near the stove to hear the reading of the letter and she felt they must all be looking at her, but she kept her eyes down, quietly listening. Erik read, and she nodded, as the others did, when Finn said he was making a home in the new land, and that he was glad he had emigrated. She felt a twinge of resentment that he had done so well without her. He went on to say they were expecting a second child in June, and that he hoped to send pictures when he could. She would very much like to see what his wife looked like. She would like to see Finn, too, if he had changed. He had not responded to her letter telling him of her pregnancy and her marriage to Ingebrigt.

"Mette?"

She yanked herself back to the present. Kristi was looking at her.

"I said, we should sort the wool from the shearing tomorrow."

"*Ja, ja,* first thing after the morning meal."

"Come children," Synnøve said abruptly. "Have I told you how the fox got the white at the end of his tail?" She motioned for Anders and Kristina to come sit beside her and began telling them the story which Mette had heard many times, but was happy to hear again.

That night in bed as they lay side by side looking up into the dark, Ingebrigt asked her, "Does it mean anything, then, this news?" She moved her head slowly from side to side, then realizing he couldn't see her, said, "No. I'm glad he has found a wife." It was good it was dark so he couldn't see her face. He turned toward her and began to pull her nightdress up. Even though she was tired, and wanted to think about Finn and the letter, she could not say no. It seemed he needed to be with her in this way almost every night, and she was discovering she did not always feel the same way.

"He has a wife, he's not coming back," he grunted in her ear, pushing deeper.

Their third child was conceived that night. Mette knew it. She was the child born of the news of Finn's marriage. They named her Synnøve after her mother, but called her Eva.

Ingebrigt was right, Finn was never coming back.

1885

Ingebrigt walked through the field of barley. Occasionally he squatted to examine a plant. The day was hot and dry, the sky clear and blue, not a cloud to be seen. He rubbed his chin and looked up, hoping a cloud had appeared since the last time he looked. No rain for three weeks and no sign of rain. The barley and rye stood half a meter high, the potatoes and turnips had flowered, but if it didn't rain soon, they would be in trouble. The window to grow the crops they depended on for money, for food, was so small. Every day counted. The Lord demanded trust, but when weeks passed and still no rain, they worried. Sometimes people turned to the old ways and buried this or that, or made a small offering to the Ancients. They put out special offerings for the *nisse*, the farm spirit, pieces of flatbrød, a dish of butter or cream.

Everyone remembered times when there wasn't enough to go around, when a family had to stretch a crop of potatoes over two seasons instead of one. It was hard to see the children holding their stomachs, having to settle for a piece of flatbrød and a bowl of porridge that was more water than grain. While Ingebrigt was squatting between the rows of barley, he prayed. He prayed and prayed. He took a handful of dirt and threw it. He did not want to be a man who could not provide for his family.

Ingebrigt had been right when he convinced his *far* that he and Mette should live at Jonsbrygga. They were needed there, especially Mette to help Kristi. Ole Ellingson had retired, and the farm passed to Erik, but since he didn't have a wife, Mette was on her way to being *husmor* of Jonsbrygga, which didn't sit particularly well with the old man. He had softened somewhat towards her, but he still hadn't completely accepted her. Once it seemed he might have, when he commented that her rommegrøt was good.

Norwegian law didn't allow Ole to merely pass ownership of the farm to the eldest son, it had to be recorded as a sale and a property tax paid to the government. Ole valued the farm at a price Erik could reasonably afford, and the appraisers deemed fair for tax purposes.

The farm's coffers were set aside for this purpose, to be used for the purchase, but still Erik had to take out a loan to pay the tax.

"For God's sake, man, go out and talk to someone!" Ole yelled at Erik. "A woman isn't going to walk through the door and ask if she can marry you." Erik listened with half a smile, but did nothing.

Ingebrigt was next in line. Should Erik die or move away, the farm would then pass to Ingebrigt, but he was in no rush. He liked things the way they were. He, Erik and Elling made a good team. None of them, though, not the brothers, not the women, not Ole Ellingson himself, could make it rain.

With times as they were, America crept into Ingebrigt's thinking. He didn't dare share his thoughts with Mette, knowing how she would react, but now with the crops at risk and their future uncertain, he began to ponder the idea. Maybe Finn and Lars had it right, and he was wrong.

While they waited for rain, out of the blue, a letter from America appeared. It was another hot day with a hazy sky, when Ingebrigt returned from the village with the letter. Mette was bent over the large wooden tub scrubbing clothes, and the strong smell of lye soap mingled with the fresh sea air.

"A letter from America," he said, holding it up. Usually a letter from America was something of an occasion, but he had an uneasy feeling about this one.

Mette wiped her hands on her apron and looked eagerly at the envelope. "From?"

"Ingebrigt Geirarne, of all people. To me."

Her face clouded. Mette had never met the sender of the letter, whom Ingebrigt was named after, but she had heard of him, and she knew that Finn had hoped to locate him when he got to America. He was Ingebrigt's step-grandfather, the second husband of Ole Ellingson's mother, Mari Lassesdatter, who had died many years ago. The story of her marrying a much younger man still went around at parties when the brandy was being poured. It was said that Mari Lassesdatter was a clever woman and good-looking, too, even at the age of forty when she was a *gamel jente*, an old girl. The men would illustrate this by hefting large imaginary breasts. Her first husband had died in the plague, as had his brother, and many wondered why she hadn't died, too, being so close to those that did, and then who should get the farm but her?

It wasn't but a year after that that she married Ingebrigt Geirarne, twenty years her junior, just a lad, and that set the parish jaws flapping. He was in service on the farm, and after her menfolk died, she leaned heavily on him, and one thing led to the other. Stories were pulled out of the air after that, some went so far as to say that she'd put a spell on him, that she was a *hulder,* a cow spirit, and they even claimed to have seen the tail beneath her dress. Geirarne fled to America, they said, when he found out what he had married. The more practical story was that he left when Mari Lassesdatter told him in no uncertain terms that he would never get any part of the farm, husband or no, it would stay in her family.

Mette sat down on the bench facing the sea and Ingebrigt sat beside her.

"It's a wonder he's still alive," Mette said. "He must be as old as Odin."

Ingebright sat looking at the envelope for so long, Mette wanted to grab it from his hands.

"We should wait to read it until after evening meal," he said. "So all can hear."

"You can read it again," Mette said.

Ingebrigt thought a bit, then took out the letter and read.

Dear Ingebrigt,

Now you are finally getting a letter from me. I admit with shame that I should have written to you long ago, and I have no good excuse. I hope you and your family are in good health. I can tell you that, except for my arthritis, I am well, may God be praised. He has chosen to give me a long life. You may have heard from others that I have settled here in Illinois, not far from your brother Finn, and I see him from time to time.

I ask your forgiveness in leaving your grandmother, but I hope you will realize that there was not much for me in Nornes where a man without land does not do well. I do not regret coming here as it has been good for me, although I miss Norway. I was not able to marry again and have lived as a bachelor all these years. That is why I am writing to you now.

Mette stiffened.

I have a hired man working the farm as I am too old to do much more than milk the cows, and even that is difficult. You are my namesake, and to you I am offering that you come to live here, and to take over the farm when I lay down my wanderer's staff.

Ingebrigt paused and looked at Mette who said nothing.

If you have married and have children, I will send tickets for the passage of all. I am sick and tired of darning socks and would welcome a woman in the house. God has been good to me and this is something I can do in memory of your grandmother. Well now, it's time for me to quit. The Lord be with you. Greet relatives and friends, and all who ask about me. I hope to hear from you soon.

Ingebrigt folded the letter and put it back in the envelope. He took a large pinch of loose tobacco from the pocket of his waistcoat and filled his pipe slowly and carefully.

"*Ja,*" was all he said. "*Ja, ja.*"

Mette turned to see what the children were doing. Anders and Kristina were playing a game, running to and fro, and Eva sat near the house banging rocks together. She looked down at her calloused palms and said something under her breath.

"Heh?" said Ingebrigt.

"Why does he not offer it to them that's there?" she said louder.

"I'm his namesake. That's as it should be."

"Then he should sell the farm and send the money to you, if he wants to give something to you." She stood up abruptly. "That's as it should be."

Ingebrigt nodded. Why did this letter come now, just when he'd been thinking about America? It seemed more than just a coincidence.

Mette straightened her shoulders and clasped one hand over the other on her belly. "You said you would never go to America," she said, looking out at the sea. "*Here I was born and here I will stay*, is what you've always said."

"*Ja-ja, sann,*" he said. "But I have never had a farm offered to me before."

"You should remember that Ingebrigt Geirarne went alone to America, with no wife," Mette said.

Ingebrigt blew a stream of smoke skyward. "The wife does as the husband does in this family."

A gull screamed, then another.

She stood. "America. It's like a great troll, luring people away with promises of gold and treasures. Maybe you should go talk to Terje Fimreite who came back without a kroner. Life wasn't so good for him." Any talk of America agitated her. "I can't sit around all day talking. I have work to do."

Ingebright scowled at her, then turned and walked to the house.

The next day, a breeze from the west, clouds began to gather and towards evening, the sky darkened. Hope rose in their hearts. Ingebright sniffed the air and smiled. After the evening meal, there was the low rumble of thunder in the distance. They cocked their ears. Then everybody left the table to go outside. Soon raindrops pocked the dirt and then more, and then it began to rain hard. They turned up their faces to feel heaven's blessing. Their prayers had been heard.

"It's still coming down good," Ingebrigt said that night in bed.

"Do you think the letter brought the rain then?" Mette asked.

Ingebrigt grunted. "God brought the rain and my answer."

They both slept well that night, the sound of the rain on the roof, and knowing they would not have to go to America. At least not yet.

1887

Mette sat near the stove and nursed her newborn. A boy finally, christened Ole. After three girls, they were beginning to think there was a curse on the family. Girls are necessary, but the farm depends on the boys. But here was Little Ole, at last one named for Ingebrigt's father, healthy and sucking for all he was worth.

They had five children now. She was making a baby every two years. If she continued this way, she could have seven or eight more children before she became an old woman. She shuddered at the thought. She knew having children wasn't going to be easy, nothing ever was, but she hadn't foreseen the constant worry, the endless fear of what could happen to them.

Each was different, too. Sigrid, the one after Eva, was so independent and brave, not shy at all as she had been as a child. Brown curls framed her face and her blue eyes were full of curiosity. She was almost two and always picking up this or that to examine it. More than once, Mette had had to run over and slap something out of her hand just as she was about to put it in her mouth. Her favorite word was "*hvofor,*" why? and she would say it all the day long, no matter what had been said to her. We must eat now. *Hvofor?* Time for bed now. *Hvofor?* Put your dress on. *Hvofor?* Metta had had to tether her because she tended to wander off, and Mette feared she'd walk into the fjord. *This one,* she thought sadly, *this one will go to America, I know it.*

As the children grew, work was assigned to them. That was the main thing, to do the work, to keep the farm going. Anders, already nine, was learning from Ingebrigt and his uncles. He took care of Mœrkei, feeding and brushing him, and could drive the cariole by himself, if necessary. He worked beside the men in the fields. Kristina and Eva, as young as they were, six and four, were beginning to knit. They could pick stones from the ground, and were learning to milk. It wouldn't be long before they went to the summer pasture.

Mette buttoned her blouse and hoisted the infant to her shoulder. She patted and rubbed his back while she walked. She sang softly to him. *Sove nå, sove nå, i Jesu navn.* Sleep now, sleep now, in Jesus' name. Jesus watch over this child.

☙

The lamp gave off a smoky, dim light. November, and even midday, it was dark. The wind blew hard and the snow drifted against the house. Mette kept a careful watch on little Sigrid, who slept fitfully on the bed near the stove. She had the coughing sickness and Mette well knew the consequences of that in one so young. The older girls, Kristina and Eva, sat with Kristi and carded wool, while Synnøve spun. The whir of the wheel and the rasp of the combs provided a soothing, monotonous sound. All felt what lurked in the room.

The brothers were outside preparing for the fall butchering, but Ingebrigt sat on the bed whittling a doll for the little girl. Every so often he'd look over at Mette who nursed Ole. She'd changed since their courting days ten years ago. While it was plain to see she treasured her children, she worried too much over every little pain, cough, cut or bump. It was as though a piece of her was in each of them, as though what happened to them happened to her. She had always been fearful, but with more at stake, she had become worse.

The coughing put them on edge, especially when she struggled for air. They had never heard such sounds from a child; it was as though she were being strangled. It was too much in one so young. Her little body was exhausted. When the coughing subsided, everyone waited until she took another choked breath, but they hated that, too, the gasping for air.

The good Gudrun came. She was run ragged because Sigrid wasn't the only child in the parish with the cough. She flew to Sigrid's side like a great black bird, took off her cloak and sat beside her. Her presence filled the room.

"Let me see, let me see. Poor child." She felt Sigrid's feverish forehead and her throat, as the little girl whimpered.

"Put this in water for her," she said to Mette, taking a bottle from her bag. "It should make her vomit. That might help." Mette did as she was told. Sigrid started coughing, so violently, it made Gudrun wince.

"*Mor*," the little girl cried and then began to cough again. Mette rushed to her side. Sigrid's dark curls were damp and pressed against her forehead and Mette brushed them away from her face.

"A wet cloth, please, and maybe a little brandy," Gudrun said, and Ingebrigt jumped to get it. The children gathered near, and Gudrun told them to move away so Sigrid wouldn't feel crowded.

Nothing Gudrun gave her seemed to help. Before she left, she put a hand on Mette's shoulder. "There's not much I can do. It's a bad sickness. I wish it weren't so." She put on her cloak. "She's in God's hands."

A day later, nothing had changed. Gudrun had suggested they give her watered down barley soup, but she couldn't swallow, and she was beginning to grow so weak, each cough ravaged her tiny body. Ingebrigt didn't know what to do. He couldn't make Sigrid better, and he couldn't ease Mette's fear. All he could do was pray with the others.

Just a week earlier, the four children had been playing in the snow together, throwing snowballs at each other and sliding down the hill on skis he had made for them. Mette smiled as she watched the little girl toddle after the older ones bundled up in a handed down winter coat that was too big for her. She looked like a little elf. Kristina had held her on her lap as they slid down the hill on a piece of elm bark. The only thing to complain about that day was the cold.

When she was through nursing, Mette laid little Ole, the swaddled infant, on a goatskin in the cradle that hung from the roof beam, and wearily pushed herself up from the chair to attend to her weak and feverish daughter.

"*Kom*," she said. She picked her up and Sigrid wrapped her legs around her waist and rested her head on her shoulder while Mette walked with her, and tried to soothe her by patting and rubbing her back. When her little body convulsed with coughing, it was all Mette could to do keep her in her arms. She looked out the window at the dark sky, the silhouette of the mountain, and beseeched God. *Hjelp denne jenta*, she prayed. *Help this little girl.*

When the coughing suddenly turned to a choke and then stopped, the room tensed. The scrape of the carders ceased, the creak of the rocking chairs, the voices, the footfall of the children. There was just the dull thud of a log dropping in the stove and the crackling of the fire.

"*Nei*," Mette said. "*Nei*." She began to shake the child, Sigrid's small head jerked forward and back like a ragdoll. Ingebrigt hurried over and picked her up by the legs and shook her upside down. "Sigrid," they both called to her. "*Pike*." Ingebrigt lay her back down on the bed and put his ear to her chest, then Mette stuck her finger into the girl's throat, but she was gone. Mette picked up the body and held it to her, and rocked back and forth.

"*Nei, nei*," she cried. Her wailing frightened the children and made little Ole cry. The grandmothers, who had seen too many children die, held their aprons to their faces. Kristi thought to open the door so Sigrid's spirit could fly to heaven.

Ingebrigt took the body from Mette's arms and held the child close before laying her on the bed. He closed her eyes and brushed a bit of damp hair from her forehead. The children crept over, and when Mette tried to move them away, he said, "*Nei*, let them." Kristina pet Sigrid's head, then kissed her sister's forehead, and began to cry. Anders patted her arm, then let his hand stay there. Ingebrigt wiped his eyes with his sleeve.

Eva, who was four, peered closely at the body and asked her mother, "Is she sleeping?"

"*Ja, ja*, that's right," Mette said, wiping her eyes. "She is finally sleeping." She kissed the warm forehead. "She is sleeping."

Eva stood beside her sister. She nudged the body, gave it a little push to wake her, but Ingebrigt stayed her hand, and said quietly, "Let her be."

But she persisted. "Sigrid," she said into her ear.

"*Nei, nei*. She can't hear you," Ingebrigt said impatiently. He pulled the child away and gave her to his mother. Kristi took her in her lap, her arms enclosing her. "*Være stille.*" Be quiet.

Ingebrigt put the little wooden doll in her hand, and started to pull the blanket over her, but Mette stayed his hand so he wouldn't cover her face.

"What am I to do," she cried. "What am I to do?" She lay her head on Sigrid's chest, the thin nightdress absorbing her tears.

"Ssshhh," Ingebrigt said, pulling her away. "Look how peacefully she sleeps. She no longer suffers."

She no longer suffered, but she no longer lived. Mette kept her eyes on her daughter, willed her chest to rise, to open her eyes, but she was as still as stone. How could this happen? She'd been a good wife and mother, a good daughter, she hadn't gone to America with Finn, she'd stayed to take care of her mother as God commanded. She'd done everything God wanted. Now He would take her daughter from her? Mette tried to stand, but fell to her knees. She felt the presence of the Ancients. She heard them whispering, murmuring as though from a great distance. *Sometimes children die, they said. There's nothing to be done.* She felt Ingebrigt beside her, his strong arms lifting her, lifting her up.

☙

Who knows how near me is my death? Mette sang the hymn with the others. The women were dressed in somber black with small white shawls on their heads tied under their chins. The men were in their Sunday dress, their hands and necks washed, their hair combed. The coffin was painted black and sat on two stools against the back wall. A candle burned at either end. The coffin lid was closed, but not yet nailed shut. A wreath of spruce leaves intertwined with ribbon and tinsel lay on top.

The guests arrived at eleven and had a bite to eat to hold them over until the larger meal after the service. On the table atop an embroidered cloth were flatbrød, cheese, pickled herring, smoked meat, coffee, funeral beer, and corn brandy. Mette sat in the corner, her eyes were vacant, her expression empty. She saw the people but she did not feel present.

Why had Sigrid died? went through her head over and over. Was it God's punishment? Was it the badger sow she had seen one winter day while pregnant, who decided to take the child for herself? Or maybe it was Ingebrigt's long dead grandmother who was angry that they hadn't named Sigrid after her. Flushed and troubled, she chewed her lip as she received her guests. She recognized the familiar and beloved faces in the room, but they seemed blurred and not real. She felt hands on hers and heard their condolences. *She is with God. She no longer suffers. She's in a better place.*

Pastor Bergson, in robe and ruffle, already a bit tipsy from drink, stood before them, beside the coffin. "Now the grave is a comfort to me, for Thy hand shall cover me," he read. It was cramped and warm in the house with so many bodies, and made Mette feel queasy.

Though I must now depart, depart not Thou from me, she sang, but her voice sounded tinny and far away.

There should never be coffins so small, Mette thought. *Never again.* It came to her suddenly and like a revelation from God: In order not to have more children die, they should not have more children. They were already blessed with four strong healthy children, two boys and two girls for whom she was more than grateful. She wasn't sure how, but there had to be a way. She would never again bring a child into the world only to see her die before she'd even lived.

After the Lord's Prayer, Mette sat, her head bowed, and added her own prayer. *Dear Father in heaven, I know Sigrid is there with you now and I know she is better off there than she ever was here. I thank you for the children you have given us, but I ask you humbly, as your servant, if it be Thy will, to not send more. Please help Ingebrigt to understand this also. In Jesus' name, I ask this.*

The hammer struck the coffin and she jerked to attention. Again, then again. She tried to get up, to go to Sigrid, but she felt dizzy.

When she finally stood, she stumbled and almost fell. Her mother came over and took her by the arm.

"*La henne gå.*" Let her go.

After the men had lifted the coffin from the stools, Ingebrigt ceremoniously kicked both stools over to ensure they would not be needed for that purpose again.

The burial would have to wait until spring when the ground was soft enough to receive her. Until then, the coffin would be stored at the church. They could have kept it in the barn, but Mette couldn't bear to think of her lying so near, in the cold. Instead, she preferred to think when she saw the little coffin being borne off on the sleigh that Mœrkei was taking her to heaven. Mœrkei pulled the sleigh up the hill and then disappeared over the top, into the clouds. Mette raised her hand in farewell.

                                            ೞ

Ingebrigt kept an eye on Mette. She got up each morning and did all that was required of her, but it was as though part of her went with Sigrid. It didn't help that it was dark almost all day and bitter cold. He hoped as life came back to the earth, it would also come back to her. She spent most of her time at the loom. The loom had it's own room, an extension built long ago on the south side of the house, in the years when Kristi was a girl. Because Mette spent so much time in there, they began to refer to it as *mor's* room.

One day in April after Ingebrigt had finished the midday meal and was smoking his pipe, he heard something he hadn't heard in a long time. He cupped his ear to make sure, holding his breath. Was that humming? He walked over to the room and peeked in.

"You're weaving then," he asked.

"*Ja, ja.* A coverlet for Sigrid."

A small chill rose in his chest. "For Sigrid?"

"*Ja*, for the coffin," she said. "I am almost done."

He blew out a breath. "*Ja*, that's good." The burial was coming up, and it was proper to drape a coverlet over the coffin. Ingebrigt did not have an eye for such things, but what Mette was weaving was unlike any coverlet he'd ever seen. He knew Mette was skilled, just look at the *åkle* she'd made. That had been a proud moment for him, standing next to his father, when Mette unrolled it and placed it on the bed. He had gone to her and cupped her elbow in his hand and nodded. "*Veldig bra*," he'd said. *Very good. Very, very good.* He looked at his father, who also nodded.

But he wasn't sure what to make of this one.

"It's...different," he said now about the coverlet. The weft was gray thread and the warp was wool dyed blue, but Mette had brought in something else, neither wool nor thread, and had weaved, what looked like, a white bird in flight.

"Is it a bird?" Ingebrigt asked.

Mette ran her hand over the weaving. "Yes, a white bird. I used pieces of her christening dress.

"That's what that is."

"The owl guided me."

"The owl?"

"Remember the owl we saw..." but she stopped there. "The owl my mother told me about, that was present at my birth."

"You can't mean an owl flew in here and told you to do this."

"The owl's spirit, husband, guided me." She began tying the threads of the coverlet. "I know you think I'm not right in the head, but I do know much about weaving, and many times the patterns come from places I cannot explain."

"From God you mean."

"Yes, sometimes, and sometimes from....other places."

Ingebrigt could not tell if she was mad or sane. What she had done was unusual and he supposed it was all right to do something different once in a while, as long as one didn't change everything, and even he could see it was skillfully done. But this talk of an owl was nonsense, and he was glad he was the only one to hear it.

That evening, when he came in for the evening meal, she was almost like her old self. She was at the stove frying herring. She turned to him and smiled, a real smile, the one that revealed her chipped tooth.

"After the funeral, I will keep Sigrid's coverlet for when she returns."

Ingebrigt nodded. He could not say what she meant by Sigrid returning, but he knew well enough to let it be. He decided right then whatever she did at the loom was up to her. He understood the loom was to her what the horse and plow were to him.

1889

Mette had not yet spoken to Ingebrigt about not having more babies. It got harder the more she put it off. She reddened with shame when she thought of speaking aloud about such things. It seemed that what was done in the dark should stay in the dark. When he came in from a long day of work and sat exhausted at the table, she couldn't see how she could ask him to stop doing one of the few things that gave him pleasure.

She thought back to the early days of their courtship when they'd talked about having children, how eagerly they'd looked forward to it. They'd hoped God would see fit to send them six, as that seemed the perfect number. Her breath quickened a bit when she thought of how he'd take her by the waist, how badly he wanted to be with her in that way. He'd said then it didn't matter to him if they had any children, as long as he had her, but she knew he didn't mean that. Children were more important than cattle, especially boys. Jonsbrygga would not do very well if it didn't have people to run it.

She nursed little Ole as long as was proper, even after he'd started to walk. Everyone knew that was one way to prevent a baby. She turned to the old ways, and at sunrise, burned a lock of Ingebrigt's hair, praying that the Ancestors would take away some of his need. She turned away from him in bed and pretended to sleep, but that rarely stopped him. One night as he moved next to her and began pulling up her nightgown, she spoke.

"*Vente.*" *Wait.* She was thankful it was dark. She spoke in a low voice so the others wouldn't hear. "I've been thinking of Onan, in the Bible, the one who..."

Ingebrigt shifted his weight and lay on his back.

"...spilled his seed on the ground."

"I wondered if maybe sometimes you could do as he did."

"This is because of Sigrid."

She nodded in the dark.

"Then you must also remember that the Lord slew Onan for that," he said. "We must do as God says, and He has said that wives must submit to their husbands, as we submit to the Lord. You cannot go against the Lord."

He was right, but it angered her nonetheless.

"So you will not do as I ask?" she hissed.

"A man has his needs."

"If you had to give birth, maybe that would change your mind."

"Keep your voice down, the others will hear."

"After this one, we'll have six. Once you said that was enough."

"These are not our decisions to make. We cannot pretend to be God."

Ole Ellingson called out, "Be done with your talking now."

Mette hoped he hadn't heard what they'd said. She turned on her side away from Ingebrigt. He let her be, but she knew it was just for that night. Men were different from women when it came to that. It was as though they couldn't stop themselves. She'd seen many a cow and sheep being mounted, how they stood patiently, bored almost, chewing their cud, blinking, waiting until it was over. Like them, she had to submit to the male.

Neither God nor the Old Ones came to her aid; or else they'd heard and decided to punish her for her blasphemous plea. Not only was she pregnant again, but after four months, she was certain she was carrying two.

ଔ

It was a year for weddings. When Elling announced he was going to marry Brita Pedersdatter of Fimreite in October and move in with her family across the fjord, Ingebrigt embraced him, more out of gratitude, than good wishes, although he surely meant that, too. Even with Elling gone, there would still be nine in the house and they were packed in like herring in a barrel. They could always fit in another baby or two, but children got bigger. As it was, the two older girls, Kristina and Eva, slept on mats on the floor. Anders was in the loft with Erik. Ingebrigt, Mette and Little Ole were in the chamber, and the three old folks, Kristi and Ole in one bed, and Synnøve in another, were in the main room. Ingebrigt didn't see where they would put another soul. That was another reason why people ran off to America, there just wasn't room for everyone.

Ingebrigt pondered these things as he sat on a rock near the boathouse mending a fishing net.

"It's a fine day," Erik said, coming up behind him.

"That it is. Do you want something?" Ingebrigt asked as he continued to work on the net.

"No, I came to talk to you," Erik said. He was in a good mood. He took a flask of brandy from his pocket, uncorked it, took a drink, and passed it to Ingebrigt who looked at him oddly. "What's this? In the middle of the day?" Erik nudged him, so he took a slug and handed it back. Erik drank, too, then put his arm around Ingebrigt and said, "Congratulate me, brother, I'm getting married."

"The devil...to Kari Knutsdatter?"

"That's the one."

"Is she right in the head?"

Erik snorted. "She's a good woman."

"Is there a child coming?"

"*Nei, nei*, it's not like that. She'll wear the crown at the wedding. She's but nineteen, but she has agreed to be my wife."

"But where will we put her?"

Erik clapped his hand on his brother's shoulder. "That's where the news gets better. I'm going to live with her in Slinde. I'll be forty soon, it's about time I left home, don't you think?"

"But that means..."

"...that you are the new owner of Jonsbrygga."

Ingebrigt put down the net and stared at him. "Let's have that bottle again."

"We'll wed in June. I'm pleased it has worked this way for you, Ingebrigt."

"And for you, too," Ingebrigt said.

They both took another long drink. Ingebrigt swallowed and exhaled loudly. Owner of Jonsbrygga! The master of his domain! He felt proud, sure enough, and Mette would be pleased. More than pleased, the wife of a landowner, that was something for a dairymaid.

ɞ

It was a big day in September, the transfer of the farm from one brother to another, important enough for old Ole Ellingson to get up off his bed, shave and put on his Sunday suit, and join Erik and Ingebrigt for the trip to the bank. The farm had been passed down four generations, from Ole Ellingson's great great grandfather in 1754 to his great grandmother, who'd passed it to his grandfather, whose wife, Mari Lassedatter, mother of Ole Ellingson, inherited it when he died, then to Ole, to Erik and now to Ingebrigt.

There was such a commotion in the house that morning, it was as if they were preparing to leave for the summer pasture. The women hovered nervously about the men, making sure they had whatever they needed. The children were jumpy and chattering like magpies until Ingebrigt put a stop to it. Little Ole ran in circles chanting *ho ho ho* like a pirate, and Mette, five months pregnant, shuffled to and fro, making sure they had everything they needed. She took a brush to Ingebrigt's coat. He needed to look respectable if they were to loan him the money to pay the tax to the government.

"Enough," he said, jerking away from her when she tried to rub the dried blood off his chin where he'd knicked himself shaving. He straightened his tie and took his Sunday cap from the peg.

She handed him the list of provisions they needed from the village. Little Ole needed shoes, but not this trip. Erik arrived from Slinde right on time to fetch them. The whole household paraded down to the shore to see them off, the children waving wildly, Mette wringing her hands.

"God be with you," Mette called after them. "Don't stay too long."

Mette prayed all would go well, that the boat would not turn over and God would keep her men folk safe. She did not know what she would do if something happened to Ingebrigt. In the afternoon, she kept checking, looking east, hoping to see the shape of them approaching.

She was busy with the evening meal when she heard Kristina shout that they were coming. She ran down to the shore to greet them and to help unload the boat. Judging by the good nature of everyone, it had gone well. Before pushing off, Erik gave the Mette a bag of almond cookies that he'd purchased at the bakery shop in Sogndal. This was an unexpected treat and Mette accepted the gift shyly but with joy. She made sure everyone got one. This was a day for eating cookies.

"*Mette Hansdatter er husmor av Jonsbrygga*," Ingebrigt said grandly as he dropped the documents on the table and hung up his coat and hat. *Mette Hansdatter is mistress of Jonsbrygga.* Ole Ellingson growled, "Looks like your plan worked." Mette reddened. Ingebrigt heard it, too, but didn't say anything. Mette picked up the papers, unfolded them and scanned them, ran her thumb over the embossed seal and his signature. Her mother came up behind her and patted her shoulder, with a side glance to the old man. She had all along said that Ingebrigt was the one for her, and now, look, she was the wife of a landowner. Mette folded the papers and put them in the box above the doorjamb.

"It was as I said," she said in a low voice to Ingebrigt. "There was no need to go all the way to America to own a farm."

A little smile crossed his lips, too. "*Ja, ja*," he said. "And here I can read what I signed." He sat down at the table and Mette brought him a cup of coffee.

Ole Ellingson had gone to his bed in the corner, where he leaned against the wall, smoking his pipe and glowering at her. Nothing she could do would win his favor. She had to let it be. She pulled her shoulders back, and returned to preparing the meal.

1890

The twin girls were born in January with spring still a long way off. Icicles hung from the eaves and the snowbanks glistened in the few hours when the sun shone. Magpies in their little black and white suits lined up on the fence as tame as pets, waiting for a crumb.

Mette had felt as though she were carrying a boulder in her belly. Her back had ached from the load, and she used the chamber pot with great difficulty, which she had to do often with the babies pressing against her bladder. Sometimes her mother would have to help her. When the babies moved, she could see their little hands and feet punch against her skin.

On the cold January day they were born Mette and Kristina had just brought in buckets of snow for water. Mette arched her back and then grabbed the table edge. Even though she'd given birth five times, she was still afraid when she felt the first pang. Ingebrigt ran for Gudrun. The grandmothers knew what to do and immediately began to prepare for the birth. No menfolk were allowed anywhere near, including Anders and Little Ole.

By the evening meal, the babies were there. Mette laid on her bed, both babies asleep next to her, her breasts heavy and painful. The room smelled of birth. *As if there weren't enough to do.* This was why Gudrun was required to be present at every birth. If one were in a position where two babies might be seen as more of a hardship than a blessing, one might perhaps want to prevent a baby from taking its first breath. She didn't want to have those thoughts, but she couldn't stop them either, so she was glad that Gudrun was there writing down in her book that two children had been born to Mette and Ingebrigt Nornes on January 24, 1890. As was the custom, they named the first one Sigrid after the one who died, and the second was named Marie, after Ingebrigt's grandmother.

But now that they were here, she felt mostly pity mixed with a heavy tenderness. *Stakkars.* It was so cold, Mette feared they might freeze to death. The stove was stoked day and night. If one sat too near the fire, one burned up; too far away and one froze. Both girls could fit in the cradle easily, they were so tiny, and Mette placed it as near the stove as she dared. They looked like two little kittens and brought tears to her eyes. She quickly wiped them away before anyone could see.

She dared not speak to anyone about her worries. She wished Anna were still near, but she had moved to Sogndal long ago, and then to Kaupanger. She was afraid Kristi and her mother would think her un-Christian if she spoke of not wanting more children. But why, when she had prayed so hard to not have more children, had He sent *two?* What was His Plan for her? Through Him all things were possible, and it was not up to her to question Him. Still, she pitied these little ones, to come into such a cold, hard world where so many bad things could happen to them when they were not yet strong enough to fight. Perhaps it would be just as well if they did freeze to death. But she quickly pushed that sinful thought out of her head and mumbled to them. *Gud velsigne deg.* God bless you.

1892

Summer came at last, blessed summer. The long days and sweet smells, the green grass, the shouts from the mountain and the singing of the birds. Mette's fears ebbed somewhat in summer. The dark dread that she carried around seemed to lift a little. She felt a small bright hope that they would do well, everyone would have enough to eat, and they would earn enough money. The girls picked wildflowers and put them in jars on the windowsills. Forget-me-nots and orange hawkweed brightened up the room.

In June, they made ready to move to the summer pasture. The house was buzzing with activity as Mette and the women packed the churns, milk pails, kettle, frying pan, pots and all the other things necessary for the summer. Then there was the preparation and packing of the provisions: the flatbrød, dried meat, flour, coffee, sugar, and salt for the cattle. They would bring their knitting, of course, and cloth to embroider.

Eva, who was eight, was going to the mountain pasture for the first time, just as Mette had done at that age and as her mother had done before her. Eight suddenly seemed too young to Mette. She tried very hard not to spoil her and Kristina's adventure with her worries, but she knew the dangers of the mountain. The possibility of wild animals attacking the creatures, the dreadful storms, how cold it would become at night later in the summer. But she also knew the freedom of being away from home, the alpine air on a summer's day, being with the other girls. She would have liked to go, too, but she had Ole who was four now, the twins, Marie and Sigrid, who had turned two in January, and her latest, Inge, who had been born on the first day of the year, a good omen. She was pretty enough with dark hair and blue eyes, but they had hoped for a boy. She reminded Mette of her heavenly daughter Sigrid so she didn't dare get too close, in case God snatched her back.

The morning of departure, Mette rose before the others, and found Eva already up and sitting at the table swinging her legs impatiently. "Why is everyone sleeping so long?" she asked. She had been just like that as a girl, eager to get going. To be with Finn.

She made the coffee. "Remember you are to be a good girl. You are to listen to Kristina and the other dairymaids, and do as you're told," she said. She'd already said these things to Eva, but it didn't hurt to remind her again. "I don't want to hear that you didn't behave." She undid her messy braids, brushed her hair and rebraided it. "Remember to say your prayers every night. You must be careful and always pay attention to your herd."

"I know," Eva said. "I will be a good herder."

Ole begged to go, but four really was too young. He followed Ingebrigt around like his shadow. "I can watch the goats, and if any wolves come, I will stab them with my knife," he said, and brandished the tiny pocketknife Ingebrigt had given him. Ingebrigt put his hand on his son's small shoulder and said, "Not yet, boy, we need you here."

On the day they left, almost the whole parish came to see them off, since the group included the neighboring farms as well. Ingebrigt blew the *lur* to call the cattle that bounded over as though let out for recess with Guldros, the bell cow, in the lead. Ingebrigt and a neighbor headed up the procession. They would bring the provisions up to the *sæter* and then return with the horse. The sheep and goats came next herded by Kristina, Eva and other young girls and boys from the neighboring farms. The dairymaids, their kerchiefs loose around their shoulders, brought up the rear, bearing wooden yokes on their shoulders from which hung pots, kettles and other utensils. They would have to walk five miles up the mountain like that, but they bore their burdens cheerfully.

Mette waved as they left, her eyes fixed on her daughters, who ran happily along, leaving the path occasionally, running behind bushes, on side paths, to bring wandering sheep and goats back in line. She hoisted Inge higher on her hip, as Marie and Sigrid pulled on her skirt. Ole jumped up and down waving at the procession. Mette watched until they were out of sight, long after the children lost interest.

Now the fields had to be plowed, the rye, barley and flax seeded. The earlier they planted, the higher the yield, but too early and a late snow could kill everything. As soon as the frost left the ground and the soil was dry enough, they began. The air smelled of freshly turned earth. But the days were long and wore them down. The potatoes and turnips would go in later, after the crops had been planted. In July, the haying would begin. They hoped for rain, but not too much. There was never enough summer.

Ole wanted to help with everything and was always by her side. Mette noticed in him an eagerness, a willingness to work. She felt very proud of this one. He was a handsome little boy, his fair hair fell on his forehead, as fair as a girl's. He loved to hear stories, too, as his uncle Finn had, whom she rarely thought of anymore. Last she heard, he had six children, all of whom were Americans and spoke only English. She clucked and mumbled under her breath, "Yankees."

But there were still days when she thought of her youth, the days on the mountain, how they had time to lie on their backs and look up at the sky. When she thought of that, her work would go down and she'd catch herself staring off. But that did not happen often; there was far too much to do than to sit around daydreaming about something that happened long ago.

In August, after Inge had been put down for a nap, Mette joined Kristi and her mother pulling flax plants. The small field was not far from the house so she could hear the high teasing voices of Ole and the twins as they played. Next year Ole would be old enough to help them with this task. The sun was hot on her neck and her clothes stuck to her skin as she yanked the plants from the ground.

A scream pierced the air. Her heart jumped and she waited. Then a loud frightened, "*Mor*." Her foot caught in her skirt as she turned to run, and she fell forward. "*Faen*!" she yelled as she stumbled to her feet. Mette Olesson did not curse so she had a conscious second where she hoped no one had heard her shout the devil's name. She ran to the sound of the crying which was near the house where she found Little Ole sitting on the ground, blood running down his leg. The twins sat beside him wailing. She picked him up and brought him inside and sat him on a chair.

"What did you do?" she demanded, angry and afraid.

"I was showing them how I'd kill a wolf," he cried.

"And your leg was the wolf?" She wet a cloth to wash the wound, but she could see it wasn't that deep. She relaxed and shushed him.

"It's not so bad, just a little cut," she said, relieved. She found a rag in her mending bag and wrapped the leg. She took the knife away from him and put it on a high shelf.

"That's enough playing with the knife," she said. "When you get older, you can have it again." That made him cry even more.

She went back to the flax. When Ingebrigt and Anders came home for the mid-day meal, Ole was limping around with his bandaged leg, and after they heard what had happened, they teased him about fighting wolves. Anders said if Ole didn't know how to use a knife, he'd take it for himself.

"No," Ole screamed. "It's my knife."

Ingebrigt, tired of this, barked, "It's *my* knife and I don't want to hear another word about it."

The next morning, Ole complained that his leg hurt. There was a bright red circle around the cut and it had begun to swell. Ingebrigt swabbed it with a little brandy, which made Ole scream. Mette made a poultice of milk and oats and slathered that on it and retied the rag, and that seemed to make him feel better. But by evening it did not look any better.

"If it's not better by tomorrow, we'll have to get Gudrun," Ingebrigt said, and swabbed it with more brandy.

The next day the red circle had widened and it looked worse than ever. Ole was flushed with fever and moaned from his bed on the floor. Anders hitched Mœrkei to the cariole and took off for *Norum Kyrke*. Gudrun returned with him, in her own cariole.

She looked at the wound and tsked, shook her head.

"You must wash your hands before you touch the wound," she instructed, "and only use a clean cloth." She took out a small brown bottle of her own concoction of ammonia and camphor, and doused the wound with it, and then wrapped it in a clean white linen cloth. She also gave Ole a hard candy, which he took shyly. Mette watched, her hands folded over her stomach. Gudrun left the bottle and another clean cloth with her, and told Mette to change the bandage at least once and bathe the cut with the mixture. She would return in the morning.

Mette did not sleep that night. She sat outside in the low sunlight and prayed. She tended to Ole the best she could, doing as Gudrun had instructed. She sat beside him, stroked his damp hair, sang to him as she rocked back and forth. She didn't know what to do. Flies buzzed around the wound and she waved them away.

These things take care of themselves, she thought. She knew and trusted Gudrun. She had helped them many times, and most of the time, not counting Sigrid, it had worked. It was just a cut, not even that deep. She stood over him as he slept, put a cool cloth on his hot damp forehead which seemed to her to feel cooler than it had in the morning.

Inge and the twins were eating their porridge that morning when they heard their mother cry out. Inge, who could sit up by herself now, sat on the floor and watched her mother move about the room. When her mother cried, she cried. She watched her go out the door.

"Ba," she called after her, raising her tiny fist. "Ba."

Mette stepped out of the house, wiped her hands on her apron, and looked north to the church, which sat high on a green hill so it could be seen by all, its white steeple pointing to heaven. A passerby might have thought she was getting a breath of air, enjoying the warm summer day perhaps. The air was sweet with the scent of wild roses.

She walked with purpose to the shore, stumbled once, righted herself, then walked into the water without hesitating. She was mildly aware of the cold water seeping into her shoes. She kept her eyes on the church, which promised hope and peace and eternal rest. That's all she wanted, rest. She just wanted to put her head in God's lap and sleep.

She struggled forward, her long skirts making it difficult to move. The water was at her waist, kelp caught at her buttons. She looked to the west, to the setting sun, the long river of the fjord going on and on to America. She stumbled and went down, her head under the cold water, and came up coughing.

She heard someone call. *Mor.* Mama.

On the shore, Marie and Sigrid jumped up and down, waving at her. She turned to look at them in their thin dresses, their bare feet. Behind them was the house with its sagging roof, and inside, another dead child. She plowed forward. She had to get to the church.

The girls shouted at her and the grandmothers were there, too. It dimly registered that something must be wrong. But something was always wrong. She waved back.

The water was getting deeper, her feet left the bottom. She kept walking, moving her hands and legs, but she didn't know how to swim. She went under. She was going to drown, she thought. She was going to go to the bottom of the fjord. Then a boat, a hand pulling at her.

"Mette Hansdatter," the voice said, "get in the boat."

She turned to see who had come for her. There was the dark shape of a head blocking the sun, with a halo around it. God had come. She smiled up at him. "*Takk,*" she said. "*Takk, takk.*" She began to cry, to unload her grief. But God dragged her into the boat, and began to shake her.

"What's the matter with you, woman," he shouted. "Have you gone mad?" And then he put both his hands on her shoulders and said in a bitter, low voice, "This is in God's hands, not ours."

She made her eyes focus on the man, whom she recognized as her husband, who glared at her fiercely and impatiently. She crouched on the bottom of the boat, like a dog, her arms covering her head. Her heavy wet dress smelled of fish and sweat and dead babies. She wept until she vomited, and then she raised her head and howled.

1894

Two winters had come and gone since little Ole's death, and another spring was on its way, a dawdling spring. At Easter, which was early that year, the birch trees were just budding. A late spring worried Ingebrigt; it worried everyone. The fields had to be planted. Easter was a precarious time anyway with the spirits being out and up to no good. One kept as quiet as possible during Easter week and tread lightly. When the wind howled and the rain beat against the house, Mette held her pregnant belly and looked anxiously through the window.

They did not talk of what happened the day little Ole died. It happened. Ingebrigt did not accuse or berate her. He showed restraint in this and an unusual patience. On that terrible day, he had had to pick her up from the boat and carry her to the house, she remembered that. The children had never seen such a thing and it frightened them. Marie and Sigrid tried to run to her, but the grandmothers kept them back. Anders held the baby Inge who cried loudly and could not be calmed. Mette had not even looked in her direction.

She left them for a while. They saw her curled on the bed, her face to the wall, rocking, but she was gone. She went to a place far away. Maybe it was heaven. Everybody had it good there. It was summer all the time. It rained when it should and stopped when it had rained enough. They were all there: her heavenly children, Sigrid and Ole, too. They ran to her and she knelt to catch them and held them close so as to never let them go. There was all the fish and cheese and meat they could eat. There were bilberries, raspberries and cloudberries growing alongside the road, and strawberries in the meadows. They picked them whenever they wanted and ate them off thin china saucers with sweet cream and sugar. But then it would shift, it would turn cold and begin to rain and they couldn't find shelter and what they thought was a mountain was a crouched troll and when he stood, he was mighty and tall with fearsome green eyes, and they'd begin to run, and she'd wake, panting and afraid again.

She heard people far off. Elin and Niels talking to Ingebrigt. She felt her mother touch her forehead and Ingebrigt talking low to her. Anna was there, too, but Mette was only dimly aware of her. She heard her comforting voice. She felt her cool hand and she grasped it. She thought of her as the white owl perched on the bed, watching her, protecting her. Anna talked of the two of them as children, of them playing, of their trip to Sogndal, of picking plants for dyes, soft soothing things that put Mette to sleep. She sang to her. But then she was gone and Mette was not sure if she had imagined her or if she had really been there.

After a month or so, with great difficulty, she finally sat up and put her feet on the floor and made herself return to the world. She knew the only thing that would save her was work. She had to get up. She looked for Ole but he was not there. Her fair boy with hair as light as a snow owl's feathers was gone.

One day that autumn when Mette was outside with the girls hauling water, she looked up and noticed, as though for the first time, the deep yellow leaves of the birch against the blue sky.

"Look," she said in wonder to the girls, "how blue the sky is."

"*Himmelen er blå*," they said, running in circles around her. "*Himmelen er blå.*" The sky is blue, the sky is blue. She put the water down and watched them run, their arms outstretched, their hair flying. Her lips began to twitch in a smile, and then she did something no one had heard for a very long time: Mette Hansdatter laughed.

ଓଃ

Ole Ellingson died that spring, just two weeks after Easter. Mette prayed for his soul, but she did not grieve. He was an old man, almost seventy, and had been doing poorly so it was not unexpected. Over the fourteen years of her marriage to his son, he had never endeared himself to her, or even tried. Once, and only once, he had nodded his approval over a coverlet she had woven for his bed. He said only a simple *takk* without looking directly at her. As a woman, her care for him was taken for granted.

He could hardly walk near the end and mostly sat on the bed in his dark corner smoking his pipe and barking orders. The children wouldn't go near him unless ordered. He had never lifted a hand to any of them, but his badger-like snarling frightened them. As the *husmor*, it was Mette's job to take care of all of those who lived under her roof, including her father-in-law, and she did what she had to, even cutting his thick, yellow toenails which Kristi couldn't see well enough to do. It would have been a sin to say she was glad he was gone, but she couldn't help thinking it.

Ingebrigt was the one to close his father's eyes, and for a while, his hand stayed there, as though in benediction, but she never saw him shed a tear for the old man. They made sure he had a respectable funeral with plenty of food and drink.

No sooner had Ole Ellingson been put in the ground, but another boy came into the world. That November, Mette gave birth to their ninth child. She hoped this new boy would turn out as well as Anders, who had grown to be a strong, hard-working lad. At sixteen, Anders had been confirmed and was ready to start his own life, and that meant, of course, talking about America. Mette wanted to dismiss it as just daydreaming, but she knew better. Even though Anders, as the eldest son, would inherit the farm one day, it was not what he wanted. The young wanted more, an adventure, a different kind of life. The old life was hard with little reward.

The second Ole was a colicky baby and cried often for no reason that anyone could tell and strained everyone's nerves. He was a bit of a runt and that both endeared him to Mette and worried her. She was afraid his weakness came from her.

Since the day of Sigrid's funeral when she'd asked the Almighty not to send them more children, she'd had four more and one taken, so it was plain to see she had been foolish to think she could meddle with the Lord's plans.

Weaving saved her. In the long winter months, when she wasn't spinning, she sat at her loom. The clack and the beat of the loom sounded from morning to night, it's rhythm a sort of music. As she wove the shuttle in and out of the yarn, she thought of the dances of her youth, of her wedding day when all the men wanted to dance with her, how she twirled round and round to the music. An arm around her waist, a hand on her shoulder. She thought of her daughters running in the meadow, their voices ringing up to the blue sky. Those were the things that fed her. She hummed to herself, her feet moved rhythmically on the treadle, the yarn went in and out, a pattern emerged, it grew, and she went on. So she spent her days.

1895

Autumn. The family had just taken a break from digging potatoes. They sat on their overturned baskets resting their backs and sipping water, the men smoking their pipes, when they saw a *stolkjære* come down the road with two people in it. They stood and shielded their eyes from the sun to squint at this unusual sight.

"It's two ladies," Mette said.

As they came nearer, the twins hid behind Mette's skirts and Inge clung to Kristina's leg. The driver pulled the horse to a halt and called out "*God dag*" to them. "*Ikke Norske,*" Mette thought. Not Norwegian.

Mette and Ingebrigt responded "*God dag,*" and walked down to the road, the rest of them shyly trailing behind. The woman driving said they were lost. She spoke in broken Norwegian, but Mette could make out that they had been on their way to Sogndal, and must have taken a wrong turn.

"Ja, you took the wrong road," Ingebrigt said, "but it's easy to get back on the main road, I'll show you. Americans, are you?"

Yes, they were from Vermont, and on holiday. They'd been in Norway two weeks and were enjoying it very much. "You have a beautiful country," said the driver who had curly black hair. At this they all beamed as if they had put the mountains and trees in place themselves.

"*Ja-ja, san,*" Ingebrigt said. "That we do. I have two brothers in America, in Wisconsin. Do you know it?"

Mette had heard of people like this, people who were so rich, they had time to travel to another country for no reason but just to visit. They could wander the countryside looking at the scenery without worry or care. The two women looked younger than she, and were nicely dressed in white cotton blouses and wool skirts. They both wore fashionable straw hats and soft leather gloves. Mette stepped forward and asked if she could offer them something to eat. It was a poor person who didn't offer a traveler hospitality.

"*Kom,*" she said. "*Velkommen.*"

They brightened at this, looked at one another, and the friend of the driver, the one with light hair pulled back in a bun, said in Norwegian, "Thank you, that would be very nice."

That took Mette back because it was not proper to accept right away. By doing that, the lady hadn't given her a chance to assure them she was sincere in her offer. They were to decline at first, so she could insist. A direct answer seemed too forward to her. While she was thinking all this, Ingebrigt helped them down and told Anders to get the horse some water.

After entering the house, Mette closed the door, and they exchanged a look she didn't understand. Did they think she should leave the door open? Mette didn't know how to tell them that leaving doors and windows open allowed unknown things to get in and other things to get out. She saw them exchange a glance and then sit down on the bench at the head of the table, obviously unaware that that was Ingebrigt's place. She was about to object, but then decided that Americans must not have seats of honor. When Ingebrigt came in, he looked surprised, but he didn't say anything; instead he sat in the chair by the stove. The grandmothers sat in their rocking chairs knitting, their needles clicking away as they rocked and watched. The children shyly pressed against the wall, silent and motionless, and stared at them.

The two women pulled off their gloves and Mette immediately noticed how white and clean their hands were. She looked at her own, rough and dirty from the field. She poured some water in a pan and rinsed them off, drying them on her apron. She stole glances at them as they looked about the room and spoke low to each other in English. Kristina laid a clean linen cloth on the table with their best cups and saucers, and Mette set out coffee and cream, flatbrød, cheese and cloudberry jam. They seemed to really enjoy the food.

She wanted to ask them so much about themselves and America, but they didn't understand her very well, and she had great difficulty understanding their Norwegian. Ingebrigt leaned back on the legs of the chair, smoking his pipe. He peered at them through the smoke and asked their names. The dark-haired one was Miss Harris and the fair-haired one was Miss Moloney. Were their people from Norway, he asked. Miss Harris, who did most of the talking since she spoke Norwegian, answered that yes, her grandmother was from the Nordfjord area, but Miss Moloney's people were from Ireland. She translated for Miss Moloney.

How old were they, Ingebrigt wanted to know. Miss Harris' eyebrows went up good-naturedly, but she responded that they were in their late twenties.

Did they have husbands? No, they did not.

How did they live then? They were both school teachers.

Did they plan to marry? Well, yes, they believed they might one day, but they were not in a hurry to do so. The two women smiled at being peppered with these questions but Miss Harris answered politely, and Ingebrigt seemed to understand her.

Mette stood by the table, ready to get anything they needed. She held her clasped hands in front of her, palms up in the shape of a bowl. Women who did not care if they married or not, who made their own living, who were free to do as they pleased, that was something to ponder. Who did not have children.

She wanted to touch their hands. They looked as soft as a child's, and their nails were smooth and even and there was no dirt under them. They must never have to work hard, she thought, or else they always wore gloves.

When there was a break in the conversation, Miss Harris pointed to the coverlet on the wall and said, "*Det er veldig hyggelig.*" That is very nice. It was the coverlet Mette had woven for Sigrid's funeral.

That was enough for Synnøve to open a trunk and pull out other coverlets Mette had woven. The women seemed to be very interested in them, but Mette could not understand what they were saying. She did understand when Miss Harris smiled at her and said, "*Dette er nydelig arbeid.*" This is beautiful work. Mette felt awkward, self-conscious. She looked down at her hands. She side glanced at Ingebrigt, who squinted at her through smoke.

Miss Harris said that if Mette could part with one of them, she would like to buy one. Mette and Synnøve looked at one another, their mouths open. What was this then? Mette was confused, "*Jeg vet ikke, jeg antar.*" I don't know, I suppose. Not the one on the wall, not Sigrid's, but perhaps one of the others. She looked at Ingebrigt who said, "Three kroner."

Miss Harris reached in her bag and counted out three kroner and handed it to Mette, not to Ingebrigt. She chose one and was clearly delighted with her purchase. "My mother will love this," she said. "Thank you very much."

"*Takk,*" Mette said. "*Mange takk.*"

Three kroner for something she did all the time.

They had to go. If they were going to reach Sogndal by evening, they had to be on their way. They thanked them many times for their hospitality — *tusen takk, takk for mat* — and told them how kind and generous the Norwegian people had been to them. Mette smiled and nodded. "*Vær så god.*" You're welcome. "*Ikke noe a takke for.*" Nothing to thank for. She shook hands with them, glad to make contact, and walked with them to their carriage.

Back in the house, she put the money in the box above the doorjamb. To be paid for her coverlets. She could hardly believe it. Real money. She picked up the cups they had drunk from and held them for a moment. Rich ladies from America had drunk coffee from her cups. Pretty ladies who thought she did "beautiful work." *Beautiful work.*

But she didn't have time to think long on it. The others had returned to the field, and she still had rows of potatoes to dig before the day was through.

ରୁ

Over the long winter, she thought of the two women often, how they came to Nornes so unexpectedly, out of the blue, like rare, beautiful birds. They flew in, sat at their table, then flew off with a coverlet in each of their beaks. Or sometimes she'd imagine that they'd sailed from America right to their doorstep. She saw them standing in the prow, one gloved hand holding down a hat, the other waving at them. She wanted to weave a coverlet just for them with something of America in it, something of Norway, a bird, a ship maybe.

She sat at her spinning wheel, her mind a million miles away. She imagined herself sailing to America just to visit them. She wouldn't be afraid. She'd have a nice dress, a valise, a hat like theirs. Somehow she'd find where they lived—she assumed they lived together—and she'd show up at their door. "*Husk meg?*" she'd ask. Remember me? They'd be so happy to see her. "*Kom in, kom in,*" they'd say. They'd have coffee out of flowery china cups and eat soft white biscuits or whatever they ate in America, something sweet and good.

She wondered if their visit really had been an accident, or if angels had sent them. Or maybe they were angels, come to pay a call on them. Maybe none of it even happened. Maybe she just imagined it.

As she spun, her foot moving back and forth on the treadle and the wool slicing across her palm, she wondered how she would have changed if she had joined Finn in America, or if she and Ingebrigt had gone when his grandfather made them that offer. She'd speak English. Maybe she would be wearing hats and gloves and fancy clothes, too. She hoped her American relations would come back to Norway one day so she could see how they turned out. Those moments at the wheel when she could daydream were precious, so precious. She appeared to be there, spinning, but she was far, far away.

1896

Another baby on the way. It was always the same. Ingebright would move against her for warmth, then he'd fiddle with his underwear and she knew what was coming. He'd pull up her nightgown and in the time it took to light a pipe, a baby was started. In the dark, by the light of the stove fire, she could just barely see a pale knot in the wood which she'd stare at, its circular pattern, the shades of the swirl, as he pushed against her.

She didn't know what she wanted to do more, punch herself in the belly or punch Ingebrigt. There were days when the sight of him made her want to run like a madwoman from the house. The way his lordship sat in his high seat smoking his pipe and reading the paper while her belly swelled. She was going to be thirty-seven that August and this would be her tenth birth. Her tenth! Some people couldn't have one and she was on her tenth. Her womb was like an old sack, stretched out and sagging. Her back ached. Her joints ached. Her teeth ached. She could barely see well enough to thread a needle. By May, she began to worry that there were two in there again, and the knot in her chest tightened.

She woke one morning, opened her eyes, and said to herself, *I should speak to God in His House.* Ingebrigt was already up waiting for her to make the coffee. He'd started the fire. She ground the beans and got the coffee going. She put porridge on the table for him, then tied her kerchief under her chin and said she'd be back for midday meal. Her mother would mind the children. He narrowed his eyes, but didn't protest.

She liked the cool of the morning, the freshness of the day before it got trampled on. The road was in shadow, the sun still behind the mountains. She walked at a quick pace, her skirts making a *thwup thwup* sound in the silence of the morning. Every once and a while she'd hear the soft cooing of the mourning dove or the shriek of a blue jay. She breathed deeply of the smell of the forest.

It was dark inside the church with the faintest scent of incense. Her wooden shoes echoed from the floor to the rafters as she walked up to the altar. She dropped to her knees, her folded hands on the rail.

Our Father who art in heaven, she prayed, *hallowed be thy name.* After her prayer, she paused and looked at the ornately carved wooden altar with Jesus on the cross in its center. She pressed her lips to her clasped hands. *Dear Father in Heaven,* she prayed, *Who is all things. Is it your will that we have more children than we can care for? Perhaps it is sacrilege, but I do not want more children. My body is tired. I am too old. And now I fear there are two more coming. I pray for strength.* She bowed her head on her folded hands and her shoulders began to shake.

And then she felt Him, His presence. Jesus was there, His hand on her shoulder, but she did not dare look up. "Mette." His voice was low and pleasing. *"Your reward comes later. Your Heavenly Father will take care of you just as he cares for the lilies in the field and the birds in the sky. It is not for you to ask this, Mette. Your children are God's gift to you. They will take care of you. You must have faith. I know of earthly suffering, Mette, and this will pass, as all things do."* And then he placed his hand on her head and blessed her.

She looked up but it was just her. Jesus was still on the cross. She wiped her eyes with her apron, pushed herself up, and walked back to a pew where she sat for a time. It was cool in God's house, she would have liked to stay there all day. But that would never do. She adjusted her kerchief and got up.

May the Lord bless you and keep you. May He make His face shine upon you and be gracious unto you. May He lift up His Countenance upon you and give you peace.

She'd be home in time for the midday meal, just as she'd said.

☙

The worry did not end. Her fears pressed against her heart. Sometimes she'd have to stop whatever she was doing and grab on to something to steady herself, or she'd go to the animal shed and lie in the hay just as she did as a girl. The smell and sound of the animals and the hay soothed her. She wished that she could see the *nisse*, the barn spirit, but he never showed himself. Sometimes she'd see signs of him, a flash of a red coat around a corner, or a dent in the hay where he'd been. Just as she asked God, she also asked the *nisse*, to help, to protect them, to make sure there was enough.

She'd run her hands over her bulging stomach, feel the kick of new life, and think of what lay ahead. It never got any easier. She feared dying while giving birth and leaving her children with no mother. She feared not being able to feed her children, of illness, of them suffering. Of them being snatched by the *hulderfolk*. Or being cursed by a spirit because she hadn't done something or she did something she wasn't supposed to.

Where would they put another child, let alone two? Kristine and Eva would soon be gone, that was true. Kristina was already confirmed and Eva would be in the spring. Both would find work on more prosperous farms. It was hard to even think of them not being there, they were such a help to her. She dropped her head into her hands. Her girls leaving home.

She didn't like when her mind took a dark turn, but she couldn't help it. She had thought of it, even considered going to Oleanna Larsdatter. It was whispered that she had the Black Book, a book of magic and spells. She'd heard that Oleanna could make a potion of cooked juniper berries, a soup made from a blue stone, that could rid the body of the baby, but it might also kill the mother. She thought on this unholy solution, turned it over and over in her mind while she worked, considered the possible result and the consequences, and decided it was a risk she couldn't take. If anyone ever found out, if Ingebrigt ever found out; never mind that, if the *lendsman* ever found out, she could be put in jail. Or worse, she could die, and leave her children motherless.

A few weeks earlier, they had heard the terrible news of a woman in Slinde who had jumped off the roof of her cottage hoping to kill herself. The woman survived, but she had been about four months pregnant, and the fall had killed the baby. The poor woman, Mette thought. She must have felt she had no other choice. She and the grandmothers shook their heads, tsked. They were saddened, but they understood. They all understood.

One summer's day, about a month or so after that, Mette found herself alone in the house, which was very unusual. The older girls were at the summer pasture, the grandmothers had taken the children to pick berries, Ingebrigt and Anders were in the field. At first she was just glad to have the place to herself, and then slowly, an idea came to her.

She peered around the yard to make sure she was alone, called to the loft to see if anyone was there, and satisfied, closed the door. She reasoned that if all things came from God, then her idea must also have come from Him. She got up on the table using a chair as a step, said a quick prayer, and jumped off. She felt her belly, then did it again, and again. Chair, table, jump. Soon the urgency of what she was doing took over, and she did it faster and faster until she sat in a heap on the floor, exhausted and bruised, crying into her apron. The door opened then and sunlight shone in on her.

Her mother stood there, frowning at her. "Have you gone crazy again?"

"Mind your own business," Mette said.

☙

"Boy."

Ingebrigt stood at the foot of the stairs and called up to Anders. That was all he had to say. Anders was out of bed and down the stairs by the time Ingebrigt left the house. Ingebrigt considered dawn the best time to fish. Not only would it give him the rest of the day for field work, but he felt he caught the fish off guard that early. If they had a good catch, Anders would take it to the market to sell along with the cream.

It was cool and still at that hour, the sun just barely over the horizon, the smell of the sea filling their senses. The two men worked silently side by side, loading the net and buckets. Just as they were about to push off, Mette called to them, holding aloft the *tine* of food Anders had forgotten. She was very pregnant and it was almost comical to see her waddle towards them. With her hair pulled tightly back and her big belly, she looked like an upright seal. Anders ran over and took the box from her.

The oars sliced into the water as Ingebrigt rowed them to a good spot east of Nornes, not too far from the shore, the measure being water no deeper than the net was wide. A seagull followed them, keeping an eye on the bucket. When they found their place, Anders readied the net. At eighteen, he was better at casting than his father, and Ingebrigt was proud of his ability. Anders stood in the boat, finding his balance, then coiled the handline over his wrist and folded and draped the net over his hand, picked up part of the weighted hem, and hurled the net into the water, all in less than a minute. It spread into a wide circle, like a flared skirt, then fell on the water and sank.

Ingebrigt nodded at him. After a bit, Anders pulled on the handline and hauled it in. Five herring. "*Ja ja, gut,*" Ingebrigt said. "*Gut.*" After an hour and with eleven herring in the bucket, they took a break. Mette had packed flatbrød, cheese, sardines and water for them, a good breakfast.

They sat across from one another and ate silently for a while, then Ingebrigt said, "We'll finish the north field today, and plant tomorrow."

Anders nodded, and stuffed a sardine in his mouth.

It was pleasant out there on the water, the sun coming up, just the two of them. Ingebrigt leaned forward, his elbows on his knees. "Have you got a girl then?"

Anders dropped his head. "*Nei*, not any one in particular." He cut a chunk of cheese and handed it to his father.

"Oh ho! *Many* girls then?"

"*Nei,* not like that. I don't want to start anything." He ate a piece of cheese. Then, "*Far*, I want to go to America."

Ingebrigt felt an urge to strike him. Not now, not on this day when the fish were biting, when they were enjoying each other's company. That was the one thing he had hoped he would never hear from his boy. He rubbed his leg, and looked east, to the glacier which was just catching the morning sun. "You do, do you?"

"As soon as I have the money."

"And when will that be, do you think?"

"In a couple of years, I hope." He rubbed the side of his hand against his cheek, using the stubble to scratch it.

Ingebrigt lit his pipe, shook the match out and threw it into the water. "A lot can happen in a couple of years. You don't want the farm then."

"*Nei,* Ole can have it."

"It's not good enough for you." He rested his pipe arm on the other and peered at his son.

"That's not it. I want to see America."

Could he stop him? *Should* he stop him? Ingebrigt couldn't say his brothers had been wrong about going. They *had* done better there, even though they always said how much they missed Norway.

"Better not say anything to your mother until you know for sure. That's the last thing she needs to hear."

Anders lit his pipe and both sat silently and smoked.

Then, "*Far*, there's something I've always wanted to ask you..." He paused, obviously struggling to find the words.

"What?"

Anders didn't look at him when he spoke, but at his feet. "Am I your son?" he asked quietly.

Ingebrigt cocked his head, as though he hadn't heard him correctly. "Why would you ask me that?"

"If I am your first son, why was I not named Ole?"

Ingebrigt shook his head and looked out at the fjord. He remembered that day he'd first seen Anders. How he'd come in out of the cold to the warm room where Mette sat holding him. He was overjoyed that she'd given him a son. It proved she would be a good wife. And then he had to tell her that awful news.

"Your grandfather didn't think your mother was good enough for me, she was a servant. We weren't married yet when you came, and he, well, he refused to give his name to a bastard, even though I'd courted your mother for a year before you were born, so you are my son, there is no doubt about that. And you are not a bastard." Ingebrigt began to ready the net. "Your grandfather was a stubborn man."

Anders blew out a puff of air. "That's why he was always so gruff with me," Anders said. "But why is *mor* so...so nervous all the time?"

"She's pregnant. The first months are always hard for her."

"But even when she's not. It doesn't seem right that someone her age is still..." He blushed and looked away.

"Don't put your nose where it doesn't belong, boy." He threw the net far into the fjord where it unfurled and landed gracefully. He knew it must be strange for Anders to think of his parents that way. He remembered when he first realized what those sounds in the night were. He was thirteen when Elling was born and it made him feel ashamed to think of his parents doing what he'd seen the animals do. But that was all part of growing up. Sooner or later you figured it out.

He knew what Anders meant, of course. He'd known for some time that Mette was not herself, but he thought she seemed to be getting better. But now this feeling that she was carrying another set of twins was disturbing because she had been right when she predicted Marie and Sigrid, and, God knew, another set of twins would be hard on all of them, but it would be the hardest on her. He rubbed his leg. He'd really gotten into it when he married her.

He pulled up the net. Nothing. Anders took over and threw it out again. The two settled into silence after all that talk, but now Ingebrigt worried about the next loss for Mette: America was going to take another man she loved.

☙

Mette's old friend Anna was coming to Jonsbrygga. Mette hadn't seen her in many years and she nervously awaited her arrival. Anna had moved to Kaupanger, farther away than Sogndal. They wrote occasionally but neither was very good at it. Mette sometimes had imaginary conversations with her, especially after the deaths of Sigrid and Ole, and Anna comforted her in their talks, made sense of things, if sense could be made. She had come after Ole died, but Mette had been too sick to be aware of her.

Anna was a milliner now with her own shop. She had married well to a livery owner. *It's hard not to love a man who is good with horses,* she had written. Mette had wanted to go to her friend's wedding, but the distance, children to take care of, and her being pregnant at the time, wouldn't allow it. With her marriage to Knute Jacobsson, Anna had at last accepted that God wanted her to stay in Norway. No more talk of America. She had two children, a boy ten and a girl twelve, and Mette envied her for that.

Mette wanted everything to be just right. She brought out of storage her best cups and saucers and her silver, and laid the table with an embroidered cloth she had just finished. She couldn't wait to tell Anna about the American ladies.

Now that Anna was a town person, Mette hoped she wouldn't think her too backwards. She checked her reflection in the mirror, and ran her hand over her face. She looked old and tired. She was always tired. When she smoothed her hair back, she suddenly saw how much she looked like her mother.

Anna arrived in her carriage in the early afternoon and Mette watched her from the window before going out. Anders held the horse while Ingebrigt offered his hand to help her down from the carriage. She was a little heavier, but not much, and looked very fashionable in a wide-brimmed straw hat with small blue and white flowers around the crown, her brown hair in a knot at her neck. She wore a white blouse and gray skirt. Mette worried that she had changed, but when Anna turned and she saw the face of her old friend, tears sprang to her eyes, and she hurried out to welcome her.

"We're two old ladies now," Anna said as they embraced. The children, Marie, Sigrid and Ingeborg, stayed near Mette and looked shyly at the new person. Ole clung to Mette's skirt. Anna offered them a bag of sweets but they were too bashful to take it, so Mette did, and let them each choose one. Now the visitor was not quite so frightening.

Mette wanted to be alone with her friend, but Kristi and Synnøve peppered Anna with questions about Kaupanger, and the children, no longer shy, ran about, and Ole pulled to sit on her lap. Anna was going on to Slinde to stay with her father after their visit, so time was precious. After they'd eaten, Mette suggested they walk by the fjord, just them.

Anna linked her arm in Mette's. "It's a hard life for you, Mette, isn't it, with so many to care for. How are you?"

Mette said nothing for a while. She did not want to complain to her friend. God had given her a good life, a home and family, she had nothing to complain about. She had no more work than her neighbors, yet why did it feel she might crumble under the weight. She looked off and started to say that she was fine, but her voice broke. Anna quickly handed her a handkerchief which she pressed to her eyes. She was not going to cry in front of her friend.

"I hadn't thought it would be this hard, Anna. Why do you suppose it must be so?" She put her hands on her belly. "Now I have another, maybe two more, coming, and I feel such a weakness, dread, for what lies ahead. I don't see how I'll ever find peace in this world."

Anna nodded, listening.

"I think sometimes I'm losing my senses. Remember how we used to play, how we'd pretend we were mothers with our babies, and we'd make imaginary bread and porridge and it was such fun. It's not fun, Anna. It's too much."

"You must pray for God's comfort when that comes over you, for He has given you much to be grateful for. You have good, strong children. I see you in them. And a good husband who provides for you. I only wish Kristina and Eva had been here.

"Do you still have the hat?"

Anna nodded. "I've worn it several times and always think of you. That poor hat never did make it to America." She breathed deeply through her nose. "How lucky you are to live right on the fjord. I don't suppose you run anymore."

Mette patted her belly. "I would have a hard time doing that, at least now."

"I remember you as a girl in Fimreite running barefoot along the shore, your braids flying. You were so fast, you beat everybody."

"I wish you lived closer," Mette said.

"You must come to see me next," Anna said. "I will make a hat just for you."

"The critters will think I'm very stylish."

The day was warm, the sun still had a long way to go to the horizon. They sat on the bench into the late afternoon and talked of many things—of childhood memories, of husbands and children, of work and play, of Finn and America, of what they'd lost and what they'd gained. That was a day to hold onto, to remember in the darker times. The fjord seemed prettier that day, the mountains greener, the sky bluer.

As Ingebrigt walked back from the field to the house, he heard his wife laugh, something he didn't hear often. He saw the two women hunched together. Their voices rose and fell like the chirping of birds, with the occasional bark of a laugh. But then it was time for Anna to go. When she was settled in her carriage, Ingebrigt handed her the reins. He put his hand on hers.

"*Takk*," he said. "*Tusen takk.*"

ೞ

The labor came on suddenly, almost two months earlier than expected. Mette was scrubbing clothes when she felt the first pain.

She put a hand to her belly. It can't be, she thought. But a second pain came, and then a third, and she knew it was time. Whether she was ready or not, the baby, or babies, were coming. Twins often came early so her feeling was probably right, although she prayed it wasn't. She stopped what she was doing, and went to the house, already sweating in the August heat. She gripped the door frame and waited while another contraction passed. Her mother knew immediately what was happening, and told little Ole to tell Anders to get Gudrun.

Mette dreaded every birth, but this one more than the others. There was a darkness in it she didn't understand. Maybe it was that they were conceived right after last year's slaughter when the smell of blood was still on them, or maybe this time she would be taken.

"*Jeg kan ikke,*" she said to her mother. I can't.

"*Men du vil,*" Synnøve replied. But you will.

They could have used the help of the older girls, but they were still at the summer pasture. Mette removed the hay and ticking from the bed, there wasn't time to wash the boards. She got the birthing blanket from the trunk to lay over the wooden frame. Kristi started water boiling on the stove, she knew Gudrun would insist on it for washing her hands. Synnøve went out to the *stabbur,* storage shed, to retrieve the cradle, diapers and swaddling clothes. They'd been through this ritual so many times.

"Aaaaaah," Mette cried, as she fell back on the bed with another contraction. "*Brennevin,*" she said to Kristi who stood by waiting for orders. Brandy for the pain.

Gudrun came through the door just then, with a panicked Anders and Ole behind her. "Go," she said to the boys. "We'll call you when it's over." She took off her kerchief and pushed up her sleeves. She looked around for the water, which Kristi quickly brought her. She examined Mette, and as she did so, she frowned.

"There may be two in there," she said. She suggested that Kristi bring a cool wet cloth for Mette's forehead, which was glistening with sweat, and then poured her another brandy.

"*Den kommer,*" Mette said. It's coming.

"I see, I see, bear down. I see the head." Mette groaned and pushed out the baby amid a pool of blood and fluids. Gudrun picked up the bloodied baby by its legs and ran her finger around its mouth and throat. "It's a boy and looks to be about a month too early," she said, and placed the baby between Mette's legs. She waited for the umbilical cord to stop pulsing, then tied it in two places.

"Cut straight," Mette cried. A cord cut on the diagonal could harm the child.

Gudrun cut the cord. They would burn it later. She felt the belly for the placenta, and possibly for the other one. But Mette was already pushing.

"There's another one," Mette said. But this one wasn't ready to leave the womb. Gudrun inserted her hand into the womb.

"There," she said, talking to herself. "He should come now, just a little repositioning."

Mette pushed and groaned, and out came another boy.

It was too hot, she couldn't get a breath. She fainted.

ෆ

When she woke, she was alone. There were no babies beside her. She tried to think back through the fog of pain. She'd had twins, she remembered that. But were they alive? Her mother came to the bed as though reading her mind.

"They're in the cradle. You have two boys, thanks be to God, but they're too small, daughter, too small." She looked hard at her, directly into her eyes, her lips pressed together.

Mette turned away. She heard the voices of Ingebrigt and Anders so guessed it was evening. She only wanted to sleep. Blessed, forgiving sleep. Synnøve brought the swaddled babies to the bed, and lay them beside her. Mette glanced at them. The ancestors would have thrown them over the fortress wall. One began to squirm and mewl, hardly a cry, then the other. Should she feed them? Should she help them live or let them die? She closed her eyes.

Ingebrigt came beside her. "Doesn't look good."

"*Nei, nei.*"

"Boys, too. What should we call them?"

She turned on her side to face the wall. "You name them."

ෆ

The darkness stayed in Mette, a darkness like the one after Ole died. She nursed the little ones because her breasts were full and painful, but they weren't good at it, having a hard time breathing and suckling at the same time. She felt a kinship with the animals, doing what every mother does, but she resented it. Ingebrigt named them Lars and Erling, but she didn't know which was which, and why should she? They were not going to be here long.

The next Sunday, when the babies were just four days old, they took them to the church to be baptized. Mette did not feel well enough, but Ingebrigt insisted, and she knew they couldn't put it off. Even if the Church said unbaptized babies would go straight to heaven, they needed the insurance that baptism gave them. Unbaptized, they were vulnerable to the hulderfolk, and even though she had little feeling for the infants, she certainly wasn't going to let *those things* take them.

She sat on the bed that morning in her Sunday finery, tired and weak, but ready to go.

"Ole, girls" she said. "*Kom.*" Sigrid, Marie, Inge and Ole lined up in front of her so she could inspect them. She smoothed the girls' hair, the grandmothers had braided it for them. They looked nice in their Sunday clothes even if they were a bit worn. She brushed the shoulders of Ole's jacket and then pulled it straight.

It was a tight squeeze to get everyone in the carriage. Mœrkei swung around to assess the size of the load, and shook his head, jingling the harness bells. Ingebrigt held the reins as Anders first helped the grandmothers in, handing them the babies once they were seated, then Mette, who groaned taking the first step. She was still very weak, her hair pulled back and covered with a white wool scarf that almost matched the color of her pale skin. Her hand shook as she reached for the side of the carriage. She muttered under her breath as she hoisted herself to her seat. The girls stood, and Ole sat up front with Anders and Ingebrigt.

The babies were quiet during the journey. The others were quiet, too, preparing for their visit to the Lord's house. The juniper scented the air, the snowy glacier rose majestically on the horizon. These things gave Mette solace, things bigger than their paltry lives.

The nine of them, the grandmothers first, then Mette and Ingebrigt, then Anders and the four children, made quite a procession as they walked to the front of the church. Mette looked up at the Lord Jesus Christ who opened his arms in welcome. She remembered that day long ago when he'd come down to talk to her but now He was just painted wood

When it was time, the pastor beckoned Mette and Ingebrigt to come forward to the baptismal font, and asked them, "Whom do you present for Holy Baptism?"

"We present our sons, Lars and Erling," Ingebrigt said.

The pastor read the baptism text from the hymnal, then he dipped his fingers into the basin of water and dribbled it on the heads of the sleeping babies, each in turn.

Lars and Erling Ingebrigtson Nornes, you are baptized in the name of the Father, and of the Son, and of the Holy Spirit. Lars and Erling Ingebrigtson Nornes, you are sealed by the Holy Spirit and marked with the cross of Christ forever. Amen.

Amen, they repeated, their heads bowed. No matter what happened now, they'd ensured their lives in heaven. The healing baptism water was bottled and given to them, a useful gift to be applied to future ailments. Mette handed the babies over to the grandmothers.

ೞ

"*Våkne opp,*" Ingebrigt said to Mette, giving her a little shake. It wasn't like her not to be up. It was already five. She should have been up an hour ago. He shook her again. She turned abruptly on her side and squinted at him. She propped herself up on an elbow, looked around at the room, then down at the babies who slept beside her, and fell back on the bed.

"*Ja, ja,*" she said.

Ingebrigt didn't like that she still brought the babies to bed with them after they'd been baptized, but her fear of the hulderfolk was stronger than overlaying. She'd taken all her children in their bed just after birth, when they were most vulnerable, even these two, whom the hulderfolk probably wouldn't want anyway.

"Seems to me you'd want them taken," Ingebrigt said. "The way you are."

Mette just shook her head like he didn't know a thing in the world. "You would throw open the door and invite the hulderfolk in?"

No, he didn't want that, but she knew as well as he, that the hulderfolk could do them no harm if they'd been baptized. Still, she insisted and that didn't fit right. On the one hand, she had as little to do with the babies as possible, and then on the other, she wanted to protect them. He couldn't figure her out. He thought of talking to Elling's wife about it, to see what she thought, but he didn't want to hang their troubles out for all to see. She fed them the way a sow feeds her piglets, lying on her side and letting them suckle, one at a time. She didn't do it so much for them as for herself, to relieve her full breasts. She secretly felt it was a waste of time. Even her mother's stern admonitions did no good. It felt as though a black spirit had flown into the house, an ill omen that would bring them harm.

Ingebrigt was never sure what he'd find when he entered the house. Would she talk or be silent, on her feet or in bed? Lately, she'd taken to lying down in the afternoon, something she'd never done before. Once he came home and she was sitting on the floor, playing a game with the children in the middle of the day! It wasn't her playing with the children that was odd, it was another odd thing on top of so many odd things. He often saw her rubbing her forehead so he suspected she had a headache. She seemed to avoid him, too.

The two older girls were back from the summer pasture and they took up much of the work, the grandmothers some, although they were too old to do anything that required strength. Kristina and Eva were now in charge of the milking and churning, all dairy related chores, and cleaning the cowshed. But now with autumn coming, there was more to be done. Everyone was needed to help with the haying and the harvesting of the crops, the potatoes and turnips. Ingebrigt didn't know how much he could depend on his wife.

She had been there for the sheep shearing. She was good with the sheep; they responded to her. She prepared them by calling them by name and talking to them while she ran her hands through the fleece, making sure it was clean of all straw or dirt. They had already been washed, but she felt for anything that might have been overlooked. Mette was teaching Kristina, and she was patient with her, showing her how to hold the sheep, how to keep the points of the shears clear of the skin. She never wanted to see blood, ever. If there was blood, they were doing it wrong. They were going too fast or too carelessly. When she was done clipping, she showed Kristina how to allow the sheep to stand slowly so in its eagerness to get away, it wouldn't get tangled in the fleece and tear it to pieces. She herself rolled the fleece, examining it again for any impurities.

That night, after the sheep shearing, she had a dream. She'd gone to sleep as soon as the sky darkened, but near morning, she sat up and called out, waking Ingebrigt. He shook her to wake her up.

"What is it?" he asked. 'What's wrong?" He heard the others stirring.

She looked terrified. "The babies, they were going to shear them, I held them...I couldn't stop them." She covered her face with her hands.

"The babies are right here, they're fine. Look."

She lay back down. "What does it mean, father," she asked Ingebrigt. "Does it mean something?"

"It's a dream," he said, lying back down. But he lay with his eyes open. He hoped it didn't mean anything.

☙

The twins were still alive a month later. If they weren't lying listless in the cradle, they were crying because they had the colic, their little legs and arms jerking erratically. It wasn't really crying, they weren't strong enough for that, but a kind of bleating. Gudrun came by with her medicine bag, and clucked and tsked over them, looked into their eyes and put her ear to their tiny chests. She had no medicine for them, she said, there wasn't anything they could do but wait and see if they gained strength. Their heartbeats were slow and weak, she said, and their systems weren't developed enough to digest the breast milk properly, which was why they were colicky. She, too, was surprised that they had managed to take in enough nourishment to keep them alive. Gudrun tightened her scarf under her chin and patted Mette's hand.

"They're in God's hands," she said. "It could be they'll live after all."

That was not what Mette wanted to hear. After Gudrun left, she stood over the swaddled infants. *"Du må gå nå,"* she whispered to them. *You must go now.* Why did they insist on life? A normal child was demanding, but these two, they wanted too much. They were small, but so big in worry and fear. Even if they lived, they may not grow up to be completely right. Signe Hansdatter's boy, he had come too early, and was never right in the head. Some even thought he might be a changeling. He was an idiot, what they called tetched, and even at the age of fifteen, he acted like he was five.

She went back and forth, from the instinct to protect them, to wanting to be rid of them. Even if she did everything to keep them alive, they would be a constant strain on her heart and on her nerves. She did not have the strength. When the bad thoughts came to her, she pushed them away, made the sign of the cross, said a prayer. She shuddered at such a thing. She sang it out of her head. *A mighty fortress is our God*...she sang, and she could see this made the others happy. She was singing, she must be well. It seemed reasonable in her mind, reasonable to want to put them out of their misery. Why prolong their agony? Wouldn't it be a blessing? Wouldn't everyone think so? She knew what the Old Ones would do. But God, would He punish her or would He understand and forgive her? From where did this thought come? From God Himself?

The potato and turnip harvests didn't leave her much time for thinking. The crops that year, like everything, had suffered from not enough rain. The potatoes were not plentiful and harder to find. At the end of the day the cart was only half filled, and this, of course, was not good. As *husmor*, it was her job to make sure the larders were full for winter, that there would be enough food for all, humans and animals. If the next day's pickings were the same, it did not bode well. That night, Mette crawled into bed, aching in every bone and muscle. The October nights were turning cold so she brought the babies to bed with her to keep them warm. She was not so heartless as to let them freeze.

She drifted into a heavy sleep and was back digging potatoes in a dream field, but in this field, there were only stones. When at last she found a potato, she bent down to dig it up, but it pulled back. She pulled harder, but the potato wasn't in the earth. It was held by one of the twins who was as strong as she was. *I had it first*, he growled. Then the other one was there, and it was her against them. They began to claw at her skirt and she couldn't get them off. She woke into half-consciousness, panting, and heard Ingebrigt snoring on his side, his back to her.

That was the sign she'd been waiting for. She was in danger, they all were. She had to do it. Quickly, instinctively, she rolled from her side to her back. She felt them beneath her, but there was little struggle. Had they even awakened? She folded her hands on her chest and prayed, *Father, into your hands I give my children. Receive them, Lord God, take them to your bosom.*

She kept her eyes closed and lay until there was no more movement, then she turned on her side, kissed the head of each, and cradled them to her bosom.

೩

Ingebrigt woke first that morning and saw Mette sleeping on her side, one arm flung over the face of one baby, the other baby face down. A bone-deep fear took hold of him. He moved her arm and recoiled. The little face was drained of color, the head turned sharply to the right, the other was face down. Neither showed any sign of movement. He turned the one face up, and gasped at the oddly fixed expression. He put his head to the boy's chest, then the other. There was no life in them. He slowly got out of bed and looked around. Had something come in the night? A demon? He stumbled to the privy, hoping when he returned, everything would be as it should. Mette would be awake and nursing the boys. But when he returned, it was just as he left it.

Ingebrigt poked Mette. "Mother, wake up. The babies are...something has happened...they're..." He choked on the words.

She blinked at him as she came to consciousness, and then sat up and looked at the swaddled infants. She put her hand to her mouth and began to cry.

"Do you think you...?" His looked at her with disbelief and sorrow. "Oh blessed Father in heaven, could one of us...?" He couldn't say it.

"*Være stille*," she said. Be quiet. "Don't let the others hear you." But already there was sounds of movement as the others woke.

"Heh?" her mother called out. "What is it?"

"God has taken the babies," she said softly. She carefully swaddled the bodies and clutched them to her bosom. She kissed their little heads. "*Stakkers, stakkers*," she said softly. Poor things.

She rocked back and forth. "We knew they weren't long for this world, we knew it, ah, but now that they're gone, I wish.... but it's God's will."

Ingebrigt felt as though all breath had left him. He stood back and tried to make sense of what he was seeing. Did she not realize what had happened? The wife he knew would have grieved loudly, called on God, shed more tears than that, run into the fjord, something, but this woman was calm. He didn't dare think...no, his wife would never do something like that. Never. It must have been an accident. Perhaps even he had unknowingly done it.

Mette sat on the edge of the bed holding the babies, and called out to the others to get up, to witness. The group of them, confused and just barely awake, stumbled over, shivering in the chilly semi-dark. Anders held Ole, and the three younger girls climbed on the bed whimpering. It was obvious to all, even the children, especially the children, that whatever she had to say was not going to be something they wanted to hear.

"God took Lars and Elling last night," Mette said calmly, and then hushed those who cried. "We knew this day was coming, but let's not mourn, let's be glad they are in their heavenly home with Sigrid and Ole and grandfather, where they will be fine and healthy. Let's pray for their souls. *Our father who art in heaven, hallowed be thy name...*" The ones who could, knelt on the floor, while the old ones sat.

Ingebrigt, still in his long underwear, prayed with them, then sat on the bed, his head in his hands.

"Why do you not mourn?" he asked her.

Mette put the babies on the bed and stood. "You know well enough that those two were not meant for this world. Why God sent them only to live two months, I do not know, only He knows. What I *do* know is that they are better off where they are. Do you have so little faith that you grieve for them?"

"But what happened? Did they just stop breathing, both at the same time?"

"Yes. They were sickly," Mette said, peering hard at him. "That is just what happened."

ଓଷ

Mette placed the two intertwined wreaths laced with ribbons on the coffin of her sons. As she knelt at the grave, she found a sense of peace within her, that her babies had the protection of the ancestors, that they were safe, that they no longer felt any pain. *Suffer the little children to come on to me*, the Lord Jesus had said. She saw Him, the Shepherd, in his white robe and with his staff, holding the boys, as

He held the little lamb. She saw them strong and healthy and happy to be with their Heavenly Father.

Lars and Erling Ingebrigtson Nornes, born and died 1896. Rest in peace.

༄

In late November with the waxing of the moon, Ingebrigt and Anders began sharpening the knives and axes for the slaughter. Round and round the grindstone went with Anders turning the wheel and Ingebrigt holding the knife to the stone. As soon as one was done, another was started. The shrill sound, the scrape of stone on steel, rang in the cold crisp air and grated on the nerves of every living thing. Even the birds flew away. "A time to kill," the Bible said, and it was that time.

Around then, a fortnight or so after the funeral, the sheriff, Lensmand Johannson, came by to talk to them. It surprised and worried Ingebrigt since everyone in the parish knew the boys had not been well so there should have been no reason for suspicion. They had had a church burial with the congregation present, they had not tried to hide what happened. When they saw the sheriff's carriage approach the farm, Mette straightened and smoothed her hand over her front, and went inside. Ingebrigt walked out to meet him.

Karl was from Fimreite, a friend of her former master. Mette had known him since she was a girl. He was short with small beady eyes under thick dark eyebrows and wore his cap pulled low on his forehead. Ingebrigt thought he looked a bit like a ferret. Mette invited him in and offered him coffee. She pulled coats and scarves from their pegs and told the three girls to take little Ole and go outside for a while, even though it was terribly cold. She made sure they were warm and bundled up, mittens and boots on. She pulled Ole's cap down and wrapped a scarf several times around his neck so just his eyes peeped through.

"Go help your sisters with the creatures," she said. "Don't come back until we call you."

Karl greeted the children kindly, and shook each of their hands, then went over to Kristi and Synnøve who sat in their rocking chairs, and greeted them. Ingebrigt told the old crones to mind the children while Karl talked to them, and they grudgingly put on their coats and shuffled out the door with a backward suspicious glance at the lendsman. After they'd left, Karl took off his cap and sat down.

Mette put coffee on the table in front of him.

"I'm sorry to hear of your sudden misfortune," he said, blowing on his coffee to cool it.

Ja, ja, takk takk. But it was not sudden," Mette said straightening her apron. "They were early, you know, and poorly...so we knew it could happen." Then she said as though she had run out of patience on the subject, "They were too small, no bigger than your thumb."

Karl seemed amused at her use of that expression. He had spoken to Gudrun and so knew of the ill health of the boys, but for them to die at the same time "seemed unusual," he said. He leaned back in his chair and studied her.

"*Ja, ja,* but that was as it should be," Mette said, surprised that he'd find that unusual. "Praise God for that. They came together into the world and He saw to it that they left together."

"Tell me how it happened," he said and pulled a small notebook and a pencil from inside his jacket.

Ingebrigt began, "I saw them first..."

Karl interrupted him. "Let your wife tell it."

"But, I don't understand, there is nothing to tell," Mette said. "They were born too early, they were sickly and they died. What more is there to say about it?"

"Just tell me for the record," he said. "So I know for sure."

She looked to Ingebrigt and then at her hands. "I don't remember so much. I was tired that night, I know that. We had picked potatoes all day, so I went right to sleep and slept all night, which isn't how it usually goes. It was Ingebrigt who had to wake me and he told me the babies were gone. I didn't know, I hadn't heard..." Her voice caught and tears sprang to her eyes, which she quickly wiped away.

Karl looked at Ingebrigt and he nodded. She spoke the truth. He did have to wake her and he did tell her the babies were dead. He could honestly say that nothing had awakened him. He didn't offer anything, only answered Karl's questions.

"So you woke in the morning to find the that both babies had died during the night and neither of you heard anything. Is that how it was?"

"Ja ja, that's right," Ingebrigt said, and Mette nodded.

"They were about two months? Isn't that unusual to still have them in your bed?"

"It was cold, I didn't want them to freeze." She clasped her hands in her lap.

"And what did you see when you woke?"

Ingebrigt answered. "As though they were sleeping, except they were very pale and there was no breath." He swallowed hard.

Karl took a sip of coffee and put his cup down, and looked at Mette. "You've heard of overlaying," he said. Ingebrigt stiffened.

Mette tsked. *"Ja, ja, stakkers."* Poor little ones. "It's a terrible thing. Terrible."

"Could that be what happened?"

Mette dropped her head and muttered under her breath.

"What was that?" Karl asked, leaning towards her.

"God will surely punish us," she said more loudly, keeping her head down, "if that was what it was. I pray that did not happen. I pray to God for that."

Karl tapped his pencil on the table while he studied her.

He asked how many children they had, even though he knew, and if they had lost others and how they had died, and Mette answered, with Ingebrigt verifying what she said. Karl looked about the room, particularly at the bed and asked if that was where they slept. Mette nodded. He went over and looked at it, pulled back the coverlet Mette took such pride in, looking for what, Ingebrigt didn't know. He moved towards Karl to protest, but then feared he might think he was trying to keep him from seeing something.

"Seven children, four adults, many mouths to feed," Karl said, and Ingebrigt knew what he was suggesting.

"We manage," Ingebrigt said, rubbing his bad leg. Mette looked out the window as though she'd seen something of interest.

Karl wrote something in his book. "That's it then," he said and looked up at them from under his thick eyebrows. He put the book and pencil back in his pocket, finished his coffee, and put his cap back on. He shook their hands and offered his condolences again. Ingebrigt walked out with him.

When the men reached the carriage, Karl took his horse by the bridle and led him towards the road. "I could get a writ to examine the bodies," he said in a low voice, "but I won't." He climbed into the carriage and picked up the reins. "I'm not sure your wife knows what happened. She might have done it on purpose, I've seen it before. But right now she's in a state...where she hasn't...how do I say it?" He searched the ground. "She's not all there, if you see what I mean. If she did it, she's made it in her mind as something she had to do for the well-being of the others."

Ingebrigt said nothing.

"Gudrun has stated the babies were not likely to live long, so we'll leave it there." He held out his hand and Ingebrigt shook it. "I'd keep an eye on her though."

Ingebrigt didn't respond. He should have objected to Karl speaking about his wife in such a familiar way. He should have defended Mette. He watched until Karl turned to the main road, then he slowly walked back to the house. The girls ran up to him and asked if they could go in, they were cold. Little Ole was crying, he wanted to come in, too. His toes were frozen.

"Just a little while longer," Ingebrigt said.

Karl had put in words what he had been circling: Mette didn't grasp what she'd done. It sickened him, but had they been animals, he would have done the same. They used up too much time and effort when there was little to spare. If she had asked him first, would he have consented? He rubbed his face and looked up at the infinite sky. People are not animals. No, he would not have consented. It was a sin, a grievous sin, and he feared how they would be punished. He held out a small hope that it was not true.

Mette was where he'd left her, darning a sock.

"He's gone then?" she asked.

"Yes, he's gone." He watched her for a while and then pulled up a chair and sat in front of her.

"Stop for a moment..." He put his hand on hers. "You must tell me the truth now."

She kept her eyes down, and mumbled something.

"Mette, you must..."

"You know what happened, you saw," she said.

"But *how* did it happen, Mette Hansdatter? Did you have anything to do with it?"

Kristi stuck her head in then to see if they could come in, and Ingebrigt shouted. "*Nei!*"

Mette folded the sock in her lap, and said finally, "I did what any good *husmor* would do."

A black shadow fell on them, dark as ink, dark as the heart of Satan.

"Do you know what you're saying?" Ingebrigt asked.

"They are with God," Mette said.

"They might have lived..."

"Yes, that was the risk." She looked hard at him, the way she had that morning when he'd asked her if they'd died on their own, and she'd said yes.

Mette Hansdatter, his fairest, sweetest girl. She wasn't so old that he couldn't still see the girl he courted—her plaited hair, her flushed face. He saw her laughing at something he'd said that wasn't even clever, and on their wedding day, how she'd danced round the bonfire, with the sparks flying high into the dark sky, her face full of light and joy. That girl drowned the day he pulled Mette from the sea, the day she howled like a dog out of grief for Ole.

Ingebrigt sat back in the chair and looked at his wife, then at her hands and the gold band on her finger. He remembered what he'd said when he gave it to her. *You can be sure of me.* That was still true, even now. For better or worse, he'd said. But this, this was something he wouldn't have dreamed of, not his Mette.

"I pray the day does not come when we have to put you away for what you've done."

"God was with me, Ingebrigt, you must know that. I was not alone."

It was all he could do not to grab her and shake her, to make her come to her senses. He stared up at the ceiling as though seeking God's help, then walked to the door and turned to face her.

"The twins died a natural death, that is what the record shows, and that is what happened. We will never speak of this again."

☙

Mette stood in the cold shed, her arms crossed over her chest, and watched as Ingebrigt and Anders inspected the sheep. She would rather not be there at all, but as *husmor*, they needed her advice on which animals were to be butchered. They considered the age first, but also inspected the sheeps' eyes and mouths, felt the thickness of their flanks and the fullness of their breasts to see how healthy they were. She nodded when Ingebrigt said the two old ewes, Rose and Lady, were likely candidates. Mette had raised them from lambs, they were a wedding gift from Niels and Elin, but she understood they were past their best years, that their productivity had declined. She didn't react one way or the other. They trudged to the cowshed next, picking their way over the frozen mud. Mette was relieved when they passed over Guldros, her favorite. But what did it matter, the cow's time would come, if not this year, then next year, or the next.

Besides determining which of the animals would be the least likely to make it through the winter, they had to consider the amount of fodder stored and how much meat the family would need. Thanks to her, there was still a pound or so of meat left in the *stabbur* from the last slaughter. As a good husmor, she knew it would not do to run out. She had made it stretch over the year, rationing out a little here and there. That was her job. She would like Rose and Lady to live, too, but that didn't matter when it came to putting food on the table.

She saw the faces of the dead boys everywhere, in the snowbank, in her porridge, behind her eyes when she tried to sleep. She'd sing or pray, recite Bible verses, anything to block them out. The image of them lying on the bed, unnatural and pale, the life gone from their tiny bodies, would never leave her. She wished she could carve it out of her head. She sprinkled linseed around the house to keep them from haunting her.

When it was decided the two ewes would be the ones, Ingebrigt kept his eyes on her. He was always watching her.

The next morning, the day of the slaughter, she rose with dread. It was still dark as pitch, dawn would not come for a few hours. Kristina had made coffee and a basin of melted snow was heating on the stove. The men were seated at the table in their jackets, smoking by lantern light. The solemnity of the task ahead of them made for little talk. Mette dressed slowly. She let the children sleep, there was no reason for them to be up yet.

Finally, Ingebrigt tapped the ashes from his pipe, and pushed himself from the chair. *"Ja, ja,"* he said quietly. "Better get on with it." The two men pulled on their gloves and tugged their caps low to cover their ears. A cold draft blew in when the door opened.

Mette sipped her coffee, nibbled at flatbrød, waited. She braced herself for the cries of the sheep, hoping they wouldn't come, knew they had to. And they did, out of the dark into her heart, cries so like a child's. She gripped the cup. Then it was quiet. Then Ingebrigt's sharp whistle signaling it was over. The women, except for Eva who stayed behind with the children, trudged out with the buckets and basins. Anders had started a fire and over it hung a cauldron filled with melting snow. By firelight, she could make out the creatures on the slaughter bench, the steam from their warm bodies rose in the cold air, blood soaked the snow. Magpies perched nearby, studying their every move, keeping an eye out for a dropped morsel. There would be little left for them when they were through.

Mette brushed her hand over the belly of one sheep, then the other. *"Min babyer,"* she murmured. My poor babies. *"Stakkars."* She dug her fingers into the fleece, then pressed her forehead on the still warm body of one of them. Flickers of concern passed over the eyes of the others. She began to keen, a low thin wail, bent over, her hands on the sheep. The keening turned to silent weeping. She pulled away and covered her mouth with a hand sticky with blood and lanolin, the other pressed against her belly. "My babies," she said again.

Her mother came beside her. "Go," she said. "Go to the house, we'll manage without you."

Ingebrigt jerked his head toward the house. "Go now."

She stayed. She wiped her face and hands with her apron and joined them at the table. She looked at each of them, Ingebrigt, Anders, Kristi, Synnøve, Kristina, each in the eye. *"If any provide not for his own, and specially for those of his own house, he hath denied the faith, and is worse than an infidel."* She picked up a knife and began her work.

☙

Jonsbrygga looked as if it were made of snow, with the roof covered and the snow banked against it. A plume of smoke rose from the chimney against the gray sky. Icicles hung from the eaves and glistened in the sun. Mette had seen a pure white stoat slink near the cowshed and told Anders to keep an eye out for it. The fur would bring a good price.

Advent was upon them and there was much to do before *Lussia*, December thirteenth. They didn't believe it anymore, but it lingered, deep down, the fear that the demon spirit Lussi would punish them if they weren't done with the Christmas preparations by then.

It was cold and dark; the sun was out only a few hours a day. When Mette sat in her chair in the evening doing her sewing chores, her mind drifted away and she imagined she was a bird and could fly away to someplace warm. She'd seen pictures of Israel in the Bible so she went there, perched on an olive tree, for they had those kinds of trees, and watched the dark-skinned people, so different from herself. Once she was so deep into that world, that Ingebrigt had to shake her to get her attention, and when she looked at him, she wasn't sure where she was.

Mette went at the cleaning with great industry, as though to rid the house of the twins' spirits. Replacing the hay in the beds and airing the bedding was first. The sheep covers were hung near the fire to get rid of the vermin and each piece of bedding was taken outside and shaken. She imagined she saw whatever was left of the twins disperse in the air, like a flutter of tiny moths. Then all the blankets were hung over the fence to freshen them up and to freeze anything else that might still lurk there.

Built-up grime was scraped from the walls and a fresh coat of whitewash applied. They brought out the Christmas coverlets from the trunk where they'd been stored since last Christmas, and hung them on the walls. The girls swept the floor from corner to corner, opened the door, and with one big movement, the accumulated pile was swept outdoors.

"How many more days?" the children asked over and over, running in circles. Little Ole had turned two in November, and Inge held up four splayed fingers when asked how old she was. The twins Marie and Sigrid were already six. Mette put their frenzy to a purpose. When they replaced the hay in the beds, she had the children jump on them to even it out. She let them strew the juniper on the floor. She found ways for them to help with the baking.

"Like this?" Inge asked as she pressed a small ball of dough into the special pan for *sandkaker*.

"A little more," Kristina said, "so it's even with the pan."

The three smaller girls were allowed to stir the batter for *pepperkaker*, gingerbread cookies, and to cut the rolled-out dough into shapes. The house began to smell like Christmas with the sweet and spicy smells of ginger and juniper. Everyone began to feel the spirit, even Mette. She felt stronger and began to look forward to the holiest day of the year. Even though they were still a few days away from Christmas, she allowed all the children to have a cookie, and she allowed herself one, too.

One day after she'd done her morning chores, there was enough light to gather pine branches in the forest. It wasn't too cold so she bundled up the four smaller children to come with her. It was a fine day, the sky was as blue as the Virgin Mary's robe and the children were in high spirits, especially little Ole, who's little cheeks were as red as holly berries. It wasn't often he saw his mother in such a gay mood, and he clung to her coat. Mette sang and they all joined in, clapping their hands.

Vi klapper i hendene,
vi synger og vi ler,
så glad er vi, så glad er vi.
Vi svinger oss i kretsen og neier, og bukker.

We clap our hands,
we sing and we laugh,
so glad we are, so happy we are.
We turn in circles and curtsy and bow.

Their laughter startled the birds who took off from the trees, flapping their wings and cawing, and that made them all laugh more, as they raised their hands and called to them. The ravens looked at them curiously, bobbing their heads as if to say, *What's going on here? What is this noise you're making?*

Everything was almost ready for the holiday. She had just taken the cod from its lye solution and put it to soak in cold water for a few days, when she suddenly felt sick to her stomach. She ran outside just in time. Up came the porridge from her morning meal. She thought it had something to do with the lye, but then everyone got sick, except Ingebrigt, and they hadn't been anywhere near the lye.

It would have been comical if it weren't so awful. They lay on their beds, holding their bellies and groaning, or staggering to the privy. Soon the house stunk of vomit and excrement. It lasted only two days for most of them, but it was harder on the grandmothers and the children, especially on little Ole. When all the rest of them were back to normal, Ole still languished. He lay on the bed, pale and weak, barely able to lift his head. Christmas was just five days away.

The good Gudrun swooped in, in her long black cape and white wimple, carrying her black bag.

"What has he eaten?" she asked, putting her hand on Ole's forehead, and then on his stomach. He flinched and began to whimper.

Mette explained that they'd all been sick but she didn't know what caused it. "Maybe the fresh meat? We don't have it so much."

Gudrun frowned, took off her cloak and sat beside Ole. "Could he have gotten into something?"

"I don't think so."

"Does it hurt here?" she asked Ole, and gently pressed on his stomach. He winced and weakly nodded. She asked for a cup of water, added a valerian tincture, and held a spoonful to his mouth, but he retched and jerked away. She took out a piece of hard candy from her pocket.

"I bet you'd like a sweet," she said, with a sly smile, but he shook his head, which frightened Mette more than anything. Little Inge stood by the bed and pet her brother's small damp head, jealously eyeing the candy.

"We must get something in him." Gudrun said, straightening. "Water, soup, something. He needs nourishment. If he can't keep anything down, I can't say."

Ingebrigt stiffened, and he glared at Mette.

Gudrun gave all the children a piece of candy. Then, as she was leaving, she turned and said, "He must eat something, drink. He must."

Mette put another blanket over the small boy who lay curled on his side shivering. This could not be happening again, God would not allow it. He was sure to get better, just as they all had. She wished she could make the boy be himself again, do that tiresome thing he often did of repeating the last word someone said. She longed to hear him say just one word in his cheerful sing-songy way. She sat beside him, opened her hymnal and quietly began to sing. *Du Herre, som er sterk og stor... Oh Lord, thou art so great and strong.* She would feed him with scripture. Inge pulled up a stool and sat beside her mother. She hummed along and pretended she knew the words as she rolled and unrolled the hem of Mette's apron. In the fading light, the crones' knitting needles clicked, their rockers creaked. The spinning wheel hummed as Kristina spun.

Ole slept. It was late evening, past supper. Mette pulled her cloak and scarf from the wall and went to the cowshed. She rooted in the cold frosty hay. The cows swung their heads to look at her with their big eyes. She liked being with the creatures. She wished she could be a cow, with nothing to do but eat and shit, no cares in the world. She liked the cold, she didn't deserve to be warm, she didn't deserve to live. She was so tired of it all.

She didn't know how long she'd been there, if she'd slept or not, when she saw a lantern come towards her. She pulled her scarf over her face, and used her heels to push deeper into the hay.

"*Nei*," she said. "Let me be."

"You'll freeze to death."

"I want to freeze to death," she said.

"Stand up," Ingebrigt said, gripping her elbow, trying to pull her up. "Ole is gone."

"No, he's sleeping, I covered him."

"Mette Hansdatter, for God's sake, stop this. You must stop it."

There was anger in his voice, but something else. He was tired, he was in pain. She didn't need a lantern to know these things.

"You have done this," he said. "It is because of your wickedness that our son is dead. You must come now." He turned and left.

She saw the dark shape of him and the lantern recede back into the night. She shook her head. That was a terrible thing for him to say. She'd just been with Ole, she'd covered him, he was sleeping. He'd see for himself when he got back. Ole might even be better, he probably was. She imagined him sitting up and chattering. *Mor, I'm not sick anymore,* he'd say, and then she'd be angry at Ingebrigt for telling such an awful lie. She heaved herself up and brushed off the hay. She went to Guldros and lay her head on the beast. She had no tears. She had vomited them out along with everything else when she was sick.

In His infinite wisdom, God would be merciful. He wouldn't take another of her boys. He would be merciful.

"That is how it will be, won't it, Guldros?" The animal lowed softly and swished her tail. Mette gave her a pat and slowly walked back to the house under a sky so clear and full of stars, it made her hopeful. But the bitter wind pulled at her cloak and stung her face reminding her she had no say in such things.

☙

When Mette returned to the house, all was quiet but for the sounds of sniffling and noses being blown. They all looked at her with such sorrow she feared that what Ingebrigt had said was true. Inge pressed her face into her mother's skirt. "Ole won't wake up," she cried. Mette saw where they had laid him, on a pallet over two chairs, a blanket over him. Two kerosene lamps dimly lit the room, one on the table, one on the mantle. The long shadow of the cupboard fell over his small body.

Mette quickly took off her coat and rushed over to the boy. "*Min sønn,*" she said, throwing off the blanket and kneeling beside him, putting her lips to his forehead. "*Min sønn.*" She picked up the lifeless body.

"*Stakkers,*" she tsked as she walked with him. Poor thing.

Ingebrigt pulled out his handkerchief and blew into it.

Mette faced them. "I left for a little while, just a little while..." Her voice rose. "Couldn't any of you have done something?"

They stared at her.

"Am I to go to all the trouble of bringing children into the world only to see them snatched away over and over again?"

Ingebrigt came forward and said low to her. "What is the matter with you?" he asked. "They are suffering enough."

She glared at him. "*They* are suffering? And you! What did you do for him?"

"Look to yourself if you want to cast blame."

"I've done nothing but care for the child since he fell ill. It's up to me to do everything. I make sure everyone eats, I feed the livestock, milk the cows. I clean the house, I bake the bread, I weave your blankets and knit your socks and make your meals while your lordship smokes his pipe and makes more children so they can suffer and die."

The room fell into a stunned silence. Ingebrigt stepped towards her, but she stood firmly, holding the boy.

"You are out of your head," he said.

"And why wouldn't I be?" she said. "How can I not be?"

Ingebrigt could not answer that; he could only shake his head and retreat to a dark corner.

"Pick up the boy's blanket," Mette ordered Inge, who quickly obeyed. "And put it on the pallet."

Mette lay the boy down and lifted the sides of the blanket to cover him.

"Bring me the brush," she said, holding out her hand. She brushed the boy's hair, spit on a corner of her apron and wiped his face. He was so small, such a little thing, just like Sigrid. She ran her hand over his little cheek and kissed him. "He's so small, so small."

"Sleep now," she said, kissing his soft cheek. "*Sove nå.*" She sat beside the boy. One hand rested on his chest, with the other she pulled out her handkerchief and pressed it to her eyes.

"He asks too much of me," she said, bowing her head. "Too much."

⋙

Just a day after Ingebrigt nailed the coffin shut, it was Christmas Eve. The juniper was still as fragrant, the cookies waited in their tins, and the season's coverlets on the wall proclaimed it was Christmas, but there was no joy at Jonsbrygga. Mette spent her days in prayer, either in her rocking chair, her head bowed, her shawl over her shoulders, or on her knees. She kept her Bible with her. She felt certain now that God was punishing her, for long ago asking Him not to send her more children. Why else had every boy born after her sinful request been taken? Even the twins. No matter what Ingebrigt thought, God had been there.

He was right to judge her.

She managed to get ready for Christmas services, putting on her finest dress and her *solje* at her throat. She longed for His Word in His House, to hear the story of the birth of the Savior, their only hope in this wretched world.

They bundled up for the ride to the church, warm coats, wool scarves wound around their necks, wool mittens. The older girls made sure the younger ones were dressed warmly. The carriage crunched over the packed snow as they made their way to the church in the dim afternoon light. The cold air on her face, the jingle of the bells on Morekei's harness and the creature's visible breath, were like little gifts.

God would have mercy on her.

And behold, an angel of the Lord stood before them, and the glory of the Lord shone around them, and they were sore afraid. Mette rocked gently with eyes closed as she listened to the familiar and beloved story. *You will find a babe wrapped in swaddling cloths, lying in a manger.* She could see it so plainly as if she were there. The crisp dark night, the star shining brightly over the manger, the animals gathered around, snorting and shaking their heads. Mary gently placed the baby Jesus in her arms, and Mette could feel his holiness like a light against her breast and she fell to her knees cradling him. Tears gathered in her throat, but she held them back. Please forgive me, she said to the baby Jesus.

After the service, the congregation moved to the cemetery to place candles on the graves of the departed. They stood with their heads bowed while a light snow fell silently on them. Some of the candles flickered and went out, others seemed to get stronger and glow brighter. Someone began the hymn *Stille Natt,* and they all joined in, their ragged voices rising in the cold night air.

When they returned home, the women put on their aprons and went to work. Mette was to make the *rommegrøt*, and the tediousness of the task was just what she needed. She put another log in the stove, and pulled out pots, one for the milk, one for the cream. When the cream came to a boil, Eva took up the job of sifting in the flour, while Mette stirred vigorously with a whisk. She held the *tvare* in her fist as she stirred and stirred, coaxing the fat out of the curd. Little Ole would have been standing on a chair beside her now, as Inge was, watching as, magically, the golden butter fat began to rise to the surface. Round and round she stirred. The butter was poured off and Eva slowly added scalded milk to the pot, as Mette continued to stir until her arm began to tire, and the porridge became smooth and silky, with not a single lump. *Take not thy holy spirit from me.* She poured the mixture into a big wooden bowl, drizzled the drawn butter on top and sprinkled it with cinnamon and sugar, and because it was Christmas, raisins.

Before sitting at the table, Mette poured a small bowl of porridge for the *nisse*, added a pat of butter, and instructed the girls to take it to the barn. They could not forget the farm spirit, not on this special day.

Ingebright said the blessing. The glow of the candlelight, the holiness of the season and with her family around her, she felt the presence of God. Her grief was great, immense, it was part of her, just as the blood that flowed through her veins, and she knew it would never go away. But her gratitude for what she had was as wide and deep as the fjord. God had shown her this. She felt His mercy and His many blessings, and she dared to think she'd been forgiven.

The two pure white tapered candles made just for that evening burned evenly and brightly throughout the evening and neither went out early. That was a good sign: hope for the new year.

1898

A year came and went, then another. The fields were planted and harvested; the creatures were herded to the mountain; the cows milked, butter churned, the cheese made; the hay grew, was cut and stored; they fished and hunted and kept themselves nourished as best they could; the children grew.

They went on.

They'd had another boy. "This one will live," Mette had said. "God has forgiven me." Mette risked the wrath of Ole Ellingson's ghost, but she refused to name the child Ole in case there was a curse on the name. They settled on Nils, after Ingebrigt's uncle. Except for the breast feeding, she gave over the care of Nils to Eva who was fifteen and confirmed. Mette felt she had fulfilled her obligation by carrying and birthing the child, the girls could do the rest. Indeed, it did sometimes seem that the boy was more Eva's than Mette's.

One summer's evening, Mette was inside cleaning up after supper, and Ingebrigt sat outside smoking his pipe, whittling. It was warm and clear, the sun reflected off the glassy surface of the fjord. He rubbed his leg. It always ached at the end of a day. The girls, except for Eva who had stayed home to take care of the baby, were at the summer pasture and as it was a Saturday night, Anders was up there, too. Ingebrigt remembered as a lad when he trekked up the mountain to see the girls. Very faintly, he could hear a fiddle playing.

He was deep in thought as he fashioned a piece of birch wood into a whistle. From inside the baby shrieked and giggled as Eva got him ready for bed. He heard the broom move across the planked floor as Mette swept up. She had become even more silent after the second Ole's death, except when she talked to herself, as she often did. It was as though she traveled back and forth between the real world and her own. Now, in the summer months, she'd often sit by the side of the fjord, gazing out at the water, sky and mountains, a bowl of unpeeled potatoes or unshucked peas in her lap. He knew she was far away then, off somewhere in her head. She'd say she was going to pick berries, then be gone the whole day, and come back with half a pail. What had she been doing?

It saddened and angered him that she wasn't like other women. She couldn't take hardship in stride, she was too nervous. His thoughts went back to when they were young, how he used to envy her and Finn, and his joy when she chose him. She didn't really choose him over Finn, but sometimes he saw it that way. That day when they were cutting branches in Fimreite and she brought them water, how pretty she had been, with the flour smudges on her face. What would Finn think of her now, he wondered. As though he'd said it aloud, Mette stuck her head out and asked, "Heh?"

Had he said something aloud? Maybe he was going off in the head, too.

They heard from Finn every now and again, usually a letter at Christmas with a photo. He had eight children, three girls and five boys, but they'd lost one, a daughter, to diphtheria. Mette listened to the letters with interest, but her eyes did not light up anymore. Finn wrote in every letter that he missed Norway, the mountains and the sea, but he did not regret emigrating. Life was good for them, at least that's what he said. He hoped one day to return to Norway for a visit, to see the place again before he went to his grave.

Ingebrigt brushed off the wood shavings from the whistle and wiped it on his pants. He put it to his lips and blew. The sound was high and sharp and immediately brought Mette to the door.

"What's that for?" she asked.

"To call you," he joked.

"It works then."

He reached for her hand, and held it, until she pulled away.

☙

The shriek of an animal woke Mette. The sound raised the hair on her arms, and her hands instinctively went to her pregnant belly. As she came to consciousness, she wondered if she'd dreamed it, but then she heard another loud screech, this time closer.

She reached for Ingebrigt.

"*Far*," she whispered. No matter how deeply asleep Ingebrigt was, he always responded to her voice.

"Heh?"

"Is it a spirit?" she whispered, digging her fingers into his arm.

Ingebrigt sat up and listened. "Barn owl," he said, and went back to sleep.

That did not comfort Mette. Now that she was awake, it would be almost impossible to go back to sleep, even when the shrieking finally stopped and the night was still again. She lay on her back, her hands on her chest, and listened to the water lapping at the shore. Was the owl warning her of something? Was more misfortune about to come down on them? She'd never forgotten her mother's story about the owl at her birth, and she had always wondered what it might have meant. Now as she lay awake in the cold dark, Mette realized it *had* meant something. That owl had been a messenger, a messenger of doom. She'd had nothing but bad luck. She felt a little chill as she often did when it seemed spirits were around. And the white one she'd seen with Finn, the one she felt was trying to tell her something. Hadn't he foretold then, what she feared, that America would separate her from Finn? Shouldn't she have known right then that she wasn't going with him?

She thought she heard a tapping, then a sigh. She pulled the blanket higher. Sometimes she thought she heard the twin boys crying, begging for food. Ole, too. Would his ghost look as he did when he died, so pale and thin? She felt the weight of her guilt. Maybe Ole Ellingson was screeching at her for not naming the last boy Ole after the one who died. She promised right there and then, if the one she was carrying was a boy, she'd name him Ole. She put her hand over her eyes, then over her mouth, smelling her sour breath.

She took stock of her life as she lay there, the grief she carried, the grief that was yet to come. Another baby was on the way. It seemed that was the pattern, just as the moon waxed and waned, every two years a baby. As soon as she stopped nursing, she became pregnant. When would she be too old to have babies? Their youngest, Nils, born fifteen months after Ole died, was two already and getting too big for the cradle. So far, he seemed a healthy child, but what did that mean? Nothing. That barn owl could swoop down and snatch him away in the blink of an eye.

She muttered to herself, "Nothing is for sure."

"Heh?" Ingebrigt grunted.

She turned on her side, scratched her bed bug bites. And now Anders had announced he was going to America. She knew what he was going to say before he'd said it. He couldn't look at her. She grabbed him by the arm. Have you prayed on this? she'd asked. Has God given you an answer? She couldn't stop him anymore than Kristi could stop Lars or Finn. Anders, the only son who'd made it to adulthood, and now he was leaving. It felt like a punch to her heart. But why shouldn't he go? She saw how they all regarded her differently since the twins' deaths and then Ole's, as though she were some kind of demon. Maybe she was the reason he was going.

Maybe he couldn't stand to be around her. She did not want to think about that, but that's exactly the sort of thing she did think of at that hour. *The grief that was yet to come.* She'd never see him again, she knew that much. The Old Ones murmured, *He is going, there is nothing you can do. He is going.*

Kristina wondered if she should go, too. She was nineteen and in service on a farm in Laerdal, but that was not for her, she said. She did not want to milk cows the rest of her life. She wanted to go to Bergen and find work in a hotel, or as a maid for a well-to-do family. Then, when she'd earned enough, maybe she'd go to America, but she was not sure if that's what she wanted. Mette prayed she'd find something to keep her in Norway.

Once Kristina had asked Mette if she'd ever wanted to emigrate. They were rolling out flatbrød, and the question surprised Mette since her daughter rarely showed any interest in her.

"Everyone thinks about it, I suppose," she'd answered. *I will see you there, Finn had said when he embraced her.* "But my place was here. Who would have cared for your grandmother if I'd gone? "That's too thick," she said, pointing to the dough Kristina was working on.

"It does seem rather far-fetched, you in America," Kristina chuckled.

Mette held her tongue. "America's not for everyone. If I had emigrated, you wouldn't be here."

That gave Kristina something to think about, but not for long. "I would have been born in America, that's all," she exclaimed.

"You have no sense. I wouldn't have married your father if I'd gone." She no longer wanted to continue with this subject, which was veering too close to things she did not want to speak about. "You're here now and you've got work to do. America's a long way off."

"I'm not sure I would fit in America either," Kristina said. Mette took measure of her daughter who had grown to be a very pretty woman with smooth skin, dark blue eyes and silky brown hair.

"Don't roll it *too* thin," Mette warned.

She was rich in daughters, all strong, healthy girls. She saw them lined up in her mind's eye: Kristina, Eva, Marie, Sigrid and Inge. Hard-working, good girls, all. If she had failed raising boys, she had succeeded with her girls. She couldn't have managed without them, of this she was sure, and she thanked God for them every day.

They were so brave compared to her. They dared to want more than shoveling manure and pulling rocks from the cold earth. Even if Kristina didn't go, another one might. America, robber of children.

1903

Mette pulled her thinning hair back tightly into a bun, securing the combs firmly against her scalp. She greased her hands with lard and smoothed it down. She didn't want a single hair in her way. She was a *gamel jente* now, an old woman of forty-four, and slow to get going in the morning. She'd gotten plump, the buttons on her frayed, worn dress strained across her breasts and belly. Her teeth hurt, she couldn't chew on the left side, and she needed spectacles, but that was a luxury they couldn't afford.

With Kristina in Bergen, and Eva away in service, she relied on the twins, Marie and Sigrid, who were thirteen, and Inge, who was eleven, to help her with the chores and with the boys. Nils was five already, Ole almost three, and the infant Lars. The animals had to be fed and milked, the cream separated and butter made, the meals prepared, wood gathered and water lugged in, spinning and weaving, knitting and mending, sewing, ironing, baking bread, and on and on. Who wouldn't want to go to America and live a life of ease?

Ingebrigt's mother Kristi was still with them, but she could do little for herself. Even with the help of two canes, she could barely walk. She called out for someone to help her with the chamber pot and Marie and Sigrid argued over who had to do it, until Ingebrigt commanded Sigrid to go, which she did, with a scorching look at the gloating Marie.

"Don't worry, you'll be next," Ingebrigt said to Marie.

Her mother had been gone almost a year, but Mette still found herself turning to ask her something. For a long time, the sight of her empty rocking chair could bring her to tears, but when she was alive, the constant creaking back and forth all day long grated on her nerves. Just before she died, as Mette sat with her, Synnøve put her hand on Mette's sleeve, and said simply, "You can go now." At the time, Mette took her to mean that she could leave her side, but later she wondered if she meant, now she could go to America.

America's shadow was always there. Anders left in April. He was twenty-four years old, strong and pretty to look at. She would never see him again on this earth. As she watched him leave that morning, she did not call out, she did not run after him, she did not throw herself at his feet. She did nothing to embarrass him. She stood at the door and gripped the jamb. *Gud være med deg,* she called after him, waving a handkerchief. God be with you. That was all she could say. *Gud være med deg.* My son, my first-born. She did not shed a tear until she was alone. Then, as she'd done the day Finn left, she went to the mountain and watched his boat sail away. She fell to her knees and prayed he would always remember her, and then she wept for him, for herself, for all those he left behind.

In a year, they'd received one letter from him, which said he'd made it fine, that he'd been to Wisconsin and seen his uncles, Finn and Lars, and that he was planning to go West. She stirred sugar into her coffee. She had been pregnant with her own Lars when Anders left, so the two brothers would never know one another. One leaving, one arriving. As though the infant sensed her thinking about him, he began to wail, and she called to Inge to tend to him. The crying continued and Mette called again. Where was that girl?

"Jeg kommer," Inge said, climbing down from the loft. Her hair hung loose down her back, and Mette made her bring the brush over so she could braid it. If she waited for Inge to do it, it would never get done.

There was something about Inge, she couldn't put her finger on it, but she wasn't like her other daughters. She was dreamy, preoccupied. She'd start one chore, then get distracted and do something else. Mette tangled more with Inge than the other girls. Maybe it was because she looked so much like her mother. She was stubborn, too, like her grandfather, and didn't listen as she should.

Inge went to little Lars, cooed and chirped to him to make him laugh. She picked him up and snuggled her face into his neck until Mette barked at her to just change him and bring him to her so she could feed him, she didn't have all day. She saw she'd hurt her feelings, but she hated the lollygagging that Inge was so good at.

"Yes, *mor*," Inge said, and hurriedly did her duty, then tripped as she approached Mette, and almost catapulted the baby into Mette's arms.

"Now get to work!" she snapped.

Mette opened her blouse and nursed the child while she finished her coffee. This baby was her last, it had to be. She was drying up. But as old as she was, and she felt older, she still could not rest.

1910

"I'm done now," Mette said, partly to Ingebrigt and partly to the night, as they lay in bed.

"Eh?" he asked. He was getting hard of hearing.

She turned towards him and said right into his ear. "I'm done."

"With what?"

"With babies. It's been eight years since Lars. No more."

Ingebrigt grunted and rolled on his side. *"Ja, ja.* We're too old for that now."

She smiled in the dark. Yes, she was finally too old for that. She hadn't bled in a long time and it hadn't turned into a baby. That was the sign that she was done. It would have felt more like a victory if she hadn't felt as though a demon had taken possession of her. Every day there seemed to be some new malady. Her shoulders hurt, her back hurt, she had headaches, she was nauseous. No one had died, no one was ill, but she was unsteady, shaky as though something bad had happened or was about to happen. She cried too easily over foolish little things, like pricking her finger. Or it went the other way and she felt anger. She'd been on the floor one afternoon cleaning up a mess, and when she stood, she hit her head on the table and she felt such rage, if she could have, she would have picked up the table and hurled it out the door.

The strangest thing was how she heated up suddenly, as though she were standing too close to the fire. She could be doing a simple task like making coffee or carding, when she'd suddenly become so hot, she wanted to tear off her dress and run into the fjord. She feared the devil was in her, but she was too ashamed to speak about it with anyone. What if she were possessed? What would they do to her?

Just thinking of it made it happen. She suddenly felt too warm. Sweat broke out on her forehead. She flung off the blanket and fanned her legs with her nightdress.

"What now?" Ingebrigt asked.

"I'm hot," she said.

"Are you sick?"

"No."

"There's always something wrong with you."

She thought of asking him if he'd ever had anything like that, but decided not to. All she could do was pray it would go away. Old Kristi had said to her once when she caught her fanning herself, "That seems to go with the time." Maybe it was a cleansing of the body after all those births.

She thought Ingebrigt had gone to sleep, but he put his hand on her hip, then moved down to the hem of her night dress, and began to pull it up. He hadn't done that for a while. Old age had slowed him down, too. She didn't resist. She reminded herself *again* that she shouldn't talk to him in bed, it always lead to this. She lay there, her back to him, and let him have his way. At least there would be no babies. She'd suffer the fire and the anguish, and that, as long as there were no more babies.

ಜ

Autumn. The birch turned yellow and the leaves fell, the wind grew colder and in late October, the first snowfall. It didn't last, but for a day there was a thin blanket of white over everything. Mette stopped on her way from the house to the barn just to look at the landscape, how the snow changed everything. The sharp edges became softly rounded. Soon there would be banks of snow and then it would become tiresome.

As the days became colder and darker, Mette spent most of her time at the loom, often working by lantern-light. Weaving was the one thing about winter she liked. It was a comfort, just her and the thread and the loom. There, she could arrange the threads as she wanted, in a pattern pleasing to the eye, with no one telling her what she could or couldn't do. Whatever spirit had taken possession of her had finally left and she was back to her everyday aches and pains, fear and worries.

She had a fresh new worry: Inge was going to America.

In early October, they'd had a letter from Kristina who had been in America for five years. That had been a hard day, when Kristina wrote from Bergen that she had decided to go with her new friend Ragnhild. Mette sat for the longest time, the letter in her hand, staring out at nothing. She was proud of Kristina and all that she'd accomplished. Going all the way to Bergen and getting a job as a maid for a well-to-do family, that was what she'd wanted. She even sent money home occasionally. She'd been there for a year or so and Mette had hoped that was the end of the America talk, but that was not God's plan.

Kristina had been fortunate to find a husband just a year after she arrived in Minnesota, a Norwegian from Molde, and now she had two children. She'd sent a picture with the letter, and Mette studied it whenever she could. How the world had changed, to have grandchildren who lived so far away, children she'd never meet except in letters and photos. The boy looked so much like Ingebrigt, as though he'd been shrunk, and the girl like Kristina. People often said Kristina resembled her, but she didn't think she'd ever been that pretty.

The purpose of the letter was to tell them she was expecting a third child, and she wanted one of her sisters to immigrate to help her.

Why should I hire help, when I have four sisters? America is where they should be. Women have more freedom here and more time to do what they like instead of working day and night. America is full of young immigrant women making a good living, and plenty of young Norwegian men looking for wives. I am sending a ticket, and it is up to you to decide who will use it. I will say that I expect to be paid back, but here you will find as much work as you can do.

Eva and Sigrid had no interest in going but Inge and Marie were both eager to take Kristina's offer. The selling point was "plenty of Norwegian men." Mette knew people who forbade their children to go to America, her sister-in-law Birta for one. But as she got older, her thinking about America had begun to change. It was useless to fight it when the people were going in droves. And if they could truly have a better life there, why would she not want that for them? She thought of those young women from America who had stopped by the farm so long ago. Why wouldn't she want her daughters to have what they had? She saw again their soft smooth hands. With another long winter setting in, she understood why they would want to get away.

The two girls drew straws, it was the only fair way, and Inge won.

଼

She left in April when Nornes was at its most beautiful. The air was sweet with the scent of the blossoming apple trees, the creatures were outside feasting on the fresh spring grass, and the trees were beginning to leaf. It was no easier on Mette than it had been with Anders and Kristina, but this time she decided it was not going to be a day of mourning, so she did not wear the black scarf she'd worn when the others left. She would not be long in the world anyway, and if she could die knowing her daughters were better off than herself, that was good.

Seeing Inge that morning reminded Mette of herself, how sick with nerves she had been that day she was supposed to go. Mette saw how Inge pressed her lips together and frowned. She was close to tears. She looked every bit the fashionable young lady in a new hat. She wore her hair up, held with combs. Girls no longer waited until they were married to wear their hair up, that had changed. Mette took her in as though memorizing her. She would have liked to send Finn a message through her, but she thought better of it. *Tell him I was glad you got to go.*

Everyone was up to see Inge off. The three boys, Nils, Ole and Lars, crept to the table shivering and yawning.

"Will you come home for Christmas?" Lars asked, and reached up to touch the discs of her *solje*.

"*Nei*, I won't be home for a long while."

"How will you find Kristina?" Ole asked.

"There are people who help you," Inge said. But Mette could see this worried her.

"You are a clever girl," Mette said. "You'll do fine."

Ingebrigt, who had been watching everything from his high seat, pulled out his watch and checked the time. He was going to take Inge to Hermanswerke where she would catch the ferry to Bergen.

"I'll ready the carriage," he said, moving towards the door. He picked up her valise and looked at Mette. For a moment their eyes held as they remembered that other day.

"Fear not, daughter, nor be afraid, for the Lord thy God goes with thee. He will not fail thee, nor forsake thee," Mette said as she embraced her. The sisters began to cry loudly as they took turns kissing her. The boys wrapped their arms around her waist. Everyone wept.

The sun was up, a bright half-circle rising from the mountains. The water lapped gently at the shore. Inge walked to the water's edge and looked out at the fjord. If she were Inge, Mette thought, and she believed a part of her was going with her, that is what she would do, too. Breathe in as much as she could, all of Nornes, the sea, the mountains, the sheep and the grass.

"*Adjø*," Inge said as she got in the carriage and waved. "*Adjø*." Ingebrigt clucked to Asbjørn, the pony who had taken Mœrkei's place, who pulled at the reins, eager to go.

"Wait," Mette said. She hurried to the shore and picked up a shell, a small cockleshell, and pressed it into Inge's hand. "*Glemmer ikke oss*," she said. Don't forget us.

Fresh tears sprang to Inge's eyes. "*Aldri*," she said. Never.

"God be with you," Mette said again and again and again. She said it with her whole heart, not in the way her mother had said it—as though she *hoped* God would be with her. No, not that way. She said it another way. God *will* be with you. Go safely, knowing He is at your side. He will watch over you.

The family stood together and waved until the carriage rounded the bend and was out of sight. Mette was at the front, waving a white handkerchief in her raised hand. *Farewell, daughter. I'll see you in heaven.*

☙

Just six months after her arrival in America, Inge was married. The letter, with its surprising news, was the fourth letter they'd received from her. Inge appeared to have a talent for writing letters. She wrote that she looked forward to that quiet time in the evening when she could sit down and write, and that by doing so, she felt closer to those in Norway. She did not always spell words correctly and her penmanship needed improvement, but those reading the letters assumed that would get better with time.

Her first letter came quickly, about a month after she'd arrived. She wrote of the voyage, of her seasickness, of the many Irish on board the ship and that she didn't think much of them. She didn't think much of America either, now that she was there. She was so homesick every day, she wrote, and wanted to return. That made Mette shake her head. If that wasn't just like Inge. No sooner was she there, but she wanted to come back.

But the last letter brought unexpected news. The family listened quietly as Sigrid read to them, and when she got to the part that she'd married, a gasp went up from the family, almost as one. When she read, *You would never know him to be a Swede. Otto is a Lutheran, a God-fearing man, and a hard worker,* Ingebrigt hit the table with such force, his cup fell over and spilled coffee on the newspaper.

"Faen!" he bellowed. "A Swede!"

The enemy. Those loathsome people who treated Norwegians as inferior because the countries' shared monarch happened to be Swedish, even though Norway was as independent as Sweden. Just five years earlier, Norway had finally broken all ties with Sweden and installed its own king on the throne in Christiania, a throne that had been vacant for over five hundred years. They had almost gone to war to separate from Sweden, and now his own daughter had married one of them?

Not having Inge to yell at, he yelled at Mette. "You shouldn't have allowed her to go, to mingle with Swedes!"

"And who gave her money to go?" she yelled back.

Ingebrigt instructed Sigrid when she wrote back to say from him, *I'd rather have heard you were dead than married to a Swede.*

Mette, too, was stunned. Such a thing would never have happened in Norway. How could Inge know whom she was marrying in such a short time? Inge enclosed a picture of them on their wedding day, and Mette peered closely at the Swede who was now her son-in-law. She hadn't married him for his looks, that was plain. Inge was very pretty in a fancy wedding dress and long veil that her husband had bought her, and looked like it had cost a lot of money. So that was good, he had money. There was nothing Norwegian about her dress. She didn't even wear her *solje*. Mette ran her thumb over her daughter's unhappy face and felt deeply sad for her. *Stakkers.* Poor thing.

The second announcement in the letter was that she was expecting, and then Mette understood. The Swede had taken advantage of her daughter, forcing her to marry him. The Swedes were like that, they did whatever they wanted with no thought for others. She feared her daughter was, as Norway had been, under the thumb of a Swede. The one glimmer of hope was that Inge was not one to take orders from anyone.

Sigrid read on. They had moved to a town in northern Minnesota, just a few miles from Canada. They were renting a farm for the present but hoped to buy land soon. Her husband had saved money from his many jobs so they had enough, she said, but she still had to work hard. Mette tsked. Wasn't it supposed to be different in America?

The land, she said, was as flat as the fjord on a calm day, and so windy. Few trees to stop it. Inge missed her homeland, the sea and the mountains. She missed everyone more than they would ever know. She promised she would return one day.

I am so homesick. I cry myself to sleep every night. To think you might never see my child.

When the letter ended, Marie stood up and said, "I knew she wouldn't appreciate America. She's always been narrow-minded with little interest in anything outside herself." She was not in the least deterred by Inge's letter, and was patiently waiting for her own ticket since Kristina still needed assistance.

Ingebrigt, who had calmed down somewhat, stood over her. "If you should even think of marrying a Swede, I never want to hear from you again."

Marie was not cowed. "*Far*, you need not worry about that. I would never stoop so low."

When Marie's ticket finally arrived, she looked at it first with great excitement, then great disappointment.

"What's the matter?" Mette asked Marie.

"I hoped she'd book on that new fancy ship," she said. Kristina had purchased a ticket on a cheaper line, not the Titanic.

"I'm sure the one she chose will get you to America," Mette said.

"I thought that...they say many wealthy people will be on it, and I was hoping...well, never mind." Marie had day-dreamed about mingling with the upper classes and perhaps meeting a rich man on the way over.

Marie was in Bergen, about to sail to England, when the news came that the great ship had sunk, and most of its passengers had gone to the bottom of the sea. The news made Mette catch her breath. It seemed more than just a coincidence that her daughter hadn't sailed on that boat. For once, the luck was good.

But, still, they had lost another daughter, and, along with everything else, it wore heavily on her. She began to use a cane to get around, as she wasn't always sure her legs were going to support her. Then it could not be said otherwise: Mette Hansdatter was an old woman.

1912

In the summer after Marie's departure, Eva returned home. She had been working for a widow in Kaupanger, but as the woman could find nothing she did acceptable, Eva moved back to Jonsbrygga to help Sigrid with the *husmor* duties. When Mette saw her coming down the road, her suitcase bumping against her leg, she felt a pinch in her heart. Eva, the one who had been conceived after receiving Finn's news that he had married, when Ingebrigt pushed against her, claiming her finally as his.

Eva was a plain girl with broad cheeks and wide-set brown eyes. She wasn't one to mix with others. She didn't like dances or picnics as other girls did, and now she was getting up in years, having turned twenty-eight in August. It was a lonely life for Eva. Weaving occupied her. She had become better at it than Mette and had even sold some of her weavings to a shop in Sogndal.

Neither Eva nor Sigrid seemed interested in marriage. But after Eva returned, a man she'd met in Kaupanger began coming around. His name was Sven Erikson and he was a much older man, a widower, almost twenty years her senior, with two grown children with whom he lived. He was a nervous sort, always fiddling with his coat or hat, or tapping his fingers on the table. He talked too much in Mette's opinion, and when he wasn't talking, he had a bad habit of saying "*ja, ja*" over and over, as though he had to fill the empty space. He got on Mette's nerves. She couldn't tell how Eva felt about him. Maybe she was just grateful for the attention. As it was a fair distance from Kaupanger to Nornes, Sven spent the night and Mette knew how that went. She felt it her duty to explain certain things to her daughter, so one day when they were alone, she asked her, "This Sven fellow, when he stays here, has he ever... what I mean is, have you..."

Eva pulled back. "This has naught to do with you."

"It has something to do with me as you live in this house."

"*Mor*, I'm a grown woman, it is none of your business."

"I would rather not see you in trouble," Mette said.

"As you were?"

That silenced Mette for a bit. "You may not be as lucky."

"You? Lucky?"

"Mind who you're talking to. I was lucky your father was a good man and understood his responsibilities."

In the end, it didn't matter what Mette said or didn't say. Eva might already have been pregnant when they had their conversation, because not long after that, she announced that she was "in that way." She said she would remain at home until she and Sven decided what they were going to do, and if it came to it, she was prepared to raise the child by herself. She calculated that the baby would arrive in February, and that was all she was going to say about it.

That which is done is that which shall be done: and there is no new thing under the sun.

Shortly after that announcement, when they were together in the loom room, Eva asked, out of the blue, "What happened with you and Uncle Finn?"

Mette stopped wrapping yarn and looked at her.

Eva went on. "I found his letters and a picture in your trunk."

"Why were you in my trunk?"

"I wanted to see your old coverlets."

"You could have asked me."

"It was just as easy to look myself." Eva moved the shuttle between the threads.

Mette could have made a fuss about Eva snooping through her things, but what would be the point. There was nothing to be ashamed of in the letters; nothing, in fact, to be ashamed of in her love for Finn.

"If you read the letters, you know what happened."

"He wanted you to join him in America but you wouldn't go?"

Mette pulled a long string of yarn from the basket and wound it around the skein. That was true and not true. "Finn and I were going to marry, but he wanted to go to America and I didn't." She tsked. "He talked about it night and day." So long ago, such big dreams.

"I always felt my place was here, but I went along with his plan because I..." Should she say it? "I loved him. But when the time came, I couldn't do it. I couldn't leave *mor*." That was almost true. "And I wasn't as brave as your sisters."

They were quiet for a moment. There was just the soft pat of the reed against the yarn as Eva worked.

"Two men. You must have been quite a catch," Eva finally said. "I'm glad you didn't go, I wouldn't be here." She paused. "*Far* was your second choice then?"

Mette was silent for a moment. "See how you weave the threads together to make that design." She ran her fingers across the wool. "So it is with the Lord. God brought your father and me together and I have always been grateful for that." She left it there. If it hadn't felt as if she were betraying Ingebrigt, she would have said, Yes, daughter, your *far* was my second choice.

ෆ

In late January on a clear day when the sun shone for a brief time, the three women, Eva, Sigrid and Mette set up the cradle, and brought in the clothes and other baby things that had long been stored away. Mette never thought she would see those things again, but there was life for you. Sorting through the clothes, all her babies went through her mind. Some of the clothes had been passed down so often, they were ready for the rag bin. Some things could be unraveled and the thread used again. There was a christening gown in good shape, still with the protective silver coin in its hem. Eva washed and cleaned the cradle, laid a new goatskin in it.

Eva's labor started in mid-February during a fierce snowstorm. The wind howled and rattled the walls, and found its way through the tiniest cracks, making the lamps flicker. Sigrid and Mette were put into service as they couldn't expect the birth helper to come out in such weather. Nor did they need one. Under normal circumstances, the men would have left the house, but the weather forced them to stay put. Mette drew the curtain to close off the bed from the rest of the room.

Mette knew well enough what to do. She ordered Sigrid to bring Eva a bit of brandy to relax her. She constantly reassured her that she was not going to die, that everything was just as it should be, and that the baby knew what to do. She much preferred to be on that side of the birth, but it was hard to see her daughter suffer when there wasn't a thing she could do to help her. The labor began midday and by midnight, a new life had arrived at Jonsbrygga. Mette did her job well and delivered the little boy who was a good size and normal, at least from the looks of him. He let out a loud cry that rivaled the wind. Mette cut the cord perfectly, and let Sigrid do the work of cleaning the boy up. Holding her son, Eva was as pretty as Mette had ever seen her. It was as though she'd finally found her purpose.

The next morning, Mette brought Eva a bowl of *fløtegrøt,* sweet cream porridge, the traditional bed food for the new mother, but also as an offering to the Old Ones who spun the fate of the child in their threads. With the offering, she wished for good health for mother and child. When Eva slept, Mette picked up the baby and instantly felt a wave of peace come over her, as though heaven still clung to him.

She cooed as she rocked him. Holding her first grandchild, at least the first one she could hold, was a pleasure hard to describe. It was different from her own babies. He was of her, but not hers. She could just simply enjoy him without worry, at least not a mother's worry. She praised and thanked God for this blessing in her old age.

The boy was properly christened Erik after Sven's father, and Sven was present at the baptism, even though the poor man seemed bewildered by the whole thing.

His visits became fewer and further apart after the first year. He didn't seem that interested in the boy which didn't surprise Mette. First, illness kept him away, then a need to visit a relative, then he broke his ankle. He sent a letter to Eva saying he didn't know when he would be able to walk again, that he feared he'd be lame for the rest of his life. They never saw him after that. Eva didn't seem particularly upset but as she kept to herself, it was hard to tell. To Erik, Sven had been an old man who visited them every now and then, one he shied away from, so it was no hardship when he stopped coming.

1916

They were nine now at Jonsbrygga—the aged Kristi, Mette and Ingebrigt, Eva and Erik, Sigrid, Nils, Ole, and Lars. Nils was the eldest and in line to inherit the farm, but it was Ole who took the most interest in it. He was sixteen but seemed older. He was like Finn in his love of books and had a good memory for what he'd read. His hair was the color of a wood thrush, cinnamon brown, and his eyes were deep and dark blue, curious eyes. When spoken to, his brow furrowed as he listened.

He used the table as his desk after the evening meal and pored over newspapers and the books he borrowed from the library in Sogndal. Mette was so pleased with this one, his willingness to work hard and his optimism about everything. He was the *gromgutt*, the apple of his parents' eye. The name Ole had finally found its rightful owner, she felt, and its curse had been removed.

He did so well in school that Ingebrigt wanted him to finish, take his exams, and then go on to the university in Christiania, but that was not for Ole. He had big plans for Jonsbrygga. The house and grounds had been neglected for years. He wanted to bring the farm into the twentieth century, put in electricity, better windows, new siding for the house. The barn was on the verge of collapsing.

"Listen to this," he said aloud to whomever was around. "In America, ordinary people, just like us, are using a motor car on wheels instead of a horse and buggy." He explained to them how an automobile worked and they shook their heads in wonder.

One day he returned from Sogndal with a box under his arm and asked everyone to gather around, he wanted to show them something. With great drama, he circled his hand over the open box as though about to do a magic trick, and pulled out a black square object.

"What do you think this is?" he asked. No one had the slightest idea. "It's a camera! It takes pictures!" he said with great excitement. He took another object from the box, a small cylinder and held it up between his thumb and forefinger. "This is the film. You put this in the camera, look through this thing, the viewer, and move this lever, and it's ready to take a picture!"

He loaded the film into the camera, then ushered them all outside and had them stand in a sunny spot. Mette protested that they weren't dressed properly for a photo, but Ole said he was taking a "snapshot," not a formal picture. They frowned suspiciously at the camera, and Ole snapped the photo.

"That's all there is to it," he said. "Now I roll the film forward using this key, and it's ready to take another picture. When I've used all the film, I send it back to the factory, and they develop it and send the pictures back to me. All this for just four kroner!" It didn't mean very much to any of them, because they hadn't done anything or seen anything. But they trusted that Ole knew what he was doing.

The best thing was that Ole did not want to go to America. What he wanted to do, he said, was make life in Norway as good as it was in America, to have the best of both worlds. With Ole's sure hand on the future, Mette's and Ingebrigt's old age seemed more secure.

☙

The aged Kristi died that fall, her prayer finally answered. She was ninety-three and had been confined to her bed for twelve years. She could see very little and only if it were right under her nose, and she had to use an ear trumpet to hear. She lay upstairs, out of the way of the comings and goings of the others. Eva and Sigrid tended to her, brought her food, bathed her and changed her clothes, helped her with the chamber pot, but they prayed she would soon be released. She wasn't all there in the head, often calling for her dead husband. She confused little Erik with her son Erik, who lived in Slinde and had four children. Little Erik was afraid of the old woman, who looked and sounded like a troll to him. He could only be lured to her side with a promise of sweets.

Mette went up to see her every day but it was difficult conversing with her. Often Kristi rambled on under her breath about something that happened years ago that seemed to her just yesterday and Mette would listen patiently and then remind her, for example, that Gudrun was not alive, so she couldn't come to see what was ailing her.

"We had a letter from Inge today," Mette said loudly into the ear trumpet.

"Who?" Kristi croaked.

"Inge," Mette said more loudly. "Your granddaughter in America, who used to share this room with you."

"Oh, Inge." But Mette wasn't sure she knew whom she was talking about. Mette covered her nose with her handkerchief. The old woman smelled of rot. Kristi couldn't move without grimacing in pain, and she needed help with the slightest thing, adjusting the pillow or the blanket. Mette prayed that she wouldn't end up that way, a burden to others.

Before Mette got to read Inge's letter, Kristi suddenly asked, "Why does Finn never come to see me?"

"Finn is in America, too. Remember? He left years ago."

Kristi looked confused. "But didn't you go with him?"

"*Nei*," Metta shouted. "I'm here."

She peered at Mette as though to place her, then reached for her hand. "Oh yes, of course, our good Mette." Her breathing was short. "It's been a hard life for you..." She paused. "You've been a good daughter to me, and good to Ingebrigt." She gripped Mette's hand, and a tear leaked out of the corner of her eye.

A week later, Kristi died, and while they were glad she was at last at peace, her passing was not without grief. Eva wove a wreath of pine and meadow flowers for her coffin. With Kristi went the stories they hadn't yet heard, the history and lore of the farm and its people. Now it was up to Mette and Ingebrigt to connect them to the past, and up to Ole to lead them into the future.

1920

Mette and Ingebrigt sat side-by-side on the ancient split-log bench and gazed out at the peaceful fjord. It was late summer and the low light of the setting sun glinted on the water. Northern divers swam about, dove, their tail-ends in the air, then popped up again. Mette was sure God put birds on earth to calm their nerves. They each had brought small tasks to do, whittling for him, knitting for her, but they had soon put them aside just to sit. Neither could remember the last time they'd been alone. The others had gone to the mountain pasture for the Saturday festivities, and had taken Erik with them, who'd soon be old enough to herd. The old song went through Mette's head: *Time is like a rushing stream, running to the sea.*

They'd been married forty years that May. Both were gray and their faces showed the years, lined and worn, but while Metta had grown round in the middle, Ingebrigt was almost the same size as when they married, and could still fit in his wedding trousers. Ingebrigt had had a pine armoire made for their anniversary. It was a traditional gift and almost every house had one, but it made Mette feel as grand as a queen. It was a large cabinet, over two meters high and one meter across, painted a deep oxblood. The two top cupboard doors were a pale blue, an expensive color, with a symbol of a juniper tree in a darker blue on each door. The year 1920 was printed on the middle drawer, again in blue, and the bottom door was rosemaled. Arching across the top in fancy lettering was *Ingebrigt O. og Mette H. Nornes.* It was most extravagant of Ingebrigt, but, for once, Mette didn't care about the expense.

Mette sat with her fingers interlaced across her stomach. "Eva says the cloudberries are out," she said, jutting her chin towards Fimreite.

"We should make a trip then. Cut some branches for the sheep, too, while we're there," Ingebrigt said, puffing on his pipe. A breeze rippled the water. One of the divers called, a sharp flute-like tune that rang across the fjord, and another answered.

Ingebrigt suddenly said, "I know just the thing." He went into the house and returned with a bottle of brandy and two small glasses. Metta thought that was a fine idea, too. She held the glasses as he poured.

"*Skål*," they said, and clicked their glasses together.

"That's good," Metta said. "*Takk*."

As the brandy relaxed them further, Ingebright asked, "Has it been so bad then?"

She knew what he meant. She took another drink and rested the glass in the palm of her hand as she looked out at the fjord. Into her head came the first time he mentioned that he wanted to marry her, in the woodshed, after Finn had only been gone a few months. She thought him rude and unfair to Finn. She wouldn't have dreamed then that they would eventually marry.

"No, no, not so bad," she said. "Not so bad at all. We've had our share of trouble, that's sure, but here we are."

"That we have," Ingebrigt said. "We still have a roof over our heads..."

Mette interrupted, "...and a fine new cabinet." She raised her glass.

Ingebrigt smiled. "Yes...and offspring to care for us. I'd say we've done well." He clinked her glass.

The sound of the fiddle came down from the mountain, surprisingly clear considering the distance, and now and then someone shouted. Mette tapped her foot to the music, and sang the tune quietly to herself. Ingebright nudged her, then took her hand and pulled her to her feet. He put an arm around her waist and they walked in a circle in time to the music. He twirled her gently, their hands raised, then they both twirled, arms across each other's backs. It had been many years since they'd danced and Mette wondered why.

They forgot steps, sometimes went different ways, but they did well enough. He dropped to a squat, intending to spring back up, but instead he stayed there. They grunted and wheezed with laughter. He had to use the bench to get himself back up and Mette patted him on the back.

"Too old for that, *far*."

"*Ja, ja, san*."

That recalled Gunnar Hanson, the one who had danced the *halling* at their wedding, how strong and good he had been at it. They wondered what happened to him.

"Went to America, most likely," Ingebrigt said, as he lit his pipe. He blew smoke into the air. "It was sure good for me that you didn't go." He looked ahead as though picturing something before him.

"That day, when I came to get you, and you got sick...I hoped you wouldn't go, and the Lord heard me." After a pause, he chuckled to himself.

"I used to sit right here and try to put thoughts in your head, make you want to marry me."

She smiled. "I used to do that...." but she stopped. That was Finn she hoped to put a spell on. Sometimes she confused them.

Ingebright poured them a second glass. He hesitated, then asked, "With everything as it has been, do you wish you'd gone?"

That was the question of her life, wasn't it? Certainly, one she'd asked herself many times, and it wasn't the first time Ingebrigt had asked it. Every now and then he needed to be reassured. Warm and content from the brandy, with nothing to do but rest her eyes and breathe in the salt air, her husband in good humor at her side, she could emphatically say no, she did not wish she'd gone. But ask her on another day, when her back ached from cleaning out the cowshed, washing clothes or some other labor, or when the ghosts of her dead children came to visit her, or when the great sin of the past came home to roost in her heart. On those days, when she felt the struggle of life and the weight of all she carried, then she might say, yes, oh yes, she wished she'd gone.

But now it was a warm summer's night, there was birdsong and music from the mountain. There was brandy. She put her hand on her husband's, and said, "This is where I belong, Ingebrigt Olesson. You know that."

The diver called again, long and tuneful, and then it was still.

1922

The wind banged the shutters, and snow and sleet pelted the house. Mette sat by the stove and rocked. She rubbed one hand, then the other, clenching and unclenching her fingers. They ached when it was cold. She had had to finally give up knitting, her fingers just couldn't manage it. She rotated the ring Ingebrigt had given her on that warm fall afternoon so many years ago. You can be sure of me, he'd said. She looked over at him. Like his father in his pension days, he spent most of the day on his bed, smoking and reading the paper, or mending things. He happened to look up then and she looked down.

Every now and then she'd get up and hobble over to the window to peer out at the fjord, hoping to see a lantern, even though it was too dark and snowy to see anything. Ole was out there somewhere in the storm and she would not feel comfortable until he returned.

"Don't worry about Ole," Ingebrigt and the boys kept saying. "He knows what he's doing."

"He shouldn't have gone alone," Mette said.

Eva, too, every so often would go to the window. Sigrid looked up from her knitting, hopefully.

The weather had been good when Ole started out for Sogndal. He had told his brothers he could manage on his own, there wasn't room in the boat for two and the lumber for the new barn, but Mette said they should have insisted. They were just being lazy, they didn't want to help him.

Mette suddenly wanted her mother. Even after almost twenty years, there were still times when she missed her. They could always count on *bestemor* on a cold snowy evening to tell a tale from the old days. *Kom, kom,* she could hear her say, *I'm going to tell you about the house mouse and the country mouse...*

Sigrid was being courted by the parish schoolteacher, a stern young man. Mette found him difficult to talk to as he seemed to know everything. She hoped Sigrid didn't feel that way. But she could do worse, as he was a man of position. Losing Kristina and Inge to America had been hard on Sigrid, but when Marie, her twin, left, she was bereft. She did her chores, everything expected of her, but she was hollowed out for a good while. She hadn't even seen her off, but stayed at home and cried in a corner. That was ten years ago. Once landed in America, Marie had married a man who'd also emigrated from Sogn, and they'd had a son who, she said, "wasn't quite right." Sigrid felt that's what she deserved for abandoning her.

Mette didn't know where Anders was or what he was doing. They rarely heard from him. He was forty-four and, as far as they knew, still hadn't married. She wondered what he looked like now and if he ever thought of them or Norway. She got up again, leaning heavily on her cane and went to the door. When she opened it, a gust of wind almost knocked her over. Nils rushed over and closed it. She went back to her chair and prayed and rocked. She knew this feeling, this feeling of dread that something bad was going to happen. He was fine, she told herself. He knows how to take care of himself. She was worrying for nothing. He would return.

Inge had six children already, four girls and two boys. She was just like her mother, a child every two years, but she did not have Mette's bad luck. She hadn't lost any children, none at all. Only the first, Anna, had been named properly after her husband's mother in Sweden. All the other names had been pulled out of a hat, with no connection to the family at all. She hoped the ancestors would not be angry and make trouble for them. But if they did, they could only blame themselves.

Eva was good to write and she wrote all the letters on the family's behalf. God bless Eva, Mette said often. After Sven's departure, Eva declared that she would be an old maid like her namesake grandmother. She devoted her time to taking care of her son and her parents, as any good daughter should. Erik was still their best hope, who, at ten, was Ole's apprentice.

"He's here," Eva suddenly shouted. "I see the lantern." She grabbed her coat, as did the others, and hurried down to the shore. Mette waited at the door. "Thank God, merciful Father," she whispered, and leaned heavily against the door. "Thank God."

Ole staggered into the house supported by Sigrid and Eva while Erik cleared the way. The men unloaded the lumber and put the boat away. Mette hoped when she saw how unsteady he was that he was only drunk, but she soon saw that his clothes were frozen and he was shaking so violently he couldn't unbutton his jacket. He sat near the stove while they helped him get into warm dry clothes. Mette ordered Erik to pull the coverlet from their bed and Eva wrapped it around him.

"I've never been so glad to see this old place," Ole said through chattering teeth. "There wasn't a place to dock so I had to keep going." Mette hushed him, told him not to talk, to just get warm, and she told Erik to rub his back and shoulders. Eva banked the stove and Sigrid brought him a cup of hot chamomile tea with brandy.

"I got the lumber, though, so we can start on the barn as soon as it clears up," he said. Mette hovered over him, felt his forehead.

"*Holde varmen*," Mette said. Keep warm.

"He shouldn't have gone alone," she said to Ingebrigt. "No one listens to me."

"He'll be fine, just caught a chill," Ingebright said, but he looked worried, too.

It was more than a chill. Lars and Ingebrigt decided they had to fetch the doctor, so off Lars went to Sogndal in the snowy cold. The doctor was a young man, about the same age as Lars, and that troubled Mette. Did he know enough? He wasn't from Sogn. He was a tall, thin man with curly hair and looked like a sheep, Mette thought. He wore a suit and tie and carried a black bag. When he entered the house, he first shook everyone's hand before he attended to the patient. He listened to Ole's chest with his instrument, and checked his pulse and his temperature. When he was through, he folded up his stethoscope and shook his head.

"Pneumonia, I'm afraid," he said. "He was exposed too long, but with the help of God and all of you, he may have a chance." There was nothing he could give him. Ingebright walked with him to the door and practically pushed him out, so disgusted was he by so-called "modern" medicine. "We pay all that money to get a doctor, and he can't do anything?" He hit the door after he'd shut it.

Eva became his nurse. She fried onions in lard, wrapped them in cloth, and placed it on his chest. That seemed to help some because he coughed up a lot of bad phlegm. She made him barley water and *øl-ost*, milk and beer, and fed him camphor powder. He slipped in and out of consciousness and all the while talked feverishly of the new barn and the wonders of electricity. He didn't always know where he was or who they were. Mette and Ingebrigt never left his side except to use the privy. Out of worry and not knowing what else to do, Ingebrigt sang, his deep baritone voice filling the room. Mette talked to Ole as though he were just taking a rest, hoping that might make it so. She told him the Lord was there, that He'd take care of him. She wiped his forehead with a cool cloth. How many times had she been through this?

She prayed, but she knew, and she knew Ingebrigt did, too. The Old Ones were close and whispered to her. She tried to put her trust in God *If it be thy will*, she prayed. *Let him live.* Still, the ancestors were there with bowed heads. They were waiting for him. A merciful God would not allow this, not this one who promised so much. She clutched her shawl tightly around her shoulders with one hand and with the other, she clung to Ole's sleeve. She shouldn't have named him Ole, she shouldn't have.

"Be merciful," she prayed. "I beg you, show mercy."

She fell asleep, slumped in the rocking chair, and she woke in the night to the sound of crying. Candlelight flickered on the wall, and she saw the shape of Ingebrigt sitting next to Ole's body, weeping. Erik, Eva and Sigrid, Nils and Lars, all wept. The door had been opened to let his soul out, and a cold wind blew in. The room began to move around her, darkness closed in on her, and she fell to the floor.

ɞ

She was there in body, but not in spirit. She was a bird and could come and go as she pleased. Sometimes even to America where she perched on a branch and watched her children and their children. The day of Ole's funeral, she moved to the loft, to be away from the earthbound ones, and never came down. Like old Kristi, her daughters tended to her, brought her what she needed, which wasn't much. She grew thinner as the days passed, so thin her ring rolled off her finger one day when Eva was dressing her. It bounced across the floor and rolled some distance before clattering to a stop. "You take it," she'd said to Eva. "I don't need it anymore." They heard her sing sometimes, her voice low and toneless. Sometimes they heard her talking to someone. *That name, your name, it's your fault. You cast a spell on that name out of spite for me.* They heard her cry often, and sometimes she moaned so loudly, it sounded as though she were a ghost already.

May 1922

"Finn Nornes," Mette said, looking up at the old man who stood before her, the one who had made her come down from her tree. She could not see the boy she had once loved in this old man. She supposed he couldn't see the girl in her either. He was light in the foot like a young man, but old in the face. He was dressed nicely in a suit coat and tie. Her hair was pulled back tightly in a bun, but her hand went up to make sure it was smooth.

She was very weak, and only recently had the girls been able to get her to come down from her nest, as they called it, and sit in her rocking chair. They could set her in a boat for all she cared, and push her out to sea, as they did with the Old Ones. She was through with this life.

"*Kom, kom,*" she said to Finn, motioning for him to sit. "Have you come back to stay then?"

"Oh no, just to visit," he said. "It's good to see you again, Mette. I'm sorry about Ole."

Her face went blank. "Ole..?"

Eva was suddenly by her side, her hand on her shoulder. "Would you like some coffee, Mother?"

Mette looked at her daughter and smiled gratefully.

Finn pulled up a chair and sat down. He rubbed his hands on his thighs.

"I'm staying with Elling and Brita," he said loudly, leaning towards her, so she could hear him. "They have a nice place there in Fimreite."

"Did you fly here?" she asked.

He frowned. "Fly? You mean in an aeroplane?"

"No, with wings. Fly."

He shifted in his chair. "I came by ship, steamer. They're so modern now. Took me only a week. Very comfortable."

"Oh yes, a ship, of course. Have you forgotten how to fly then?"

She saw him glance at Eva, and then he said, "I suppose I have. That was a long time ago."

"Ja," she said. "It was a long time ago, but I can still fly." She looked at her hands.

Eva put the coffee down and he nodded at her. "I understand that Ingebrigt and your boys are in Sogndal for the day," he said. Mette pulled at her sleeve and looked out the window.

They drank their coffee, and he talked. He'd come alone, he told her, his wife preferred to stay at home; one trip across the ocean was enough for her. *Hahaha.* They had eight children: the eldest was forty-two, the youngest twenty-one. He hadn't had to worry about them emigrating. *Hahaha.* He told her how good it was to meet her daughters, Kristine, Inge and Marie, in America. The three of them and their families had come to the farm one Sunday afternoon.

"What fine girls you have," he said. "I've even met some of your grandchildren. Inge's daughter Irene looks very much like you."

Once that would have interested her.

"Did all your children live?" she asked suddenly, narrowing her eyes at him.

He paused to understand what she meant, then said, "We lost a daughter. Diphtheria. She was eight."

"Just the one?" Mette leaned forward and gripped his arm. "You're lucky then," she said, peering at him. Then she leaned back and began to rock. "I lost four, six if you count the twins." But she quickly dismissed that with a wave of her hand. "They were only here for a short time."

She rested her elbows on the arms of the rocking chair, and looked out the window. "Four children taken. They're in heaven, of course, they never suffer, but it's hard, you know, when they go." She drifted off. "I'll be happy to see them again, especially my last Ole, who...I don't understand..." She mumbled to herself. "How that could have happened...I thought..." She searched his face, beseeching him. She used her handkerchief to dab at her eyes.

Finn was quiet, and then reached over and put his hand on her hand, "We don't know why God does what He does. We have to trust that He knows best."

"*Ja, ja,* that's right." She shook her head and neither said anything for a while. Then, "Do you remember the owl?"

"Owl?" He looked puzzled. "I'm afraid I don't."

"He knew my place was here."

Finn drank the last of his coffee and took her hand in his. "I thought many times of returning to Norway. There were times I was so homesick, I thought I might just as well dig a grave and lie in it. There were times I feared for my soul, but the Lord has always been with me. I promised myself I would come back here one day, maybe even to live, but now that I am here, I see that my home is in America. I had to come here to understand that."

She smiled, too, hesitated, then looked down at their joined hands. "Have you forgiven me?"

"Long ago, Mette, long ago."

Finn, Finn. She saw him as a young man striding up the mountain with a hatful of raspberries, she saw him pulling the oars as he rowed them across the fjord, and she felt his embrace before he left for America.

"*Takk for alt. Takk, Finn.*" She wanted to leave then. She was done.

"I'll come back when Ingebrigt and the boys are here."

But Mette had flown away.

She settled back in the tree and looked down from her high perch at Jonsbrygga, at her fourteen children, the ones in heaven and the ones on earth. All were there. Ole Ellingson was there, too. He lifted a hand to her in greeting, and she nodded. Ingebrigt stood side by side with Finn, the brothers who had loved her and whom she had loved. The wind picked up and she pushed off the branch and flew into it. She had been a good girl, she'd done all she could, and now she was released. She was free.

Afterword

It was spring when my grandmother Inge received the black-bordered envelope that brought the news of her mother's death. I know spring on the prairie. The dull browns and grays of winter give way to glorious color as the earth returns to life. Wild crab apple blossoms and sweet clover scent the air and foxtail and blue grass wave in the warm breeze. There is the rich smell of freshly turned soil, and the birds chirp and swoop, building their nests. There was a new life in my grandmother then, too. She was pregnant with her seventh child.

Inge has said of her mother's death, *"So Ole died, so she died of that."* Mette was sixty-two, and died two months after Ole's death. Ingebrigt lived twelve more years and died in 1934, from a gallbladder attack.

None of Mette's sons married. Anders died alone in a nursing home in San Francisco in 1967, Nils and Lars died in Nornes in 1984 and 1989, respectively. Eva never married and lived with Nils and Lars until her death in 1971. Eva's child, Erik, didn't survive as I have lead you to believe. He died of diphtheria when he was four. When it came time to write that, I couldn't do it, I wasn't going to let Mette lose the only grandchild she had known. But she did.

Sigrid married the schoolteacher, but never had children. Marie had one child, Kristina three, and Inge nine, all of whom lived long lives. Inge was ninety-three when she died, the same age as her grandmother Kristi.

Inge, as she vowed she would, returned to Norway in 1947, when she was fifty-five. She hadn't seen her siblings in thirty-five years. She recognized Eva, but not Sigrid or her brothers, who were quite young when she left. Inge had told her husband that she was going to stay in Norway, but after a week, she was so lonesome she wanted to return to her home on the prairie.

In 1985, after Nils died and Lars moved to a nursing home in Sogndal, the farm was sold to Elling Fimreite, a great-grandson of Ingebrigt's brother. We were told that the place was a crumbling heap. The two brothers had lived in squalor with no electricity, for which they refused to pay; yet stashes of money were found throughout the house. The buildings were razed and now it's a park of sorts. Grass has grown over everything.

Jonsbrygga is no more.

Glossary

Adjø	Farewell
Bunad	Regional folk dress
Cariole	Carriage for one person
Far	Father
Fru	Mrs.
Fylgja	Guardian spirit
Gaard	Farm estate
God dag	Good day
Halling	Spirited folk dance
Eldhus	A farm building with an open hearth used for dyeing, baking, brewing and washing
Hjelpjente	Midwife
Husmann/cotter	A farm worker who leases a cottage from a farmer, and sometimes a small holding of land, usually in return for services or sharing of their crops
Jenta	Girl
Lur	Birch bark horn
Mor	Mother
Nisse	Farm spirits, similar to gnomes
Pike	Girl
Sæter	Mountain hut
Skål	Toast to health
Solje	A silver brooch with dangling discs
Stabbur	Storage shed
Stolkjære	A two-wheel carriage
Takk	Thank you
Tine	An oval box made of birch bark
Tollekniv	Knife
Tvare	A three-pronged utensil made of pine used for mixing

Acknowledgements

I owe a special thanks to my aunt, Eva Mildred Pearson, whose book *I Remember, I Remember, My Viking Heritage*, opened my eyes to my maternal grandparents' backgrounds. I was in my mid-forties when I first learned about their families and where they came from. When I initially looked at my grandmother's family, I didn't pay too much attention, I just noted she was one of fourteen children. But looking further, I began to see that not all those children lived long. That sobering information along with a comment my grandmother made about her mother—*I think she was a kind of nervous person, she took everything so hard*—put me on the road to writing this book.

I love and thank my writing group, together for more than thirty years, who made this long journey with me. I would never have attempted this book without the help of these amazing and talented women—(in alphabetical order) Sheri Cooper, Terry Gamble, Suzanne Lewis, Donna Levin, Mary Beth McClure, and Alison Sackett. I love you ladies.

And a huge shout out to my dearest friend and my writing godmother, Elizabeth Berg, who encouraged me to write in the first place and who has always promoted my work. She made me believe that I could write. I owe so much to her. *Tusen takk*, darling.

Printed in Great Britain
by Amazon